Love

and Other Stories

Got this from
an old bookstore
in Brooklyn. I
hope you enjoy :)

Love

and Other Stories

TIBOR DÉRY

Introduction by George Szirtes

A New Directions Classic

Published by arrangement with Hofra Ltd., H-1061 Budapest, Andrássy ut 23,
Hungary.

"Games of the Underworld," translated by Kathleen Szasz, was originally published
in *The Portuguese Princess and Other Stories* (Calder and Boyars Ltd., 1966; North-
western University Press, 1987); "Behind the Brick Wall," translated by Kathleen
Szasz, and "Love," translated by Ilona Duczynska, were originally published in *The
Giant* (John Calder Publishers Ltd., 1964); "Reckoning" and "Two Women," translated by Dr. D. Mervyn Jones, were first published in *Encounter* (Vol. XX No.1,
1963; Vol. XXII No. 6, 1964); "The Circus," translated by Elizabeth Csicsery-
Rónay, was first published in *Hungarian Short Stories*, edited by Paul Varnai (Exile
Editions, 1983); "Philemon and Baucis" was translated by Judith Sollosy.

Manufactured in the United States of America
New Directions Books are printed on acid-free paper.
First published as a New Directions Paperbook (NDP1013) in 2005
Published simultaneously in Canada by Penguin Books Canada Limited

Library of Congress Cataloging-in-Publication Data

Déry, Tibor, 1894–1977
 [Short stories. English. Selections]
 Love and other stories / by Tibor Déry.
  p. cm.
 ISBN 0-8112-1625-X (alk. paper)
 I. Title.
 PH3213.D53A6   2005
 894'.511'33—dc22   2005000995

New Directions Books are published for James Laughlin
by New Directions Publishing Corporation
80 Eighth Avenue, New York, NY 10011

CONTENTS

INTRODUCTION

BY GEORGE SZIRTES

One of the best products of Hungarian cinema is Károly Makk's *Szerelem* (*Love*) made in 1971, which is based on a very short story by Tibor Déry. The story, which is included here, is no more than the journey from prison to home of a man convicted of some unnamed political crime. Leaving the prison he gets on a tram, hails a taxi and finds the house with the single room where his wife and child live. They are out but someone lets him in. People are kind. Eventually he goes out in the street again and sees his wife and child coming up the street. They greet each other and go in. That is all. There are no murders, no car chases and no major twists. The man simply breathes in his wife's scent while he is waiting for her in their tiny room. Out of this and another perfectly simple story also included in this book, "Two Women," Makk made a wonderful feature-length film. There was, he felt, enough in them, and indeed there was.

Tibor Déry knew what it was like to be in prison. He had served three terms, all on political charges. Born into a middle-class family in Budapest in 1894, at the height of national optimism, two years before the great Millennial celebrations of the founding of the Hungarian state, and when Budapest was the fastest growing city in the world, he saw confidence crumble and come crashing down at the end of the First World War when the Austro-Hungarian Empire was broken up. By the terms of the Treaties of Versailles and Trianon, Hungary lost two-thirds of its territory and one-third of its population.

Déry had studied at the Academy of Commerce and spent a year in Switzerland, studying languages, but had already begun writing and was politically active, supporting demands for

higher wages and joining the Communist Party that pro-
claimed a Soviet Republic on 21 March, 1919, and announced a
dictatorship of the proletariat three months later. Déry was a
member of the Writers' *Directoire*, which nationalized private
property, including his father's block of flats. According to
some, his father committed suicide as a result. The Bolsheviks
were finished by 1 August. Red Terror was succeeded by White
Terror and the rule of Admiral Horthy. This was the time of
Déry's first imprisonment.

After prison, Déry, who was married by this time, worked
abroad for some years, in journalism among other things, and
played roulette in Monte Carlo. He returned to Hungary in
1926. He wrote papers, articles and stories that he found difficult to publish so undertook translation. In 1934 he took part
in a workers' uprising in Vienna and the following year was arrested again, in Hungary, this time for translating a banned
work by Andé Gide. The jail sentence was only two months.

During the war he worked in the underground both figura-
tively and literally, hiding out in cellars and bomb shelters. His
partly Jewish background would have made life very dangerous
for him. Straight after the war he joined the Communist Party
again, and shortly before it assumed control of the country, he
was awarded a major literary prize. A lot of his work, old and
new, was published. However, the nature of the dictatorship,
with its tendency to prosecute, imprison and execute friends as
well as enemies, led him to join with those who opposed it in
1956, and when the revolution failed he was condemned to
nine years in prison, of which he served three. Because of the
high regard in which he was held, his imprisonment had considerable symbolic value. He was cleared of all charges on his
release.

In this respect, then, the story of "Love" is written from
hard-earned personal knowledge, and the conditions of life it
describes are meticulously rendered. Among those conditions—

poverty, overcrowding—the reader will note the virtues of generosity and, naturally enough considering the title, love. There is nothing sentimental in the love that is presented in the story. It is comprised of fidelity and tenderness and is seen as part of a social compact founded on simple actions and shared assumptions.

These shared assumptions—so difficult for a writer of our own age to conjure—spring out of the physical state of siege endured by the population of Budapest during the latter stages of the war and its psychological equivalent in the period of dictatorship that followed it, but were also part of the climate of international humanism that produced E. M. Forster in England and John Steinbeck in America. The biggest international success of Déry's own writing career was his novella, *Niki: The Story of a Dog*, which appeared in Hungary in 1956 and was soon translated into various languages. It is an apparently simple storyline embodying a sharp critique of hard line Stalinist dictatorship. Here, too, the values are clear, as are their anthiseses: trust versus suspicion, freewill versus coercion, logic versus paranoia, generosity versus pettiness, love versus fear. In the West, no doubt, *Niki*'s success was helped by the fact that its author was in prison, and was therefore available as Cold War material. The uses of *Niki*, and, more to the point, of Déry, might very well be sentimental in ways the book itself was not.

Who would not vote for good if it were opposed to bad? Who would not prefer love to fear? But the conditions under which Déry wrote and the conditions under which he was read in Hungary were very different from the conditions in which he was read abroad. Déry's Hungarian readership was in a position to check the truth. His readers could tell he had a first rate ear for dialogue and a keen eye for physical detail. That was what people sounded like: that was what their streets, workplaces and accommodation were like physically and psychologically. And, they understood that his fiction—particularly his short stories, where he seems to have written with greater freedom than in his novels—was about them. They recognized themselves as ordinary people living under extraordinary circumstances, and could see their dilemmas reflected in Déry's prose.

In most respects the mature Déry was only following the party line of Socialist Realism as interpreted by another epigone of the brief 1919 Bolshevik state, György Lukács, who wrote an introduction for one of Déry's books, and who, like Déry, was associated with the revolutionary government of 1956. Everyone was more or less obliged to follow the party line, which actively demanded values often shared, but not demanded by, international humanism. The writer was to write about the lives of ordinary workers and to embody an optimistic vision of their capacity to be brought to a better material and intellectual condition. In communist societies, of course, the only possible agent of such improvement was the Moscow-based Party, and this message had somehow to be intimated to a satisfactory degree.

It was at this point that friction arose between Déry and the Party, as indeed between many writers and the Party, in 1956. For Déry's "optimistic" view of the human condition is not predicated entirely on the Party. In fact, while espousing a view of the people not altogether different from that espoused by the rhetoric of the Party, his understanding of them locates them in opposition to all prevailing circumstances generally, including the circumstances of the Party.

In other words, Déry's people are alive and act as independent creatures. They are raised to heroic stature not by ideology, not even by any consciousness of themselves as heroes, but by circumstances that occasionally require them to act heroically. This form of heroism is the one recourse they have.

Not that they always behave in a heroic manner. The cast of characters inhabiting the bomb shelters and cellars of the latter stages of the siege of Budapest in 1944 in the stories of the "Games of the Underworld" section, originally published as a book in Hungary in 1946, include a variety of types ranging from tough old widows, humble servants, self-absorbed middle-class whiners and right-wing dignitaries through to outright fascists, and the reader knows that, on the whole, by and by, the tough old widows are going to be a lot more sympathetic than the right-wing dignitaries let alone the fascists. Of course they are, and should we be obliged to lay out a map of virtue, we would have little difficulty in allocating Déry's bomb-shelter society high- or low-ground status by class. Nevertheless, the stories we read here are so packed with convincing voices and intimate physical detail that there is rarely a point at which we stop believing Déry's account of *in extremis* reality. This is partly because the acts of heroism are forlorn or incidental, not a matter of ideologically fuelled derring-do, and because the corresponding acts of wickedness mostly come down to petty loathing and brutal idiocy, which, in its effects, is as tragically incidental as the good.

The one false note is the entry of the Russian soldier with his "laughing blue eyes" at the end of "Fear." The boy with laughing eyes was associated more with rape, pillage, abduction, murder and terror than with laughter for most people, and what he ushered in is well documented by now. That could hardly be said after 1949, though it is interesting that the figure of the Soviet liberator is already present in Déry in 1946, some time before he became subject for public statues. What it shows is that for many, particularly for the hunted Jews, the figure was indeed a liberator. Who, after all, was to know in 1946 what would happen within three years? In 1946 Hungary was still a democracy with a range of political parties. To set out on an investigation of who said or wrote what, when, why and to what effect in the years straight after the war, would be a very slow and thankless task.

But Déry was as aware as anyone of the effects of the laughing Russian's heritage. In a story of 1955, "Behind the Brick Wall," he describes conditions in a Stakhanovite factory where the employees are so poor they are reduced to stealing. The central character, Bodi, is there to enforce workers' discipline, and as a direct result of his actions one worker hangs himself and the rest grow to hate him. Not that Bodi is presented as any kind of villain. Bodi, like all actors in Déry, is himself incidental. He is merely carrying out his task. According to Stakhanovite principles production was boosted by raising the norms required of each worker, Stakhanov being the ideal worker on whom the practice was modeled. By 1955, Stalin, the power behind such principles, was dead and the dictator he had supported in Hungary, Mátyás Rákosi, was, temporarily at least, relegated to the background. It had become possible to criticize the excesses of the previous six years, and "Behind the Brick Wall" is very much a direct and devastating critique, not so much in terms of ideology as of practice. As ever in Déry the incidental is symptomatic. The incidental is where people live and die.

"Reckoning" is a remarkable story to be published in 1962 by one recently released from prison. It concerns an elderly professor who sets out for Austria in the wake of 1956, traveling by train, bus and on foot, only to turn back and die. Hundreds of thousands undertook such journeys, including my own family, whose experience precisely echoes that of the professor, up to the point of turning his back. The woman whose heart is too weak for the journey might have been my mother, except my mother made it. The story is remarkable in that it shows overt sympathy for those on the side of the doomed revolution, which was quickly labeled a counter-revolution after its failure and remained so in official parlance until 1989 when Imre Pozsgay, a liberal member of the still ruling Party, let slip the term "revolution" in the course of a broadcast interview. But there was a considerable gap, long before then, between official and unofficial view of events.

The professor may be presumed to stand for Déry himself, if only as a moral argument, moral argument being half the story, the other half being an authoritative account of the circumstances under which people made their way to the border. In moral terms, the story is written by one who stayed behind, for others who stayed behind. It had, therefore, like all Déry's good work, to stand up to the test of recognition: Is this why people left? Is this how it was for them? Is this why they chose to stay? The professor has helped a revolutionary student, at some risk to himself, by looking after his machine gun. He admonishes the student even as he helps him, and throughout the rest of the story goes on admonishing people while helping them. The issue of the heroic and the incidental receive special attention here. One of the escapees, a "stout, pale-faced doctor" the professor had known in Budapest, offers the professor a seat (which he rejects), arguing: "What would the world come to, my dear professor, if everybody was a hero? . . . Let us not expect more of human nature than it can give."

But the whole point of Déry's literary output is precisely that everybody is a hero, if only an incidental hero in a world of incidents or, to put it another way, the hero is everybody. Déry rejects the doctor's account of human nature, which, in the doctor's words, "turns one's face toward heaven and with a heart full of gratitude begins to praise the authorities of the time." The delicacy and risk, for Déry, lies in asserting the centrality of heroism and of locating it in the figure of the professor and his shudder of moral disgust. Because not everyone in the refugee group is a casuist, like the doctor: most are human beings in impossible incidental situations. Nevertheless, says Déry, true heroism lies in staying. The moral argument is extended, and possibly muddied, by the fact that the story was published as early as 1962. There were important political changes backstage and a deal was struck. The story therefore existed in the public sphere where its meaning and authority lay open to the acute bifocal reading of the time. Then, as now, reading was conducted as much between the lines as in them. In other words, the publication of "Reckoning" was and remains an overtly political act. It may be argued—and often is—that no literature is entirely apolitical, but post-1956, within the framework of an effective but wounded communist authority, "Reckoning" is a very special case indeed.

For us, at this distance, it is as literature, not as politics, that Déry's stories demand to be judged. Déry had a particular ear for the way women spoke, and a particular sympathy for their own quiet and remarkable heroism. It is their voices that come over most clearly in the cellars of 1944 Budapest (the men mainly lying dead in the street), and it is in "Two Women," the parallel piece to "Love," that Déry's hearing is most acute and most sympathetic.

The story is titled "Two Women" but there are in fact three: the elderly woman dying in bed, her daughter-in-law who comes visiting and the housekeeper. The husband, who haunts the story by his absence, is, like the man in "Love," in prison for very similar non-reasons at much the same time. His mother doesn't know this. Now sly, now tyrannical, now vulnerable, now admirable, the old woman is fed on the lie that her son is brilliantly successful and in Hollywood making a movie, surrounded by swimming pools and body guards, and that he will be home soon. The wife, who is responsible for this story, fabricates letters and brings presents as if they were from him. The housekeeper plays along with not just this illusion, but with others too. The truth is that the young woman is impoverished, that the son isn't coming home. She has decided that if her mother-in-law is to die she will die happy. The exchanges between the two main characters are witty, repetitive, desperate and wholly convincing, and in the end the old woman does die without knowing the truth. The cost of the lie is borne by the wife who is utterly selfless in maintaining it. She is, in effect, performing one of those incidental heroic acts that fascinated Déry, all the more so because the act itself is morally far from simple and because we are never given the reason for the younger woman's devotion. The incidental heroic, the story argues, does not spring from reasons, but from instinctive imperatives. The author trusts that people are capable of acting on such instinctive imperatives, that the imperatives represent the best in people and that people are capable of acting on them.

In some ways, the set-piece element of Déry is what will appear most dated. It doesn't take much looking to discover the main structural elements of the set. These elements are stern, unbending, and as old-fashioned as those we find in Déry's contemporary, Sándor Márai. They are what make Déry a writer of his time. But Déry is not trapped in his time because his ear, eye and instinct—his own imperatives, if you like—are, in his best work, vital, energetic and large beyond their context.

That great modern English curmudgeon, the poet Philip Larkin, famously, and in some ways uncharacteristically, wrote, "What will survive of us is love." In Déry, an altogether kinder and more tested writer, it is love that survives, love as in the story bearing that title, as in the actions of those who trust their better instincts. And, on the whole, in Déry they can and do.

and Other Stories

RECKONING

SOME TIME before the main entrance was closed, the student smuggled the Tommy gun into the flat of the Professor of Medicine, hiding it under his mackintosh. He felt no twinges of conscience. He was not even particularly excited. His only fear was that if his emotions carried him away, he might offend the old man. The monumental bare anteroom, which he had known previously only in its daytime form, with corners that vanished into darkness and unapproachable walls, now in the glaring lamplight suddenly assumed its hidden geometrical shape: it was disagreeably obvious and unfriendly. He hung his head; instead of looking into the professor's face, with its expression of amazement, of one demanding an explanation, he watched, with eyes downcast, the old man's feet which seemed movingly aged and helpless in his clumsy black-laced shoes. The old man was still a head the taller.

"I am disgusted with you, my young friend," said the professor. "I would not have believed you capable of such guile. You turn up a minute before curfew, relying on my not throwing you out on the street after the main entrance is closed."

"Gently, sir," said the student.

"And what right have you to presume that I agree with you?" asked the old man. "And in particular, that our understanding is so perfect as to extend to this vile skin-punching instrument. For what cause could there be, other than the understanding you presume, for your wishing to conceal it with me?"

"Your house will not be searched, sir," said the student.

"Will yours?"

"That is what I have run away from," said the student. "I jumped out of the window."

The old man laughed mockingly: "From the ground floor, eh? And not from the fifth floor?"

The student had no doubt how their conversation would end, he was only afraid that in its tortuous course he might lose patience. He already imagined he felt anger slowly accumulating in his nerves. "So you have come to me direct from the ground floor or the fifth floor, my young friend," said the professor. "It is moving, the brotherly spirit which made you wish to share the danger with me."

"One word and I'll take the thing away, sir," said the student, gazing into the old man's well-loved, gaunt face.

"First, I am appalled by the cool cunning with which you have trapped me. It will take you far in life. Why are you smiling?"

"Perhaps the real cause of your rage is that I've dirtied your floor, sir," said the student with a suppressed laugh. The snow, which had formed a hump on his back, had begun to melt, and trickled to the floor in the folds of his mackintosh. Round his feet, a small circular puddle, shining in the electric light, had already formed. He knew what painful care the old man bestowed on external cleanliness. It was common knowledge in the university that it was not advisable to have black nails or a dirty shirt when you went to get a certificate signed, or even when you sat in the front rows of the lecture theater. And now too, late in the evening, alone in his bachelor flat, the professor had opened the door to the student in a blinding white collar and cuffs, and the trousers which showed beneath his long silk dressing-gown had been pressed to a sharp crease.

"I'll wipe it up before I go, sir," said the student with a faint, quivering undertone of mockery.

The old man gazed at the Tommy gun protruding from under the mackintosh.

"I am disgusted with you, my young friend," he said. "Even if, for some reason unknown to me, you have the right to assume my sympathy with your trouble-making, how tactless and impertinent to force me to admit it. What is more, you not only extort from me this admission, against my inclination and taste, but you sink so low as to demand instantly—without my approval—my help, my personal participation. You want me to take a risk, defy the law, go to prison, and, in the last resort, to die a martyr's death as well. . . . I am misstating the case, you are not demanding this of me, but forcing it on me directly, appealing to some incomprehensible, stupid moral laws . . . you are forcing me to go to prison, perhaps to the scaffold, and all this a minute before the entrance is closed, in my own flat, while you smile like an idiot and send streams of slush trickling all over my anteroom, which I had polished yesterday . . . and finally you have the nerve, as the climax of your puerile prank, to offer mockingly to wipe up this puddle. You make a child wipe it up, if it wets you, don't you? Perhaps you'd even polish it if I asked you?"

"I repeat, one word and I'll take the skin-puncher away, sir," said the student.

"Have you no eye for nuances, my young friend?" asked the professor. "Can you not distinguish between approval and identification? Do you not know that if a man of sixty-two agrees with a man of twenty, the consequences are not the same for both of them? That what is befitting for you is perhaps not befitting for me? That it is for the young man to act, for the old only to judge? Has the passion for play so robbed you of your reason that you cannot distinguish between the obligations of youth and the rights of age? What a wretched picture of the world you seem to have, if you can in all good faith lay a claim to sacrifice my life, or even hazard it, for your insignificant, shallow twenty years. . . . Yes, it is so, no use looking at me with that stupid sparkle in your eyes! If you dare to exchange a reality in the present, which I have earned, for a handful of promises, with a gay wink, and without a thought, where is the guarantee that you will make them good? Show me just one such dream, which really has as much weight as a thrush's whistle! Till now I liked you for your frankness and courage, though I never esteemed your intelligence very highly. But now I have found, with regret, my dear embryo friend, that you are a crafty coward."

I see, thought the student, he's wearing me down till I get tired of it and take the thing away. Never mind, we're not taken in. But his forehead and ears had reddened.

"Coward?" he asked.

The old man twirled his old-fashioned thin silver pencil between his fingers with the same pale, dignified look as in his lectures. By now the wind had quite covered the glass front door with snow, the draught kept on belching up the chimney; in the huge, bare anteroom it grew colder almost from minute to minute.

"A coward, because you don't like facing reality," said the old man. "Mothers are not sacrificed for embryos."

"For a crafty embryo . . . ," said the student.

The professor pointed to the bulge in the mackintosh with his pathetic, thick, white index finger. "Do not jest, please," he said, rebuffing him. "You do not have enough humility toward the world for that. Your choice of weapon already proves your guile. How unmanly it is to use a weapon, with which you can punch a hole in the skin of your fellows, virtually without personal danger! Turning out corpses on a conveyor belt—is that the ideal of modern youth? With a vile thing like this, you can make away with fifty men, feeling as good as a lord, without risking your own skin. Of course you do not care that it costs you a man's honor. And you dare to bring this perforating-machine into my flat, with a grin on your face, for me to adopt it as my own? Certainly—if you bring a sword, a Toledo blade, which I could regard as an extension of your person, I might keep it as a souvenir, I might shed a tear, too, because it would recall my own long-past, youthful folly—yes, my friend, if you charged into the arena with a sword and challenged a tank to single combat, that would deserve some respect, because in the absence of other results, at least it would give us a caricature of the modern world that everybody could understand. Then, perhaps, my opinion of your intellectual powers would change. But how shall I start, I beg you, with a moral formula that brandishes a Tommy gun, which shows its baseness as soon as it encounters one weaker than itself?"

The blood rushed to the student's head. "How do you mean, sir?" he asked, blushing to roots of his hair.

"A hypocrite into the bargain?" said the old man reproachfully. "You are playing a safe game, young man. You know my irresolute nature and can be certain that I feel far too unsure of myself not to take your side against mine in my own mind—even against a wicked embryo like you. My responsibility is thereby lessened, do you understand? You knew for certain that by the end of your visit I should be the weaker. Even with your undeveloped intellectual powers, you had time to learn the psychology of reflection from my behavior. You have abused my sympathy."

The student suddenly turned on his heels and ran toward the door.

"Feri!" shouted the old man after him.

The student stumbled, and immediately ran on. But even before he reached the door, the old man, taking him unawares, seized him by the shoulder from behind, pulled out the Tommy gun from under his mackintosh and tossed it into the far corner of the anteroom. He opened the door himself, and with the full weight of his tall, bony frame flung out the amazed, terrified boy, for whom—excluding a handshake—this was the first and last physical contact with the professor. "Get out!" he shouted after him, panting slightly. "Do not set foot in here again!"

The gale fanned a flurry. of snow from the corridor into the anteroom; a moment later, the anteroom door was slammed on the hesitating heel of the student.

THE FOLLOWING week was passed in a struggle between the professor and his charwoman. At the sight of the Tommy gun lying in the corner the old woman smote her face with her hand and began to whimper, but there was no way of persuading the professor to remove the weapon from the flat, or even to conceal it. He did not even allow her to cover it with a blanket, and one day, when he discovered, on returning from his early morning walk, that she had hung it on the peg under his light overcoat, he tore down the coat in a sudden fit of anger and flung it on the ground. In his old age he could not endure even the most tactful forms of mendacity, pretence, silence, concealment, and he had been really worn out by the pressure of the preceding years. Now, for example, if he imagined himself having to smuggle the weapon out of the flat—the unlawful possession of arms carried a minimum penalty of ten or fifteen years' imprisonment at this time—if he imagined himself hiding it under his coat and stealthily taking it out of the house, in the evening, after dark, in order to meet as few passers-by as possible, but before curfew, so that the porter should not catch sight of him—and carrying it to the banks of the Danube, as far as possible by deserted side-streets, hiding there, walking up and down, peering about to see that he was not being observed from behind a heap of stones or from a window behind his back—if he imagined himself like this, with his head shrunk between his shoulders, his fluttering eyelids moving furtively like a thief's, he was seized by a physical malaise so violent that he began to retch and on one occasion brought up the potato soup which his charwoman cooked for his dinner. Was he bringing up his past or his future?

HE UNDRESSED, had a bath, put on clean underclothes and dressed again. He sat around in the unheated room by the window till midnight, contemplating the ruined house opposite, in which one dark window-frame grinned right into his eyes. In the whole street only one lamp was lit, and that illuminated only the piles of rubble and litter which had grown around it.

"Mary," he said to the charwoman, gazing at his coat that lay on the floor. "If you hide this weapon from my conscience once more, you will never set foot in this flat again."

"Oh, my God, stop tormenting me!" said the old woman. "If they find it in your flat, they'll lock you up, sir."

"Report me, then we'll get it over more quickly," replied the professor. He turned on his heels and went out of the flat.

The long, narrow street was even more disagreeable by daylight, with the occasional passer-by tripping up among the snow-covered rubble, with whirls of dust that the wind had rolled out from the ruins of collapsed houses leaping about like frogs. Close by the main entrance, a municipal dustbin stood with its lid open: it was rumored that an escaped prisoner had hidden there for two days until a police patrol had chanced to come across him in a half-frozen condition. By the dustbin, a small mound covered with snow marked a temporary grave in which the inhabitants of the street had buried some stranger. Further on, a fallen lamppost lay across the road.

By the time the old man reached Rákosi Street, a thick fog had descended on the city. Trams and buses were still not running, pedestrians filled the road as well as the pavement, pressing against each other, stumbling behind each other as they rolled in a thick unbroken stream toward the city center. Anyone moving in the opposite direction was caught up in the flood and swept into a side-street. The crowd was hurrying;

some were forcing a way for themselves by running; now and again, in their wake, the thin cries of an old woman they had pushed aside swirled about in the fog. In mute silence, with heads down and lips tightly shut, people trod the mud, which the cold wind, blowing in from the Danube, crowned with ever new clouds of dust: the gusts dislodged the dust from the rubble of the houses, stirred it in the air, then struck it down on the ground. On the way from the Eastern railway station, a long line of lorries cut through the crowd, people jumped out of their way without a word, pushed aside those walking near them, and continued their journey without a curse.

The old man was forced off the pavement. A dense crowd, compact, impenetrable, was lining up in front of a shop with shutters drawn, lashing its speedily growing tail over the pavement onto the road. "What's on sale here?" asked the professor.

"That doesn't matter, father," said a young woman in slacks, with a scarf holding her hair in place.

"Toilet paper, sir," announced a young man standing beside him: the professor remembered his face from the university, but could not put a name to it. The pressure was no less severe at the corner of Lenin Boulevard. Emke House was burnt down to the ground, only its roofless walls rose up to the winter sky; opposite, the National Theater had fortunately been hit only once, on the scene-dock side. The Corvin store, too, remained undamaged. Meanwhile the fog lifted, or had been swept on by the force of the wind toward Józsefvaros: Rákosi Street was now visible as far as the Urania Cinema. The professor cast a look of disgust at his mud-bespattered trousers, and then trudged on slowly. Repair work had already started on the Rókus Chapel; further on, scaffolding had been raised around a block of flats that had suffered minor damage.

In spite of the cold and the wind the market was set up all along Rákosi Street. Men lived on, with touching zeal, and were buying worn clothes, imitation jewelry, pans and stockings from the obliging hawkers in the doorways, who likewise wished to live on. We are as hardy as bugs, thought the professor dejectedly, and how much more intelligent! Pressing his elbows against his sides, he carefully fought his way through the crowd that surrounded the traders, and was wholeheartedly bargaining with them. Here and there they were already selling Christmas-tree decorations for the festival, which was imminent, with some extra charge in view of the difficult times. The old man would certainly have bought something if he had had anyone to buy it for. He turned onto Museum Boulevard where there were fewer people than on Lajos Kossuth Street. A vacuum has strong powers of suction: the old man cut through the deserted ruins of Calvin Square where a burnt-out tank still lay on the snow-covered road, and made his way toward the bridge. He resolved to cross to Buda. He was unaware that under the distant attraction of the silence, he was unconsciously quickening his step.

BENEATH THE arcades of the market-hall, a man was measuring out wine from a large-bellied demijohn.

"Five-sixty," he said.

"Five-sixty," repeated the professor.

The wine was cloudy, with a somewhat bitter taste. A few yards further on, they were selling plum brandy at a small table for three forints a glass. The old man drank a thimbleful of this too, but it made him neither more bitter nor happier. He was shown black or white cotton at thirty forints a spool, but he declined these offers with a hesitant movement. He learned from the conversation of those who were passing beside him that Christmas trees were already on sale on the first floor of the market hall.

"They're already selling Christmas trees on the first floor," a gray-haired woman with a kindly face said to him; she too had stopped for a glass of plum brandy by the open-air stall. "You should buy them now if you've got the money, because later on you only get the leftovers."

"They are selling them on the first floor?" asked the professor.

There were many people walking over the bridge, mostly coming from Buda to Pest. The old man nevertheless stopped in the middle and, leaning over the railings as was his custom, he yielded himself for a minute to the attraction of Death. This time he was seized so strongly that he became giddy, and he pulled himself back instantly. His was a thoughtful, irresolute nature, but he despised flirting with fate. Deep down the river whirled, dark gray; it was not yet frozen over, but near the bank films were already beginning to form, here and there an occasional small, semi-transparent piece of ice floated toward him, and disappeared under the bridge, floating on the crest of a wave. The strong wind drew all ten of its claws over the surface of the river. There were many people walking over the bridge; the professor went on. When he noticed that he was cold, he thrust both his hands—for a time—into his overcoat pockets. As the wind had blown his hat down into the Danube, his head too began to feel cold beneath his sparse gray hair, which fluttered this way and that. On reaching the end, he hesitated for a moment whether to turn left or right, then, with the houses of Béla Bartók Street giving him shelter from the wind, he trudged comfortably along in the direction of the Körtér.

WHEN HE arrived at Kelenföld Station, already pretty tired, he immediately boarded a train that had just arrived from the Southern station. He hurried, so as not to have to think. When, in reply to his question, a traveler told him that the train was going to Györ, he nodded assent. "That's right," he said, "good." The train waited in the station a long time; he could have got out to buy a ticket, but he was afraid of having to wait at the booking-office. The train was packed. But in one compartment they nevertheless squeezed together to make room for the old man.

"Going Sopron way?" asked his neighbor, as soon as the train had left the station.

"Yes," said the professor.

"For the pig-killing?"

"I don't understand you," said the professor.

"To relations, for the pig-killing?"

"I have no relations there," said the professor.

The questioner was a young man with a sympathetic face, and a pleasant smile; over the smile he had a thick moustache. "Pig-killing's not good," he said. "They send back two hundred men a day, all of whom are on their way to relations for the pig-killing."

The people in the compartment laughed. There were eight in all, in addition to the old man; they had visibly warmed to one another, since leaving the Southern Station. Most of them seemed to be people from the country: the fact that they were well fed showed that. The train went on, slowly, but still too quickly. The old man looked out through the window watching Gellért Hill as it receded further and further.

"Got a permit to go through the frontier zone?" asked the young man.

"No."

"No matter," said the young man. "You can get it at Györ. Everything for money. When you've got to Sopron . . . of course it's better if you disappear at Balfürdö or even a station earlier. Are you going to Agfalva or Magyarfalva?"

"I don't know yet," said the old man, "whether I am going to Agfalva or Magyarfalva."

"No matter," said the young man with the smiling moustache, "you'll get addresses at Györ. The thing is, though, that the cops mustn't get you before Györ. They're keeping a close eye on this train now. Do you know anybody there?"

"No," said the old man.

"Don't know anybody at Györ? How can that be?" asked an elderly, stout woman in a head-scarf in amazement. "Don't know anybody at Györ?"

"It happens sometimes, people don't know anybody at Györ," said a sour-faced, thin man by the window. "Last time I met somebody like that at Debrecen; he didn't know anybody either."

The people laughed. "Don't you know the Steiners?" asked the old woman in the head-scarf, who did not know what the joke was. "The people who used to have the big bicycle shop on Lajos Kossuth Street?"

The professor turned away his head. "I do not know them."

"Pity," said the old woman. "True, they ran away to America in November."

IT WAS growing dark quickly: through the window the snow-covered lands too were graying, but even so their radiance still filled the compartment with a slow glimmer of light. The train was unheated, but the nine people warmed one another in sympathy. In the corridor, a single weak electric bulb burned, from which the light fell on a young married couple sitting by the window; they were obviously from Pest, and were withdrawn into themselves, shut off from the conversation; they spoke, with exaggerated cordiality, only when someone addressed them directly. "Someone left us in November for Vienna," said the old woman in the head-scarf, "as if they were going to the next village, to Abda or Öttevény. He got into a taxi and it took him to the frontier for five hundred forints; there he raised his hat and walked over. My nephew went like that too, with the missus and his three kids. A week later they sent a message home on the radio that they had arrived safely, thank God."

"When the Pest train arrived at Györ," said another

woman, "the conductor went out onto the platform and shouted: '*Emigrants change, platform two.*' Don't let's forget to make a note of the password."

The people laughed. "On the Hegyeshalom train, though," said the man sitting next to the old man, the young man with the smiling moustache, "the driver stopped between Levél and Hegyeshalom on the open line, and the conductor went all the way through the train, shouting: '*Emigrants all change.*'"

"There are many going even now," said the old woman in the head-scarf. "I don't know what for. Why, I've read in the paper that there are shows on now in the theaters in Pest."

Someone opened the door from outside, let in a draft of smoky cold, then shut the door again. "Why are you laughing, may I ask?" inquired the lady in the head-scarf of the sour-faced, thin man by the window. "I'm right, aren't I? There's even a show at the Opera; true, only in the morning."

"People are confused," said the other woman, "they don't know what to do. Should they stay—should they go? It's bad either way. There's a famous sportsman living next door to me; he was sent out to the Olympic Games, in America. . . ."

"Australia," said the sour-faced man. "Melbourne."

"Could be," said the woman. "There they promised him a hundred thousand dollars if he'd stay abroad . . . but no, he wouldn't stay . . . this . . . that . . . his wife, his child, his mother are in Budapest . . . he's coming home. And he did come home too, but by then his wife, his mother, and his child had run away to Austria. Now he sits at home in his empty flat and bangs his head against the wall."

The people laughed again. "There are special cases like that," said the smiling man with the thick moustache, who was sitting next to the old man. "At my brother-in-law's, in Pest, there's a young couple living on the second floor of the house— the fellow goes out in the morning and tells his darling wife to pack—he'll get a car for the afternoon, and they'll go to

Vienna. In the afternoon a big Csepel truck draws up in front of the house, packed with people—the driver gets out, goes into the house, rings and tells the woman that her husband's waiting for her downstairs, she must come down at once. So darling goes down. The driver pushes her into the truck from behind, bangs the hood down on her, and off they go—they don't stop till Wiener Neustadt. Yes, but the driver made a mistake and rang at the first floor instead of the second, fetched down some unknown dame with his shouting. Her husband came home from the office in the evening and racked his brains wondering what had become of his wife."

They laughed again. "My God," said the old woman in the head-scarf, "what are they going to do now, poor things? The best thing would be if they swapped partners."

"The best thing would be if they hanged themselves," said an older, gray-haired man who had not spoken a word until then. "Damn all these slackers who've nothing better to do than to slink off abroad. Why don't they stay at home, blast their eyes! Why don't they help put right the damage they've done?"

"You've got something there," said the second woman.

The gray-haired man turned toward her. "I've got something, have I?" he repeated irritably. "What do you mean, I've got something? When every decent man—don't take this amiss, comrade!—when every decent man is working his head off to set the country in order, that's when they play the look-out man for these lunatics? For the strikers who cause millions' worth of damage to the country every day? For the ex-cops and county-court judges, who want to bring back the landlords and Jewish bankers on us? Let 'em open their bleary eyes. God have mercy on 'em—don't they see our necks are at stake?

THERE WAS a sudden silence in the compartment. The young man with the smiling moustache looked out through the window. He watched with half-shut eyes the slowly darkening, snowy landscape with the telegraph poles that suddenly dashed at him, and, quickly changing places with one another, had the same effect on the retina as an unbroken drumroll has on the ear. The others looked away. Suddenly the brutal clatter of the wheels broke through out of the silence. "The comrade and I know each other, I think," said the sour-face thin man. "We know each other, don't we? You worked in the police at Győr, right?—in '52 or '53?"

The gray-haired man did not reply.

"Or was it before '52? In '50 or '49?"

"It wasn't either in '49 or after," said the gray-haired man. "Most of the time under Rákosi and Company, the only place you might have met me was in a cell in the Budapest Central Prison. I was in there for sixty-two months, comrade, not a day less. And I'm not running away even now, though one lung and a kidney have gone west."

The clatter of the wheels became audible again. "My God, let's keep off politics," said the old woman in the head-scarf. "You'll only burn your mouth, sooner or later."

"Are those who clear out keeping off politics?" said the gray-haired man, with a sudden flush in his face. "Or are they the only ones who don't have to keep off politics?" He pressed his fur cap onto his head, leapt up and pushed his way out of the compartment. The young couple from Budapest sitting by the door, terrified, shrank back, drawing in their legs, and looked after him. The glass door slammed. Outside, in the smoky corridor, people were jammed tight; the gray-haired man violently forced a way through them with his elbows. The couple from Budapest turned away their heads again, and stared ahead with a remote expression on their lean faces. "Where are you going?" asked the man with the thick moustache, smiling genially, of a peasant boy who was sitting bolt upright with taut thigh muscles, and was similarly staring silently ahead, but beneath his prominent, Tartar cheekbones he smiled readily with the others when he saw their mouths opening to laugh. On his arm he wore a broad black armband, and had a small porkpie hat on his head. "Sopron," he said.

"And then?"

"No further," said the boy.

"Well," smiled the man with the moustache, you can speak up bravely here now. We're Hungarians, we stick together. You're not from Sopron?"

"No. Kiskunmajsa, Bács County," said the boy, smiling readily.

"And what are you going to Sopron for?"

"My mother has died," said the boy. "I am going to her funeral."

"In Sopron?"

"She lived there with her elder sister," said the boy, smiling, "since she lost her husband."

"And the funeral's in Sopron?"

The boy lifted up his index finger to explain. "It wasn't worth it to bring her home," he said. "Counting all the expenses it's cheaper if I take the wreath there."

Above his head, on the luggage rack, was a small evergreen wreath; everybody looked up. "You're bringing that from home?" asked the young man with the pleasant smile. "You could have got it in Sopron."

"Who knows!" said the boy, smiling. "What if that's the very place where they're sold out now? Only two people were knocked on the head where I live, so there's still some in stock."

Outside, it was now completely dark, thick yellow streaks of sparks drifting back from the engine were fanning out over the fields of snow, until an occasional stronger gust of wind beat them down to the ground. "Why are you keeping your hat on your head, my friend?" asked the man with the smiling moustache, shaking his head disapprovingly. "We're not in a pub."

"He must be taking a sparrow underneath it to Sopron, in case they're sold out of them too there," said the sour-faced thin man. The smiling young man leaned forward a little and with a sudden movement lifted the little porkpie hat off the boy's head. A frightened, faint cry was heard. Out of the hat a blood-stained wad of cotton-wool fell to the ground. On the boy's skull, which was shaved, a bleeding, black swelling as big as a man's fist bulged out; in several places there were broad cuts in the skin and the black, clotted blood, like a complicated network of canals, cut crisscross into the scalp, which had turned bloodred with the inflammation. The old woman in the head-scarf, terrified, clapped her hand to her mouth. Somebody sighed audibly in the sudden silence; again only the clatter of the wheels of the train could be heard. The young wife from Budapest stared, horrified, with round, wide-open eyes at the boy, who watched with a motionless, stiff expression the face of the young man with the moustache, who was smiling warmly.

"Hm!" said the latter, "a good-sized sparrow. Where did you get it?"

"In a pub," said the peasant boy, smiling. "Kindly give me back my hat!"

"You didn't have a scuffle with the law?"

"Excuse me, no," said the boy quietly. "In a pub. Kindly give me back my hat!"

Water had to be fetched because the young wife from Budapest had fainted. Her husband pushed his way through the people squeezed in the corridor, but either there was no washbasin in the toilet, or if there was, no water came out of it. Meanwhile his wife had been revived by the old woman in the head-scarf with a nip of brandy; by this time the boy had fortunately put his hat on his head again. "The only thing I don't understand," said the young man with the bushy moustache, "is why this journey was so urgent that you didn't even have time to go to the doctor."

"But my mother died," said the boy, smiling.

THE TRAIN slowed down, as if it wanted to have a good look around before drawing into the station. Either the coaches had turned a corner, or the wind had changed, for the streaks of smoke and the streams of sparks which till then had gone past the carriage window now appeared on the corridor side. Here, in a siding, some snow-covered railway carriages were standing, coupled at the front to an old-fashioned engine with small wheels and a ridiculously long funnel. Behind it, the main road, running at right angles to it, was empty as far as the eye could see, on both sides, with an occasional deep snowdrift behind the poplars, which were gesticulating in the storm.

"Bicske?" asked a voice.

"We've passed it already," said the sour-faced thin man.

"Tatabánya?"

But the train did not stop; it accelerated again.

"One thing's certain," said the sour-faced man, addressing the professor, "humanity is in a turmoil all the world over. You are from Budapest, sir, you've surely heard the case of the famous Budapest actor, Cservö József?"

"I had not heard of it," said the old man.

"Go on!" shouted the old woman in the head-scarf, folding, her arms over her questioning, ample bosom.

"He came down to us to Györ to run away, too," said the sour-faced man, with a bitter smile. "The roadside inn was his rendezvous with the gentleman who was to have taken him in his car to Vienna."

"I can assure you," interrupted the young man with the pleasant smile and the moustache, "I can assure you, in that inn even today you may find a means of transport which you can board without a headache. Of course there are no truck routes now, but private cars, and foreign journalists too. . . ."

"Thank you," said the old man. "How do you know I want to run away?"

The young man burst out laughing, and waved his hand.

"I am honored," said the professor. "Why don't you run away?"

"I manage in this little country," said the young man, smiling. "I've no trouble with anybody here, either above or below. But those who want to go, let 'em go."

"What is your occupation, if I am not being offensive?" asked the professor.

"Now this, now that," said the young man with a pleasant smile. "I manage for myself. You must respect the authorities, sir; but that goes for abroad as much as for here at home. On the other hand, if I understand the bigwigs here aright, why should I go to a country where they can't even do stewed veal properly?"

"My God, veal!"

"That's what I'm going to have for dinner tonight," said the young man. I've brought one-and-a-half kilos of leg from Budapest."

"And I've got two lengths of good, strong rose-colored cotton," said the old woman in the head-scarf. "True, I queued for it all day."

"In a word," said the sour-faced man, "the artist gentleman dropped in at the roadside inn and ordered half a liter of mulled wine. When his friend came with the car, they ordered another liter and later, toward evening, heaven knows where from, they got hold of a gypsy too. The artist gentleman sang and wept all night. He could not bring himself to bid farewell to his beloved country. By dawn the next morning they had embraced, staggered out to the car, and set off. They gave the gypsy alone a thousand forints because they thought that he would certainly be the last gypsy in their lives. But half an hour later they were already seen to be coming back, making straight for Budapest at one hundred kilometers an hour."

The peasant boy with the swelling on his head guffawed loudly; the others too, recovered from their previous alarm, laughed emotionally.

"On the other hand," said the sour-faced man "there are some who are dead set on this trip, with nothing more than the clothes they're standing up in, no luggage, no nothing"—the old man thought that the man was winking at him—"they're dead set on it, if I may say so, as if their lives depended on it. I know somebody else they caught on the frontier and sent back. He tried a second time, again he only got into a jam, again they sent him off with a return ticket. When he was hooked the third time, the commander of No. 2 Frontier Guard at Csorna, a good Hungarian, said to him: 'Look here, if I see you again I'll have you put in irons and throw you over the frontier myself.'"

At Komárom the train stopped for a longer time. The young peasant boy got out for a drink of water. "We'll be in Györ in an hour," said the man with the smiling moustache, yawning, when they had started again. The train rolled slowly out of the station; in the compartment, which was growing drowsy, the howling of the storm outside could be heard. When the police reached the compartment they had already gone through the stop at Ipartelep, which is not more than two kilometers from Györ. In the corridor more frequent motion, stifled, nervous fragments of talk announced in advance the arrival of the law. The sour-faced man leaned toward the professor's ear.

"If you really don't know anybody in the town," he whispered, "mention my younger brother—Brátesz György, an agricultural official of the Council. I'll fix it with him."

Since they were sitting in the last carriage, the detectives quickly completed the check. They only cast a glance at the professor's personal papers, which this time he had fortunately not left behind in the pocket of another coat, and gave them back to him without a word. With a slow whistle the train drew into Györ station. Only now did they notice that the young peasant boy had apparently got off the train at Komárom. The wreath for the grave of his mother remained on the empty luggage rack.

THE STORM grew no calmer toward evening. By the time the old man, with the aid of willing directions from the local inhabitants, had reached the roadside inn, the snow had started, lashing its thick flakes into his face and eyes. The old man's head felt cold. He resolved to buy a hat the next day. Where? The little inn was packed, but he did not see a single hat to his liking on the pegs. It is only one step from running away to stealing a hat, but it is a step we do not take!

"I cannot accept your kind offer to smuggle me across the frontier in a Belgian Red Cross ambulance," said the old man to an acquaintance of his, a doctor from Budapest, who had sat down at his table. When he had seen the professor, after a minute's quick calculation, he had suddenly leapt up from his place, left his companions, run to the professor, and greeted him with cordial, but delicately concealed joy. "I cannot accept it, because my nature is full of guile, and I do not wish to contribute to the soothing of your troubled conscience, however little it would take to do that. Further, I cannot accept it, because I do not share your viewpoint that a man can accept from everybody, without discrimination, what they can offer him. I do not wish to strengthen you in your youthful belief, or even in your experience, that you can flay seven skins off one cat. Further . . ."

The old man was suddenly silent. "Enough!" he said irritably. "Let us take it that I did not justify my resolution."

The window under which they were sitting had been completely covered with snow by the wind; it was no longer possible to see through it. No new guests arrived in the snowstorm, which was continually gathering strength. None of the earlier ones ventured into the whistling, howling blizzard outside, which was growing stronger in the chimney and, dragging the smoke with it, was pressing into the bar through the stove door, which would not shut properly. In a circle at the small tables, the people were drinking, quietly smoking their pipes. The radio was being turned off and on all the time.

"All right, dear professor," said the stout doctor from Budapest, laughing, "let us take it that you did not justify your resolution. On the other hand I am delighted to see that since we last met you have lost none of your freshness of outlook and your youthful outspokenness. So you can take a seat in my car without fear. I will not send you the bill."

"I will not take a seat," said the old man.

"You will not take a seat," repeated the doctor from Budapest. "Really, what have I done to you? Is it that once or twice I have been mistaken in my political judgment of the situation and have openly admitted my mistakes?"

"That is it," said the professor. "Why did you not stick to them?"

"Are you making fun of me, dear professor?" asked the doctor, raising his eyebrows over his pale low forehead.

"Of course," said the old man. "I have nothing better to do."

The stout doctor, after a moment's amazed silence in which he pulled back into place his tie which had slipped sideways, and regained his presence of mind, leaned over in his excitement so close to the old man's face that the latter could smell his sour breath. "Are you reproaching me for having been taken in by the infernal Rákosi propaganda machine?" he asked, panting nervously. "You know, the whole country was in step with them. Or do you resent the fact that in my justified indignation I drew the obvious conclusions and went into opposition for a short time? Or are you offended with me because I have now accepted a post in the Ministry of Health, guided by the conviction that this country must at last be set in order? Little men like me have only suffered history so far; now the time has come for them to make it themselves. I have outlined to you the reactions of a healthy soul, my dear professor."

"The reactions of a healthy soul?" repeated the old man. "And why do you want to smuggle me out? To cover yourself here too?"

"Out of respect," said the doctor, smiling. "Out of human respect. You must have a good reason for running away.

"I have," said the old man.

The stout, pale-faced doctor burst into an exasperated laugh. "Of course! You have had seventeen men executed. You have strangled two with your own hands. Still waters run deep."

The old man felt his head: his hair was beginning to dry. If he went out into the night for a walk, perhaps he would not catch cold.

"What would the world come to, my dear professor, if everybody was a hero?" said the stout doctor. "As it is, we murder quite enough people, primarily of course out of cowardice. But what a permanent slaughterhouse the world would become, if everybody clung heroically to his convictions! I will go further: if people in general had any convictions other than this single belief, that they have a right to life. This one belief causes enough nasty business, especially now! Let us not expect more of human nature than it can give, my dear professor! I regard him as an honest man, who can reconcile his needs somehow or other with current demands, that is, who so orders his little life, that as far as possible it shall not suffer through the greed of others . . . who tries, as far as possible for him, to agree with those who are more powerful than he, and does not injure beyond measure those who are weaker. A solid little life, my dear professor, under the aegis of general peace and disarmament. Let us not be frivolous, please! Let us recognize our limits! Let us whistle, if we are afraid in the dark! In my experience, every hero costs, on a conservative estimate, at least a thousand innocent victims, of whom not one would have had any other desire than to be left in peace to crow on his own little dunghill. The murderous instincts of an average man like me can be amply satisfied within his small family circle including, possibly, lodgers and good neighbors. In the depths of his heart everybody honors those who are stronger than he, that is, the authorities. They say that the Lord spits out the lukewarm. It is not true, my dear professor! The Lord expelled Lucifer and delights in him who obeys, for ever and ever, Amen."

"Is that all?" asked the old man.

The doctor from Budapest broke into a smile all over his plump, pale, spongy-skinned face.

"One complains a little, grows a little indignant, grumbles a little within the permitted limits—but having reached those limits, turns one's face toward heaven and with a heart full of gratitude begins to praise the authorities of the time. That is the true *vox humana*, my dear professor."

"Is that all?" asked the old man.

IN THE room, the choking mixture of tobacco smoke and the smell of coal became more and more intolerable. An occasional guest who had lost patience got up from his chair and peeped outside the door, but the snowdrift that immediately swept in on the floor and the tablecloth-rending gale prompted him to instant retreat. "Of course, of course, it is not easy to remain honorable," said the doctor with a gesture of resignation, pursing his thick lips. "The lightning speed of tactics with which history flashes demands superhuman flexibility. No wonder we go wrong now and then."

"I repeat the question," said the old man. "Why do you wish to smuggle me over the frontier?"

The doctor leaned over the old man's ear. "I shall not be coming back for the time being, either," he whispered. "It has come to my knowledge that my good wife reported me yesterday to the police, because I associated myself with the demands of the young people in October. As you see, my dear professor, you can feel quite safe if you entrust yourself to me."

"Go to blazes!" said the old man. He stood up and moved to another table.

In the morning, through the good offices of a waiter, he climbed onto a truck that took him for a thousand forints into the frontier zone as far as the Kapuvár bus station. Here he boarded the bus and set off as scheduled on the main road, which the gale had swept clean during the night. But scarcely half an hour later, even before Hegykö, they were held up at a bend. Half a meter of soft snow had piled up on this section of the road: the bus drove onto it, but was unable either to make its way through or to back off it. The snow started again. It fell so thickly that at about noon, when the driver, who had struggled on foot as far as the nearest village, returned with some men with shovels, the wheels were already invisible beneath the snow.

But the old man did not wait for them. With his train companions, the quiet young couple from Budapest, whom he had come across again in the bus, the wife's sister who lived at Györ, and her four-year-old son, he set out on foot. The young husband, an employee in a general store at Budapest, was carrying two heavy cases. The two women and the old man took it in turns to hold the child in their arms. The young man from Budapest lent the professor his dark blue Swiss cap. It was an hour's journey to the farm where the farmer was to take them across the frontier; but the hour became three hours' heavy walking. They turned off the main road onto one of the roads leading toward the farm and immediately lost their way. Beneath the thick cover of snow, the road could no longer be distinguished from the plowland which surrounded it. First one, then another, sank into the snow up to the knees. The child cried; only in the old stranger's arms did he calm down slightly. The woman from Budapest had to stop frequently; the heavy going was too much for her heart. It was snowing ceaselessly. The journey was easier if the wind caught them from behind, but if it blew in their faces, they had to exert themselves like a swimmer in a river going against the current. Once, the young wife from Győr fell into a ditch up to her waist; fortunately when it happened the child was sitting on the professor's back. Having waded across the ditch, they came out again onto the main road, at the same point from which they had started three hours earlier. Even in the thickly falling snow they could clearly make out, a few hundred yards further on, behind the snow-drift, the snow-covered roof of the bus, and that the men shoveling were conversing with the travelers.

"Well, here we are, my children," said the old man gaily.

ON THE main road it was impossible to lose one's way. They set off toward Hegykő, where they would soon engage someone to take them to the farm. They knocked at the first house at the edge of the village, and rested for an hour. The peasant asked for one hundred forints per head for showing the way to the farm.

It was a deserted farm, north of Balf, in the marshes of Lake Fertö, far from the main road, at the end of a cart-track, which naturally was now also covered by the snow. But the old man's party now overtook another group on the way, three men and two women, who were plainly heading in the same direction and seemed as exhausted as they were; one of the men, leaning on a stick, was limping badly. They caught sight, by a distant row of poplars, of another still longer line of people who seemed to run toward them diagonally. Behind the regular black trellis of the poplars, beneath the low ceiling of clouds, as it were in a never-ending cage, small human forms, loosely scattered, were moving behind one another in the dirty light of the snow. In the farmhouse itself there were already fifteen or twenty people sitting in the smoky kitchen, crouching on the bench by the fire and on the bed. Only on the floor could the newcomers find room.

The farmer asked for two thousand forints per head for the route, payable in advance, for children too. He was a stocky, broad-shouldered man, with a bristly face on which fatigue had drawn deep trenches below his eyes. He stood in the door in wellingtons. In his hand was a gun that even later he did not put down—and with a quietly searching look from under his gray eyebrows he individually scrutinized the new arrivals crowding into the kitchen. His son stood by the door and flashed a light into the faces of the newcomers. Behind him stood another older peasant, his brother-in-law, who also carried a gun in his hand. No bargaining, said the farmer: he himself had to pass on a large proportion of the money, and not even Christ's tomb was guarded for nothing. It was doubtful whether they could set out that night. He had not yet received a report whether the route was passable. If they postponed setting out until the next night, they must spend the day in the barn. But he could give no one anything to eat. To the question whether it was possible to cross the frontier safely, he shrugged his shoulders. If the route was free from danger, he would not be asking for two thousand forints. Three days earlier the frontier guard had shot a member of his group, and wounded another, but the others had got through. But in this snowstorm—if they could make a start—perhaps the route would be safer than it usually was at that time. The frontier guards were reluctant to risk frostbite in an ear or foot.

THE FARMER, in spite of all his surliness, appeared a reliable man; by contrast with the generally hesitant manner of the peasants, he spoke out what was up his sleeve, or at least what was on his tongue. He had scarcely finished his short speech when the group approaching from the direction of the row of poplars arrived: fourteen newcomers, perhaps even more exhausted than the others. There were many women and children among them, and they had been walking since morning, in snow that in places was up to their knees. There was now not an inch of space in the room; they sat on the earth floor of the kitchen, or lay down, leaning their backs and heads against the tiled fireplace. A mother of three children, one of whose sons had been left behind on the way unnoticed, broke into spasmodic, unrestrained weeping: at the sound of her moans, the children in the room grew alarmed and began to whimper, terrified.

Meanwhile the man who had been sent out to study the condition of the snow returned. The four men, who were joined by the farmer's wife, a powerful gray-haired peasant woman in boots, withdrew into a corner of the kitchen and consulted together in low voices; it was noticeable from their gestures and their tone of voice that they did not agree. The woman would plainly have liked to be rid as soon as possible of the wretched swarm of locusts which had overrun her house: clearly she feared that the large number of fugitives who had been converging on the farm in several groups and from several directions in the course of the day had aroused the attention of the frontier guards, and that in spite of the bad weather they would come on them by chance. The four men, however, were visibly loath to risk the journey; their reluctance was quite clearly explained by the repeated plaintive moans and howls of the storm, and by the incessant quivering of the knotted acacia trees that stood before the door. "The roads are not too good," the farmer finally announced in the sudden silence, broken only by the occasional cry of a weeping child; the frosty weather too was unfavorable; the journey could not be recommended to women or children. But if there were any among the single men who felt sufficiently strong to start at once, then they could set out in one or two groups, depending on the number of applicants. But only healthy, strong men should come, he added conscientiously, because the weak ones would delay the others; and they would be compelled to leave to their fate any who dropped behind on the way. The two thousand forints per head was to be paid in advance.

"Anybody who remains lying down on the road today will be frozen to death," said his brother-in-law beside him, gun in hand. "And if anybody slips, falls, and breaks or even just sprains his ankle, he should not count on the others being able to take him with them in this storm, and in such deep snow. So think it over well, because Christ is not everyone's friend."

Between fifteen and twenty presented themselves, including a girl in ski slacks and a short fur coat. Her hair was bound with a head-scarf and she carried a rucksack on her shoulders. She had slightly slanting eyes, and protruding cheekbones, and obstinately kept her mouth shut tight. "I have seven hundred and twenty forints," she said to the peasant. "That is all the money I have. If it is not enough for you, I shall cross the frontier a hundred yards behind you for nothing."

The old peasant thoughtfully examined the stubborn young face of the girl. "No bargaining," he said curtly. The girl remained defiantly silent and shrugged her shoulders. "If you go over alone, that of course costs no money," said the peasant after a time, turning his back on the girl.

They divided those who had presented themselves into three groups of six or seven each. The professor set out with the last one, an hour after the first party. The farmer was visibly unwilling to accept him among those going; he surveyed suspiciously the black overcoat on his tall, lean, slightly bent form, his silk scarf, and above it the wrinkles which six decades had drawn on the crumpled, narrow, bony face. "You would do better to wait another day," he said. The old man did not reply; he counted out the money into the hand of the peasant. Before setting off he bade farewell to the general store employee from Budapest and his family who were staying on in the farm, and gave the young husband the three thousand forints which he knew they were short of for their fee. He bough a quarter of a kilo of bread for the journey from the housewife for ten forints.

The cold was biting only when they came face-to-face with the wind. Fortunately it did not blow constantly all night, but sometimes desisted for a quarter or half an hour; then their lungs could rest a little, and afterward they could bear with more endurance the blows that the resurgent gusts dealt, crackling and whistling. The storm was sometimes so aggressive that they could regain their breath only by stopping for a minute or two—with legs apart, so as not to be knocked over by its force—and turning their heads back, filling their lungs with air, then turning round cautiously and setting off again with lowered heads, like bulls about to charge. There was of course no protection against the hard snowflakes which were flying with great force and dizzy speed, no means of preventing their penetrating into every opening of the bare face and under scarves and clothes, however tightly done up; eyes, mouth, nose, and ears were filled with snow, and with every new gust you noticed with indignation and surprise that in your annoyance you burst into tears again and again. By the time the tears running down from your eyes had frozen on your face, the next gust of wind had caused new ones to well up.

The storm had at any rate this advantage, that in places it had swept the road clean, or to describe it more accurately, those narrow paths and balks that led among the plowlands or crackling fields of maize which had also been blown bare. At such times there was no need to look at the ground continuously, and you could devote all your presence of mind and strength to husbanding your breath. On these sections of the road the hard-frozen, crumbling soil appeared beneath the close-shaven layer of snow; feet clung happily to its clods.

There was no sky above the heads of the walkers. Light came only from the moon. The flakes, whirling around where the ceiling might be, sometimes flying upward aslant in the form of a pillar or swooping to the ground like a gigantic swarm of moths, occasionally let a little weak glimmer of light seep through toward the earth. On both sides the broad coverings of snow stood out from the restless darkness with an even, autonomous light. The continuous roar of the wind was almost deafening. "What is the matter?" asked the professor, panting a little, of a man stumbling in front of him who had suddenly stopped and was looking about hesitantly.

"I can't see," said the man.

"What d'you mean, you can't see?"

"My spectacles are broken."

"Now?"

"At the start of the journey," said the man. "At first I got on somehow, but it seems my eyes have tired. Now I can see nothing."

"Never mind," said the old man. "Take my arm, we'll go together."

On the clear sections of the road they managed quite well, in spite of the narrowness of the path, but whenever they had to wade through a snowdrift, in which they were sometimes buried above the knees, or had to stride across a ditch, they dropped fifty or a hundred yards behind the people ahead of them.

"Trust me!" said the old man panting. "Hold on tight to me. You may as well close your eyes."

The wind roared across the plain with an Ice Age passion.

"What did you say?" shouted the man, turning his mouth toward the professor's ear. "I didn't hear what you said, for the wind."

ON SOME sections of the journey snowdrifts two or three me-
ters deep rose up; they had to go around them and then find
their way back again to the snow-covered path. The danger was
that if they dropped too far behind and lost sight of the people
ahead of them, they would lose their way. Footprints were
buried by the blizzard in an instant. Fortunately the six men
ahead of them—including the farmer's son, the leader of the
group—on one occasion halted for a longer time; from afar it
seemed as if they were examining some object lying on the
ground. It was the frozen body of an elderly man, which was
leaning against a tree in a sitting position. When they moved it
from its place, it fell on its back, with knees raised up toward
the sky, like a wooden doll. It was already stiff, it could not be
straightened out from its immodest posture, and since it was
dead, did not deserve to have much time wasted on it.

They had already, earlier on, met the scattered debris of the
great migration. A hundred yards or so behind the farm, a car
that had broken down stood upright, embedded in the snow,
which was now up to its windows. On the edge of a maize field,
the outline of an overturned motorcycle showed beneath the
covering of snow; it had probably been abandoned only an
hour or two before. They also found an empty, much-patched
rucksack and a large, open pigskin handbag, whose contents
had clearly been removed by the previous parties; only a bundle
of papers tied up with ribbon and a comb with a long handle
showed through the snow beside it.

A few minutes after they had left the body, the professor
was relieved of the task of assisting the blinded man. Seeing the
two clinging together, a youth went up to the old man and offered him his arm. "A mistake, young man," the professor said
to him, irritably. "I am supporting, not being supported. If you
would be so kind as to take my place for a while . . ."

He was tired; he found it even harder to keep pace with this
group composed mostly of vigorous young men. It was near

midnight. They had already reached the swamp around Lake Fertö, where the going was even heavier, because beneath the covering of snow there ran thin layers of ice in places, and if you sank into the snow, or if the ice underneath broke, your shoes plunged into the squelching thick waters of the swamp, which immediately enclosed them and dragged them down still further. The old man's thin city shoes submitted to these tests reluctantly. His silk scarf, wound around his neck, had long ago become wet through, and stuck to his neck like a cold compress; his leather gloves too were soaking with the snow that thrust its way into them. He took both scarf and gloves off and threw them away. His shirt and collar were drenched from above by the slush dripping on them, from below by his own perspiration.

The nearer they drew to the immediate frontier zone, the northern area, glimmering in the light of the snow, grew more and more populous. The even rustling of the reeds in the gale was at times interrupted by a heavier force, and behind the swaying stems—instead of the expected, invisible gust—the thicker outlines of stooping human forms emerged, moving forward. Naked white faces looked out of the blades of vegetation that were as tall as men. "If you recognize a God," a woman's tired voice began to speak in the darkness, immediately beside the old man, "take this little girl with you. I can't go on. A student took the child into his arms, but at a nervously harsh admonition from the leader, they were compelled to leave to her fate the woman, who had sat down on the stump of a tree with another woman. "Go, go," she said, "there is nothing wrong with me. It's just that we're dead tired, both of us. If we can rest for half an hour and don't have to carry the child, then we can go on alone."

"Where's the child's father?" somebody asked.

"Go, go!" said the woman, weeping. "Take care of the child! God bless you. Her name is Bálint Etus, don't forget it! Make a note of it! We'll look for you in a minute. You're good people, you won't leave her, will you? Under her blouse, tied to her neck . . ."

Apparently the other woman nudged her because she was suddenly silent.

"Go now!" said the other woman. "Go!"

"Where is the child's father?" asked the old man.

"Go now, God bless you!" said the other woman, weeping loudly. "The child's name is Bálint Etus. Go, please, never mind us!"

Since the leader was threatening to turn back and go home if they delayed any longer, the group moved on again. "The frontier guards don't come much down here into the swamp," explained the young peasant. "But when they patrol the main Fertőrákos Road, they sometimes shoot into the reeds at random when they think of it, so as to frighten people." The man whom his father had mentioned before, who had been shot in his group, had caught such a blind bullet in his head, right between the eyes, while a woman had been wounded in the arm.

FOR A time the snow had stopped, and the gale too suddenly slackened. The journey, however, became more and more difficult, or the people weaker: every minute they sank up to their ankles in the soft, powdered snow, or even deeper into the mud that lay concealed beneath the snow. The task of lifting your feet out of this thick, sticky dough, and of propelling them forward again, together with the snow and mud that had stuck to your shoes, cost, at every step, an exertion and concentration of the will equal to that of an athlete preparing to break the record in the long jump. The muscles, saturated in lactic acid, would not obey. No one had a dry place on his body the size of the palm of his hand; the perspiration on the brow froze onto the face, burning.

It grew unexpectedly lighter. For a minute the moon shone through the flying clouds and the leader, looking continually to his left and right and incessantly turning back in a nervous manner, urged the people to press on more quickly. In the moonlight the black human forms moving on the white plain could be seen from afar. After less than a quarter of an hour, a sudden loud barking was heard on the left, presumably from the direction of the main road, and was immediately followed by some long-drawn-out shouts. The snow-covered land resounds over a great distance, and the barking police dog was clearly several kilometers away. But the possibility had to be reckoned with, that they were on the track of the group ahead, which had set out half an hour earlier—though neither could the more favorable possibility be excluded, that they were pursuing other fugitives hiding in the reeds. The moon shone forth again. The leader listened: there were no more shouts to be heard. When the first shot rang out, he cursed himself: even on Christmas Eve they did not leave people in peace. But the dog was silent. It was possible, said the leader, that his uncle had shot it: that was why they carried guns, not for use against men. The moon shone forth again. Another shot rang out, then a third, and a few minutes later the barking of the dog could be heard again. When a police dog picks up the scent, it follows the trail silently until it reaches what it is looking for; only then does it give voice. The moon shone forth again, but this time from another direction.

While the leader consulted with the people, who had gathered around him, the old man, who had fallen twice on the way from fatigue and dropped a good way behind the others, rejoined the group. This time he had a companion: the young peasant boy with the black armband, with his little porkpie hat on his bloodstained head. He had suddenly emerged from the reeds, with a newly acquired evergreen wreath on his arm, and joined him.

"Why are you carrying that wreath?" asked the old man.

The boy was silent. "I think they let you into the frontier

zone with it," said the old man. "But it cannot be of any use to you here, my boy."

"I am taking it to my mother's grave," said the boy, smiling.

"Now you can safely throw it away," replied the old man. "They won't let you cross the frontier with it."

The moon shone forth again. At the request of the leader, the people took off their coats and trousers, in spite of the biting cold. In white pants they were less exposed to the danger of being seen from afar. Most of them folded their outer garments and carried them into the reeds; they would get a change of clothes over there. The old man dropped behind again. He was disinclined to cross the frontier in his shirtsleeves and pants. He disliked arousing pity. All his life, hitherto, he had studiously avoided stripping in front of strangers. The young peasant remained with him, out of modesty or because he wanted to keep his clothes; his wreath he had thrown away already, at the instance of the professor.

The people were by now a burden to the old man. He wanted to be alone in that solemn moment, when he left his country forever, when he rose from the grave—or entered his grave? He sent the young boy on ahead, and sat down on a heap of snow. The small group to which he belonged—the last! —was now invisible. In their white underclothes they had disappeared on the snow-covered plain. The little thin, black form of the boy, too, was receding further and further into the distance. The old man was cold. He rubbed his skull to quicken the circulation in his scalp, tapped with numb feet on the snow. He had already thrown away the Swiss cap he had borrowed; it had been soaked through. The moon shone forth again, its faint hydrogenated light floating over the dead country. There was silence.

YOU CANNOT remain alone in the Sopron marshes at night, in ten degrees below freezing, thought the old man starting up in annoyance when he caught sight of the stubborn-mouthed young girl with the ski slacks and the rucksack, coming out of the parting reeds. She had followed them as the rearguard of the last group, at a distance of fifty or a hundred yards, as she had stated, for the whole time—for nothing! She will cross the frontier for nothing too, thought the old man. "What do you want from me?" he asked, in an angry whisper, because he was so hoarse that he could scarcely hear his own voice. "What is the matter? Why are you standing about here in front of me?"

"You mustn't stay sitting down in this cold, professor," said the girl, knitting her young brows, "however tired you are. . . . Get up, please!"

"How do you know me?" asked the old man.

"Get up, please!" repeated the girl with her impatient, stubborn mouth. "My God, you haven't even got a sweater! Get up, please!"

The old man looked for a time at the girl's pale young face and infinite pity took possession of his heart. "How do you know me?" he asked, in a hoarse whisper.

"Get up, please!" said the girl. "From the university—I studied philosophy."

"To my knowledge I give no lectures in the Faculty of Philosophy," said the old man.

The girl shrugged her shoulders impatiently. "Get up, please!" she said. "I am engaged to Kovács Feri, your student, sir."

"Feri?" repeated the old man. "The one who presented me with a gun the other day?"

"Yes," said the girl.

"And now where is the beloved wandering about?" asked the old man. "Is he skiing in the Tyrolean mountains? Or at Engadine? And you now hurrying urgently after him? Why has he left you behind here?"

"For God's sake, sir, why are you running away?" asked the

girl, involuntarily lowering her voice. Her lips trembled. "At your age? Why, you'd done nothing, sir."

"Of course I had," said the old man. "I had hidden a gun."

"Don't be funny!" said the girl. "Feri hid that in your flat."

"I should have reported it," said the old man.

The girl pursed her stubborn lips; her eyes flashed with rage.

"Look here, young woman!" said the old man. "Master Feri knew precisely why he hid that vile object in my flat, because Master Feri is not blind, is not deaf, and has not contracted softening of the brain. Why did he not hide it with my colleague Snarler, or my colleague Spy, or my colleague Hyde? Why with me? Because he lives near me? Because he knows that I like him? Really! The cause of this action was his doubtless reasonable and justified conviction that I agree with him."

"But, sir . . ."

"Silence!" said the old man sternly. "You say that I did not use that gun? I as good as used it. If I did not actually use it, the sole reason was that it was unbecoming to my years, or that I did not understand the mechanism, or that it was repugnant to my taste. I virtually used it, kindly understand! I used it with my every unexpressed thought, with my every unspoken word, with every atom of my being. It was used by others in my place, on the basis of tacit consent. And I am also responsible for the occasion when it was misused—just as Master Feri—and you too, young woman—and everybody in this country is responsible for what happened, for what happened before that and will happen after this. Not only little Baldhead Rákosi is responsible! One must accept responsibility, young woman. So I should go with a ridiculous gun under my arm to the police and give myself up? That they might forgive me and send me home? I don't want them to forgive me!"

"But sir, you really didn't do anything," said the girl in despair.

The old man laughed mockingly. "I did nothing?" he repeated. "That is why I am running away."

"Professor, sir, get up!" shouted the girl. "Your face is already blue."

"Spare yourself the trouble, young woman," said the old man impatiently. "Just go on nicely ahead. We will meet in the Tyrolean mountains."

The girl continued to stand in front of him. The moon shone forth again. The wind flicked a finger into the reeds, which rustled a little; then silence returned.

"Do not disturb me, young woman!" said the old man. "Be good enough to leave me alone! What right have you to intrude into my life? Honor, charity, you say? Do you wish to use me as a ridiculous example in order to repair what a whole country has neglected for a century? No, young woman, this people has not yet atoned for the past and the future. And do you imagine that if you take my arm with that dirty little hand of yours which is frozen red, carry me across the frontier and save my valuable life, that you will be repairing anything that way? Or that I can repair anything over there? Suppose I do not wish to? It cannot be repaired, young woman, nothing can be repaired. The dead cannot be resurrected, wounds can only appear to be healed. One must live honorably, young woman, not make reparation! Or do you imagine that it will not be possible to live here honorably again? Now leave me alone, please! Offer your Samaritan services to such as are better capable of appreciating them. There must surely still be people deserving of pity, here or over there, go seek them! Go, please, before I smack your face."

HE WAITED for the narrow form of the girl to disappear among the dark reeds, then got up and set off slowly. He staggered along for another hour, or perhaps two hours. His turned-up coat collar, which was soaked through and had now frozen as hard as a board, chafed his skin till it bled. When he fell once again, he was perhaps near the frontier, only a few hundred yards away, because he noticed some yellow, vaporous sparkling above the snow, which he found after a long, absent-minded examination to be the light of a mighty Christmas tree. It was Christmas Eve, a white Christmas. For a time he remained lying on the ground. With a great effort he could still have crawled on all fours under the Christmas tree, but he had no taste for this disgraceful exhibition. Let us stay in this little country! Shots sounded from a great distance, then, somewhat nearer, the receding rattle of a motorcycle. The old man struggled to his feet, turned his back on the frontier, and symbolically retraced his steps a few paces, toward the interior. He sat on the edge of a ditch filled with snow. He was very tired. He scarcely felt the cold anymore.

He closed his eyes and yawned again and again. Incipient degeneration was his diagnosis, after feeling his pulse several times. He knew the process. Fatigue, sleepiness, breathing becomes faint. The muscles grow stiff; that too makes breathing more difficult. The amount of carbon dioxide in the poorly oxygenated blood steadily increases. Disturbances appear in the metabolism, the body's temperature control fails. Visual and aural hallucinations follow. The functioning of the heart grows irregular, with frequent extrasystole. The temperature in the rectum drops steadily; when it reaches twenty-four degrees, there is nothing practical that can be done. The liver ceases to produce glycogen, the blood sugar falls. The heartbeats grow ever fainter. The pulse becomes intermittent and imperceptible. When the blood sugar necessary for the nutrition of the organism falls to nothing, the end comes.

Translated by Dr. D. Mervyn Jones

GAMES OF THE UNDERWORLD

Christmas Eve

I T WAS Christmas Eve, 1944; Budapest was blanketed in thick fog. Few cars were about, the trains had stopped running at noon. Suddenly there appeared a great host of ravens, a cloud of them which flew in from the hills of Buda and settled in the trees of the parks. The air raids were getting more and more frequent, and as a result the streets were covered in accumulated litter.

The fog lay thickest near the river. Frances Rusko, 52 years old and a widow, an attendant at the Lukacs bathing establishment, lived in a third-floor room-and-kitchen apartment looking out onto a narrow side-street in the building opposite Police Headquarters on the Pest bank. She had been sick for three days; during that time she had left the house only once because of her gouty foot, to do her Christmas shopping. She was expecting her daughter and her daughter's fiancé for dinner.

She was a big, graying woman with a somewhat protruding stomach, a pair of man's shoes several sizes too large on her feet, red, chapped hands and arms, but her eyes shone with a mocking, youthful gaiety. She had buried three of her children, four remained: two girls who had married and gone off to live in the provinces, one boy at the front, and Evi, the youngest, who was resident teacher at a girls' boarding school. She had stayed alone for a year in the little flat that had been hers for over two decades, and had recently, in a burst of hospitality, taken in a speckled hen, Pinduri. Pinduri was a noisy lodger, but even during the winter she laid an egg every other day.

The old woman laid the table for the dinner party in the room. It was about one o'clock when Evi and her fiancé, also a school teacher, arrived. Laughing and inquisitive, the girl at once ran to the kitchen, dragging the still somewhat awkward, dejected young man after her by the hand.

"It's going to be a wonderful dinner, you'll see, Janos!" she said, and her round laughing face that even weeks of semi-starvation in early winter had not succeeded in marking, shone so sweetly and gently with happiness that it illuminated the whole kitchen. "It'll be a dinner to remember, you mark my words. What we'll have is mother's secret, of course . . . just look at her, keeping me away from the stove! Let me look, mother," she begged, "at least let me peep!"

"Get along with you!" said the old woman, her stomach shaking with laughter.

Evi wrinkled her nose. "Don't shout at me," she grumbled. "How long did you starve yourself to produce this feast, just tell me that!"

"I didn't!"

"A week?" the girl asked severely. "Two weeks? Three?" She laughed again, with such liquid, warbling turtle-dove laughter that even her fiancé, whose brother had been arrested by the secret police that very morning, broke into a smile, and felt easier for a moment.

"She used to starve the whole family for a month," Evi told her fiancé, beating her two tiny fists together in sudden anger. "The eight of us lived on soup and mush for a whole month before Christmas till we got so thin that a draft would blow us out through the keyhole, and all the time this old woman here saved every penny in her drawer to put a turkey and twenty-four loaves of nut and poppy seed cake on the table on Christmas Eve. . . . What? I'm making it up?" she cried, laughing. "Just look at her shaking her stomach! By that time we'd all got so weak that we couldn't swallow a single bite—we just stared at the laden table and wept. I suppose that isn't true either? Am I lying? What did you 'starve' together for today? Tell me, won't you let me go near the stove to look? And if I die before it's served? You wait, mother, you'll be sorry for upsetting your dearest daughter like this!"

The old woman folded her hands over her stomach and looked at her daughter. "Nosey!" she said, and her stomach heaved again with laughter. Evi clapped her hand over her lips.

At that moment a piece of plaster, the size of a leaf, detached itself from the ceiling and plopped down on the stove where it crumbled into powder like snow. A crack, the width of a finger, opened in the wall from floor to ceiling. A little kitchen stool standing by the wall jumped straight into the air like a young goat, shaking off the sieve which had lain on it. The thick explosion filled the kitchen with a cloud of dust; for a second none of them could see.

"What was that?" Evi asked. She stood there, very pale, grasping the dresser with both hands.

The old woman fingered her ear. "I thought I'd gone deaf," she said.

The kitchen stool jumped again into the air, and a shower of plaster fell from the ceiling. A pot slid slowly along the top of the stove and leapt with a loud clanking noise onto the stone floor of the kitchen. The young girl staggered, and fell against the wall.

"Lucky there was only water in it," said the old woman, picking up the pot. "There wasn't an air raid warning, was there, Janos?"

"There wasn't," replied the young school teacher, wiping

the blood from his forehead, which had been scratched by a sharp piece of plaster.

"Are you wounded?" Evi asked. "What was it?"

The teacher did not answer. Giving the girl a quick look to make sure she was unhurt, he ran into the room, opened the window, and looked up at the sky. Evi ran after him. "Get away from the window, quick!" she cried. "What are you looking for?"

The young man turned to face her. The expression on his face was so extraordinary, such a strange mixture of surprise and happiness that he reminded one of a young mother gazing at her first-born child.

"It wasn't a plane," he said quietly.

"What was it then?"

The young man swallowed with emotion. "It's Christmas Day," he said.

Evi gazed into his face with rounded eyes.

"Yes," Janos said, "the first Russian shell on Christmas Day. Perhaps salvation is at hand. Come!"

He went to the girl and took her in his arms. A third shell exploded in the wall of a house a little further away; only the light hanging from the ceiling nodded lazily in recognition.

"Let's go down into the underworld!" the old woman called from the kitchen. She had already packed their things and was waiting for them with her coat and scarf on, and a large jar under her arm. "I'm taking the lard," she said, "lest the cockroaches eat it up!" Pinduri, the hen, sat on her shoulder, screwing its head around anxiously.

By the time they had descended the narrow, gaping stairs into the cellar, the air-raid shelter was already crowded. There was no electricity, a single oil lamp threw its pale, melancholy light into the two narrow spaces placed one behind the other like the two strokes of a T, and were full of chairs, divans and bare iron bedsteads. The men stood in the lobby round a tub filled with water, wondering what to do, while the women exchanged loud excited greetings further in, near the stove set up in the first cellar.

The widow Rusko and her family settled down in the second cellar. "If we hadn't been struck by lightning," she grumbled, "it would have been ready by now."

Evi winked at her fiancé. "What would have been ready, mother?" she asked, casually, as if she were not really interested.

The old woman muttered something.

"I didn't hear you," Evi said. "What did you say?"

The old woman shrugged her shoulders. "I said it would be ready by now."

"What would?"

"Nosey!" said the old woman. "You'll find out this evening."

Both started to laugh simultaneously, the old woman pressing her hand to her belly to stop it shaking, and Evi, throwing back her head, laughed so boisterously, so zealously that her round, white throat tensed with the sweet effort, and the entire cellar fell silent and looked at them, smiling for a moment. "You can't win," Evi said, "the old dear's brain is as sharp as a bishop's; I just don't know why, with such gifts, she chose to be a proletarian."

"Nosey," the old woman said for the third time that day. "If I were you, I'd find out why my fiancé is hanging his head."

Evi glanced quickly at the young man who was gazing ahead silently, deep in thought. "That's his normal attitude," she said.

"Perhaps he's hungry," the old woman suggested.

"When he's hungry he shouts. He's sad like that only when he's happy."

"Happy?" the old woman broke into gentle mocking laughter.

"Happy as an angel in the wood-cellar," Evi said.

"If I were intending to marry an insolent chit like you, I'd have joined a funeral society long ago," said the old woman.

"He's done that," said Evi, "but that's not what makes him so melancholy."

"What then, you school-marm?"

"The fact that he doesn't know what he's getting for dinner," said the girl, laughing. "You'll drive us both to our deaths, you'll see, mother!"

The young man indicated by a fleeting smile that he was participating in the conversation with his ears, but he did not raise his head. As the first excitement abated, the talk around them grew quieter; the women rummaged in the food bags, someone was noisily sipping tea from a thermos flask; all eyes turned in that direction. A young girl settled herself under the oil lamp and began to read the Bible.

"So the siege has begun at last!" sighed a voice. Pinduri, the hen, which had been calmly preening itself on the old woman's lap, launched itself with a flap of its wings onto the young schoolteacher's shoulder, and knocked on his head with its beak.

"She wants to know why you're so silent," the young girl said.

"Obviously because he has nothing to say," said the widow, and, laughing again, dealt the young man a resounding slap on the back.

From time to time, a messenger ran up from the cellar into the still deeper darkness of the yard, to inspect the state of the damaged building. Though the gunfire abated by the evening, and the house had not been hit again, nobody suggested moving back into the exposed flats, so the women began slowly to get the place ready for the night. Pillows, blankets, appeared on the beds and, where there was enough room, armchairs were pushed together and the children bedded down on them.

The oil in the lamps burned low, and a candle had to be lit. Evi rose.

"Where are you going?" asked the old woman.

The girl bent down to murmur into her ear. "We'll go and eat our dinner," she whispered. "You stay down here, and we'll bring yours down to you."

"Go ahead, child," the widow looked at her, resting her bony old hand with its narrow silver band on the ring finger on her daughter's shoulder for an instant. The girl nodded, and ran from the cellar.

It was dark in the flat, and they had to light a candle. Evi closed the windows, put the candle on a chair behind the wardrobe, then, leaning back against the wall, she pulled the young man toward her by the lapels of his jacket.

"Is anything wrong?" she asked him.

"Nothing at all."

"Sure?"

The young man nodded.

"Has your brother come home?"

"He has."

"He isn't in trouble?"

"No," the young man said.

"Sure?"

"Sure."

Evi gave a sigh of relief. "I really was badly scared this time. If they'd caught him and found the weapons . . . Thank God it came off!"

"Yes," said the man.

Evi threw her arms round his neck and kissed him on the lips. Her pale face flushed softly like the sky at dawn, when it feels the approach of the sun. "Wait," she whispered. "The papers are with mother. They're safer with her than with me. Right?"

"Right," said the young man.

"This is our Christmas," the girl whispered. "Let's celebrate it."

She stirred up the fire in the stove where the big secret, the duck, was waiting, pink and ready, for its initiation, and in a moment the kitchen was filled with its strong, triumphant smell. A bottle of red wine stood on the dresser, and beside it were four loaves of nut and poppy seed cake as well as a white country loaf rolled up in a tea-towel.

"The old woman certainly has done us proud," Evi said, in amazement. "I wonder where she found this beautiful bird."

She served up the small, round duck, which seemed to dance in the hot, voluble, spluttering nut-brown fat around it in the iron roasting tin.

In places a light foam had collected in round spots on top of the fat, which flashed silvery in the candlelight, and in the center the duck rose, a mound of tenderness and crispness, radiating from under its pink skin. On the right, a plate of purple beetroot, on the left, the tart, dream-filled juice of the wine complemented the pink, oily duck. The thick slice of soft white bread near the plates was salvation itself.

"You see," Evi said, "this is the short, fat, big-bottomed duck one should always choose because it's the best. Don't ever let me skin it after we're married—it must be roasted in its own fat or it isn't worth eating. You can cut off the fat around its bottom because one doesn't eat it anyway, but the rest . . . ! Now just watch me!" She rolled up her sleeves to the elbow and bent her happy face, bathed in red light, over the pan. "Look," she said. "Just see how the skin has slipped up here on the leg, and how nicely the little bone has reddened? I take it between two fingers and make a clean cut around it, then I lift it a bit . . . it seems to stick a little . . . did you hear the joint crack? . . . and now it comes off in one piece as if it had never been there.

Now I lift it by its bottom and stand it on its nose, then I cut into it right and left. At such times a bit of temper doesn't hurt—it helps you to get the better of these tough tendons . . . but today I can't be angry and that's why it's lasting as long as a wet afternoon. But now you can turn away because I'm going to reach in with my hand and tear off the breast meat and then I'll lick my fingers and pick up every little crumb of meat because that's the best part of it. Don't look! Am I ready yet? No, not for ages yet! I still have to cut off the wings, scrape the burnt bits off the side of the pan because that's what tastes best, and all the time that's going on, you can faint with hunger. Here's a leg, schoolteacher—amuse yourself with it!"

After dinner, they both fell silent. They just sat gazing at each other. The girl blew out the candle and opened the window in order to air the room. An overturned truck lay under the window in a tank trap with two dead soldiers on the cab. Evi shuddered and closed the window. From the direction of Buda the guns opened fire again with a dull, distant rumble.

"We're not going downstairs," Evi said. "Come."

They lay in the bed for the first time since they had met and fallen in love. When an occasional shell exploded nearby, the candle fluttered for a moment, turning the room upside down. Toward midnight, the kitchen door opened, and the big-framed old woman stopped on the threshold with a candle held high in her hand. Soundlessly, she observed the two lovers fast asleep in each other's arms, then she nodded, turned around, and silently closed the door behind her. "Poor little things!" she murmured. She squatted down by the stove, and began to eat the remnants of the dinner. "They didn't leave me any wine, the little runts," she grumbled, and laughed soundlessly, making her stomach wobble. Pinduri, the hen, perched on her shoulder and watched sleepily as the old woman's hand moved up and down in the light of the candle.

Dawn in December

BEFORE FLARING up and jerkily stretching forth its squat little flame, bathing the rough wooden shelf and the thin female hand that rested on the wall behind it in a friendly, yellow light, the tall candle had stood silent in the thick darkness, and only a second later did it begin—as if roused to life by its own gleam—to splutter its rapid, early morning sermon. Those who were asleep beneath the cellar's low ceiling woke immediately; and, replying to the greeting of the light with a short, unthinking yawn, a raucous clearing of the throat, or a low moan, the thirty men and women sat up in bed almost simultaneously. Only one stubborn individual snored on undauntedly near the emergency exit. But he, too, fell silent when a near miss shook the walls and elicited a low tinkle from the small chamber pot that shone with a white gleam under one of the children's beds.

"They're not losing any time today, are they?" said Uncle Lajos, pulling his thick white legs quickly out from under the camelhair blanket.

"They've certainly got it in for this neighborhood!" said a younger voice sleepily.

The women remained silent. Someone lit a candle at the back of the cellar, which guttered softly, then suddenly spread an even, smooth carpet of light on to the low-hung ceiling. The crackling of the freshly lit stove could be heard from the next cellar, which was divided from the first only by a batten door. Another shell found its target; again the concrete floor seemed to shiver, and the crucifix on the wall slid to one side. The caretaker's four-year-old son sat up in bed, pointed at the shell-shocked crucifix, and broke into melodious laughter.

"Did they hit us?" asked a lanky, big-boned old maid, who

was sitting bolt upright and motionless on the edge of her bed, wiping her large bespectacled face from time to time with a red silk handkerchief.

By now the blasts were shaking the walls almost unceasingly. The vibration spread invisibly under the skin of the stones, jarring the nerves of the people as they sat dressing on the edge of their beds, like a long-drawn-out, unanswered question, slithering back and forth below their consciousness and seeking vainly for a solution. Only a feeble light came from the candles burning in the damp, close air, so that the center of the huge cellar remained plunged in almost total darkness. It was here, in the darkness, that the tearstained, unaired smell of the pillows and blankets collected thickest.

"We can't air the place now," someone said with her head thrown back, looking up at the window under the ceiling which was covered with a metal plate. A thin iron ladder led up to it.

"I asked if we'd been hit," the bespectacled old maid repeated.

"No, that one was a near miss," replied the retired colonel next to her, who was so deaf in both ears that he could not hear male voices at all, and of the female voices only the shrillest and sharpest were audible to him; despite this, he enjoyed undivided authority in all things military.

"And that? . . . What was that?" his neighbor, a young doctor who, for lack of better accommodation, slept on an operating table covered in white oilcloth, asked, bending close to the colonel's ear.

"That was another near miss!" answered the optimistic colonel.

At the back of the cellar, under the candle which was guttering on its shelf, a young girl stood combing her hair; shadows from her slowly moving arms ran up to the ceiling with wide, sweeping movements, paused there for a moment, then— as if reluctant to fall back—sank back into the muddy darkness below the shelf. Between her lips she held a thin wire hairpin. At a new, heavier explosion, the hairpin fell from her mouth and dropped, with a tinkle, onto the floor.

"What are you cooking today? Juliska?" she asked the caretaker's wife, after bending down to grope for the hairpin, cleaning it with her fingers, and sticking it back between her lips. "Beans?"

The caretaker's wife shook her head; not beans. "If I can go up to the flat this morning," she said, "I'll light the stove and make some cabbage noodles."

The young girl drew a deep breath, closed her eyes, and clapped her hand over her mouth. "Lord!" she exclaimed, "if only I could eat an apple strudel just once more—with lots of currants and a thick layer of castor sugar on top! . . . That one hit the house, didn't it?" she whispered, her lips whitening, and gripping the shelf with both hands. Someone in the next cellar pushed open the batten door, stopped for a moment on the threshold, then withdrew, reassured.

"It wasn't this house; perhaps it was the one next door," said Uncle Lajos. "Juliska, dear, if you light the stove, I'll give you a few potatoes and some vinegar to cook for me."

At the word "vinegar," the pregnant young woman who had been gazing silently at her little round belly, a soft, happy, dreamy smile on her lips, suddenly shut her eyes. From the white, hissing ball, which the word "vinegar" represented for her, a sour, acrid smell rose up like a cloud of flies from a torn carcass, covered the walls and furniture with a gray sediment, and emitted tiny bubbles that, within seconds, flew around the cellar, turned red, swelled up and dripped blood all over the floor.

"That was a hit!" the colonel informed his listeners in a booming voice; he had not noticed that someone had fainted behind him, and that the women were busy trying to revive the young woman with toilet water and wet sponges. "On the other hand, it might have been a bomb," he added thoughtfully, "one of the small-caliber ones . . . twenty-five to fifty kilos . . . the kind the Russians use. . . ."

When the shelling stopped half an hour later, the cellar emptied; only the children remained—watched over by a few women—and an old couple moved in from one of the neighboring houses. They opened the air shaft, and a young girl began to sweep the floor; the rising dust mingled with the cold dawn mists streaming in through the ventilator, and peopled the deserted room with the fresh, familiar images of household chores and cleanliness. It must have been seven o'clock. The old maid pushed her way quickly through the second cellar where the poorer inhabitants of the house had settled, ran along the long, dark corridor opening from it, climbed the winding stairs, and, reaching the yard, looked about her anxiously.

As far as she could make out in the fog, the house was undamaged, and even the door to her flat was unharmed. Her heart always contracted a little as she came up in the mornings, because she never knew whether, instead of her peaceful flat, she was not going to be met by the cornucopia of destruction. But once more she was fortunate: her flat, the only possession she had on earth, had come through unscathed except for a broken window. The old maid set about cleaning the place up; only after she had done that would she wash and have her breakfast. At this time of the morning, before it was fully light, there was always a pause in the shelling, which would last for an hour or two as if, from sheer humanity and worldly consideration, the besiegers were granting the inhabitants a small respite to clean themselves after the ugly, underworld nights.

After shaking the rug, sweeping the ceiling with her feather duster, and removing the last speck of dust from the room as it took shape in the slow December dawn, she washed herself from top to toe, and drank her unsweetened Hungarian tea;

then she took the speckled hen—which sat under the sewing machine—into her arms, and hurried down the street. In a few moments she reached the Stock Exchange from one of whose destroyed store rooms the blast had swept innumerable dead rats and bats out into the street. She put the hen down on the sidewalk, tied a long string to its leg, then, straightening her back, and with a dreamy smile on her broad face, she began her daily tour of inspection.

The streets were deserted; along Nador Street, reaching out to the distant fog-washed dark mass of the Parliament building, along the narrow side streets running down to the Danube, along the bullet-torn walks of Liberty Square, not a soul was visible, only the fog rolled on above the wetly shining asphalt. It was cold. Some distance away smoke curled out of a cellar window; like some mushroom growth of underground putrefaction it pushed out into the street and spread in thick gray bushes over the pavement.

"Perhaps they're baking bread," said the old maid aloud with a questioning expression on her face.

The hen was standing still, its feet spread wide, picking with its pointed beak at the head of a dead rat. Its feathers shone, its neck was tense; it was the only unmarred creature among all the ruins. On the opposite pavement lay the body of a soldier near a torn-up tree, its roots stretched toward the sky. A slow cold rain was falling.

The stillness of the street was so absolute that, at a louder tap of the hen's beak, the old maid was startled, and turned around to stare suspiciously toward Liberty Square. Behind her, the façade of a tall apartment building caved in, the torn green wallpaper on the rear wall swayed slowly forward and backward in the wind. For a while, the old maid watched in silence; then she picked the hen up, kissed it, and started out homeward. A reconnaissance plane roared over her head; it was only a matter of minutes before the next raid was due to start.

By the time she reached the hall, the machine guns were crackling, and the antiaircraft unit on the roof had gone into action. There was a bottleneck at the head of the cellar steps, and the inhabitants of the house were fleeing, helter-skelter, down them.

"Juliska," the old maid said to the caretaker's wife, "tell Uncle Lajos that his soldier son is dead. He is lying on the pavement in front of 28 Nador Street."

She still had to climb up to the flat, to hide the frightened hen that was nervously jerking its ruffled head at each detonation, in its place under the sewing machine. For a while she pottered around quietly in the flat, then groped her way down to the cellar where the candle had just gone out. Someone lit another.

The Horse

IT WAS dusk. A slow drizzle was falling from the low-lying clouds. Here and there a puddle gleamed amidst the flagstones of the muddy pavement.

The old man walked quickly in order to get home before dark. From across the street dense, velvety black clouds of smoke thrust their way out of the first-floor windows of a block of flats, accompanied by thin, hissing tongues of flame that bathed the still unbroken panes of the house opposite in a yellow light. The street was deserted—only a dead soldier lay amongst the glass splinters in the middle of the narrow roadway, his face hidden in the crook of his arm.

The old man stopped short in front of a dairy. A brown horse with a lighter colored mane stuck its head out into the street from the empty frame of the narrow shop entrance. "And how did you get in there?" murmured the old man, and bent forward curiously to examine the tiny premises. The horse's rump was pressed against the rear wall of the shop where an announcement printed on wine-red paper hung, and its flanks were caught between the white-painted counter on the right, and an overturned refrigerator on the left.

The old man stepped back a pace, raised his head and read the shop sign the blast had blown awry. "Milk Butter Eggs" was the inscription he could make out in the rapidly thickening darkness. He looked at the horse once more, perplexedly, shook his head, and set off homeward again. The horse pushed the door open with its head, and followed him.

They still had a short way to go. In front walked the old man, his head bowed as he listened thoughtfully to the rhythmical clatter of the horse's hoofs on the wet asphalt behind him. Once, when he turned into a side street, the hoofs fell silent as if the horse had stopped to think; but a moment later the animal broke into an excited trot in which the heartbeats of anxiety were clearly discernible. A little later, to test him, the old man turned down another side street; the horse paused behind him as before, and then followed him again in an alarmed, rapid trot.

"Blind," the old man muttered moodily, "blind in both eyes!"

The streets were deserted and silent; there was a faint rattle of machine-gun fire in the distance. Behind the Basilica a woman, bent double, ran with squelching feet across the slushy square and disappeared into a doorway. Further up, the wide street was covered in broken glass; the dark winter sky was fleetingly reflected in it, flashed, and then froze into the glass. It was getting darker every minute.

By the time they reached home, the Russian mine-throwers were heard from the direction of Buda, and a low-flying fighter plane was sweeping over the rooftops above their heads. But the horse went down the narrow winding cellar steps behind his new master with movements as practiced as if he had been assistant porter in a five-story block of flats for ten years. He stumbled on the last step only, fell to his knees, and slid on his belly onto the soot-black landing in front of the air-raid shelter. But no sooner had he arrived than he leapt up, his hoofs beating a tattoo, and, bending his head, he galloped into the long corridor that lead to the coal cellars. Only the yellow sparks rising from his hoofs shone in the Stygian darkness of the night, like the punctuation marks of a scream. He neighed long and plaintively, blood streaming from his neck and back; the low ceiling of the cellar had flayed him in three places. As he reached the end of the corridor, he suddenly stopped and hung his head.

Inside the air-raid shelter people were preparing for bed. The unaccustomed noise brought most of the men and some of the women streaming out on to the landing, where they advanced in single file, peering forward curiously toward the coal cellar. Here the shelter commander, who was walking at the head of the procession, halted abruptly, and raised his small black kerosene lamp above his head. Wildly gesticulating shadows raced down the two walls and merged at the roots like an evil tangled bush, cowering, motionless on the ground. Under the dark vaulted ceiling of the cellar the broad illuminated rump of the horse emerged clearly, enclosed in its low-roofed frame.

A woman gave a stifled cry, then men laughed. The squat, gray-moustached janitor clasped his middle in rare good humor. Someone made the sign of the cross. The air-raid warden, Audit Office Councilor Pignitzky, raised his lamp still higher, and bent forward—as if he were unable to believe his eyes—gazing nonplussed at the animal's thick fair tail.

"Look at the poor thing shaking," sighed an elderly woman. As if he could understand her, the horse looked back at her, his large brown eyes gleaming in the lamplight.

"Now you've done it, Uncle Janos," the air-raid warden grumbled.

"What on earth did you bring it here for?"

The old man wiped the sweat from his forehead with the back of his hand. "If I'd left him outside, he'd have been killed by a grenade," he said quietly.

No one spoke. People gazed stolidly ahead, their eyes darkening, their teeth cruel and compressed; they looked as if they were examining the fat, sweating rump of the animal with the dual passion of pagan guts and Christian love. The horse looked back at them with an expression of patient conciliation on its face.

"That little lamp gives a good light," said a skinny woman, unexpectedly. "It's got quite bright."

"Well, he'd have perished outside, that's true enough," muttered the janitor thoughtfully.

Aunt Mari, a cobbler's widow, stepped forward and, with a tiny shy movement drew her wrinkled palm over the animal's buttocks. The spectacles that she had inherited from her husband, and which she now wore for piety's sake only in front of her healthy old eyes—for she had no need of them—flashed with severity in the lamplight.

"Careful, he might kick you!"

"He's old—he couldn't hurt a fly," said Mr. Andrasi, the lame waiter. Thus encouraged, the old women drew even closer to the horse.

"Where did you find him, Uncle Janos?" asked the janitor.

Once again the old man wiped his damp forehead with his hand, and his sharp, cold eyes slowly examined one by one the illuminated faces suddenly turned toward him. "I didn't find him, he just came," he said. "He was standing at the counter of a cheese store looking out into the street. The houses opposite were burning, a mine had torn up the road, and there was a burned-out tank smoking in the middle of the street. As soon as he heard me he came out of the shop and followed me. That bit of the street was covered with corpses—as I was the only living soul, the poor innocent brute picked on me."

"Did you speak to him?" asked Aunt Mari.

The man shook his head. "No, I didn't."

"How did he get into the shop?" a woman asked.

"How do I know?" the old man replied morosely. "I don't even know how he got down these stairs considering that he's blind in both eyes!"

"Blind?" Aunt Mari gasped.

For a moment there was silence. Then there was the sound of loud, cheerful children's voices from the direction of the air-raid shelter, and immediately afterward, like an angry warning from Mount Zion, came the subdued rumble of a distant explosion. The horse's broad rump quivered almost imperceptibly.

"He's frightened!" cried Juli Sovany, the janitor's orphaned niece who lived on her charity, pressing her hand to her heart. "Good Lord, he's terrified!"

A big, heavy-breasted woman standing next to her wiped her eyes. By some strange process of transference, her ageing heart evoked her own blond childhood from the golden gleam of the horse's tail. In a second, sentimentality touched the women's hearts, their eyes filled with tears, their hair became disheveled, and their noses reddened; the horse's gentle, nut-brown eye transformed them, metamorphosed Gorgons, into water.

"Well! I'm not going to chase him away," said the old man slowly. "Even if the mines spared him, some dirty tramp would certainly slaughter him by the morning."

Councilor Pignitzky suddenly turned around.

"All right, let him stay," he said in his slightly cracked voice. "He'll have to be turned around so that he can stand with his head looking out. Lead him out onto the landing—that's wide enough for him to turn, then back him into the corner and tie him to the door of the coal cellar. Juli, you can clean up after him twice a day—once in the morning and once in the evening."

"Yes, sir," said Juli Sovany.

"But what are you going to feed him?" asked a woman.

"He'd starve to death outside, poor thing," said Aunt Mari, sighing.

"I'll get him some grass from Liberty Square," offered the lame waiter, who, even in compassion, tried to serve humanity according to the rules of his trade.

"We'll find something," people said to each other.

The problem of hospitality thus settled, the procession wandered back to the air-raid shelter. Juli Sovany ran ahead: she still had to warm up the janitor's dinner and make the beds. In her haste, she stumbled over a protruding stone and fell, whimpering quietly, onto her face.

Aunt Mari, the bespectacled widow of the cobbler, trotted at the tail end of the procession beside another widow who worked as laundress for the wealthy families of the nearby Nador Street. The two old women were on friendly terms. They were both short, skinny and tough; when they stood side by side talking it seemed as if two thin candles had burst into tiny flickering flames in the dark and drafty hall of the great big world. What little light they had they spent modestly and wisely on illuminating, not the baffling night, but each other.

"You noticed it too, didn't you, dear?" the laundress asked.

Aunt Mari stopped and turned the severe gleam of the dead man's spectacles onto her friend. "And what am I supposed to have noticed, Mrs. Daniska?" she asked mildly.

"The light," the laundress replied, in a whisper.

Aunt Mari nodded silently; she could not even guess what light her friend meant.

"You remember, dear, don't you," the widow Daniska continued, "before we started back, Councilor Pignitzky was holding the lamp in his hand. Then he suddenly turned his back on the horse. He held the lamp so low that he completely hid it with his body—and he is a fine figure of a man—yet the horse did not disappear in the darkness," the laundress went on, lowering her voice still more, "because the light stayed there, like a halo round its head. I couldn't believe my eyes—I looked again and again, but there was such a radiance round it that it seemed as if a star was shining over its head."

Aunt Mari did not answer.

"When I stroked it," she said after a little while, "it's skin was as velvety as the petal of a pansy."

The air-raid shelter consisted of two cellars, connected not by a door, but by a short, narrow little passage. On the right of the first cellar, a small recess opened, which the most distinguished denizens, Councilor Pignitzky, the air-raid warden, and his family, had appropriated for themselves. The common people—widowed charwomen, laundresses, day laborers, an aged barber's assistant, an even more aged porter, a woman tobacconist, the lame waiter, a retired postman, and elderly unemployed, slept in the two wide low-ceilinged cellars made of quarry stones, on beds and couches moved down from the flats. The stove stood in the second cellar, its flue leading out into the street through the walled-up window of an empty storeroom.

In the first cellar they were playing cards. A wick thrust into a tin box cast its uncertain, moon-like light from a shelf over the table. The men sat around the table on kitchen stools; one of them leaned back against the bed and could not stop sneezing. From time to time the thick shadow of an arm would race triumphantly up to the ceiling, and then sink back into obscurity.

"They're not half punishing this neighborhood today!" said one of the men, his big red face glowing like the disc of the sun, bent over his cards. He emitted a long whistle, and used his broad palm to sweep the bank into his lap.

"Let them!" murmured his neighbor, a young man in an army blouse. "They won't get us down here. Who's banker?"

The next player to hold the bank gave a cheerful, energetic sneeze. In answer, two others followed suit, then, like a thick knot at the end of a string, the stout red-faced man finished the scale in his fat, blaring trumpet.

"Card, please," grunted the soldier.

The walls shook almost continuously under the impact of the Russian heavy artillery. Loud female laughter shrilled from one corner. The sound was as unexpected in the musty, cold cellar, with its damp, greasy walls, as if a chandelier had suddenly turned on, on the ceiling. Juli Sovany was making up a bed in the far corner of the cellar; her angular behind, bent over the bed, rounded out momentarily in the light of that laughter.

In the next cellar the women were busy preparing dinner. Bean soup was boiling in a huge cauldron on the stove, shopping bags, suitcases, wrapped loaves appeared from under the beds; Aunt Mari, the bespectacled widow of the cobbler, placed a small jar of honey beside her on the bed, and waved in excited invitation to Mrs. Daniska, who was squatting on the third bed over from hers, to join her. The cellar lived on shared food, and whenever someone could lay their hands on a delicacy, they shared it dutifully with their closest neighbor. Only two families cooked separately for themselves—the janitor and his wife, and the Pignitzkys, who had their own stove in the recess in which they lived.

"Juli, when you've finished with that bed, bring me a pail of water," said the pregnant woman.

"With pleasure," replied Juli.

A squat, pink-faced smiling woman turned to her from the nearby couch. "I'll bring you the water," she offered. "Poor Juli has been on her feet since dawn. What do you need it for?"

The young woman was overcome with confusion. "I'd like to wash my hair," she replied in a low voice. "But I can fetch the water myself, Aunt Rozsi!"

A long, muffled roll like thunder sounded from the direction of the entrance; a bomb must have fallen nearby. A glass slipped from the table and rolled noisily to the wall; flames shot out from the stove. A pale, dark-haired girl began muttering the Lord's Prayer.

"You'll catch a chill, my dear, if you wash your hair in this cold," the pink-faced woman said, and sneezed. "I've got one already."

Sneezes of every pitch sounded from all around as the dust, stirred up by the explosion, irritated the membranes. In the first cellar, a chorus of male noses rang out like machine-gun fire. "Stop that now, dinner is ready!" cried one of the women. The old, retired postman knelt down on the ground, and pulled a small bottle of plum brandy out of his kit bag: he threw his head back, and poured a mouthful down past his protruding Adam's apple, then handed the bottle to the lame waiter who was squatting next to him.

"Have one for the fright we had," he said, "but go slow, neighbor, there's only a drop left at the bottom!"

"To your good health!" said the waiter, lugubriously.

"Juli, come over here!" shouted someone from the first cellar.

"Yes, sir!" Juli shouted back.

The card players put down their cards, and turned to the girl as she ran in.

"I hear they've brought a horse into the cellar," the fat, red-faced man said with a sneeze. "What sort of a horse is it?"

"A beautiful horse," Juli replied, folding her hands on her stomach.

"But who brought it?" asked the soldier.

Juli Sovany shook her head vehemently. "I don't know," she said, "I think it came by itself."

"By itself, by itself!" the fat man frowned with annoyance. "This isn't a pub that it should just walk in! Can't you talk more intelligently?"

"No," Juli replied, frightened.

"Is it fat?" someone asked. The girl nodded. The soldier clicked his tongue. "Bring it in here!" he shouted at the girl. Juli promptly turned around and began to run toward the door, halfway there she stopped and, pressing her back to the wall, turned around slowly.

"It can't be brought in," she said excitedly, "It's blind!"

"Then lead it, idiot!" the soldier bawled at her.

"I can't," Juli shook her head. "It's back is bleeding."

By now everybody was laughing.

"No one told you to sit on its back, stupid," said the fat man, getting up.

He stretched, and tapped the girl playfully on the head. "Don't forget to clean my boots before morning, do you hear?"

"Yes, sir," said Juli, and ran back into the second cellar. The men followed her more slowly. As they passed the recess, a greasy smell of pancakes assailed their noses from the direction of the Pignitzky's stove; the fat tailor, who was walking ahead, turned back and winked at his companions—it was as if the whole expanse of his big face winked.

"What are you having for dinner, Councilor?" he called into the recess.

"Only some leftovers from midday, Mr. Kovacs," a woman's voice replied. "I've used up the last of my flour today."

"Dear me, dear me!" Mr. Kovacs wagged his head. "The last of your flour!"

The men grinned at each other, walked in single file up to the stove, and sat down on their beds, each with a plate of bean soup. At such times it was forbidden to sneeze, because if someone did, the soup spilled from the plates onto one's own or one's neighbor's trousers; as a result, sniffing, flaring and violently grimacing nostrils bent over the plates. They were still at dinner when the news came—no doubt brought by the janitor who had peeped out into the street for a second—that Anglo-American heavy bombers must have been over the town because the third and fourth floors of the house opposite had completely caved in; the rubble was standing man-high in the street.

The night threatened to be stormy, and the besieging army appeared to be preparing for an attack. The men standing on the landing moodily inhaled the smoke of their cigarettes, and the more timid soon retreated to safer shelter. The dull thud of the missiles came rolling down the spiral staircase of the cellar in endless succession, like evil black pearls. The antiaircraft gun installed on the roof of the next building coughed uninterruptedly, and when, at times, there was a brief pause between two rounds, one could immediately distinguish the unearthly, brutal humming of the fighters circling over the house and the wild teeth-gnashing of their machine guns. When a bomb exploded close by, the old porter, who was smoking his pipe near the stairs got sick, vomited his dinner and then retired into the shelter to go to bed.

Inside, people were gradually falling silent in the wincing light of their oil lamps, and were beginning to accustom themselves to the approaching night. The young pregnant woman drew her footstool close to the stove, and, bending down, quickly soaped her hair; a woman standing beside her poured fresh warm water over the long, gleaming, soapy hair, while another warmed two towels in the oven so that the young woman should not catch cold. Juli Sovany was squatting by the next bed, unlacing the old tobacconist's shoes. Aunt Mari retired to a corner under the light of the candle; thanks to her youthful and unimpaired eyesight, she was able to repair Mrs. Daniska's pitifully ragged petticoat before going to bed. The pale, dark-haired girl fell asleep with the Bible in her hand; her neighbor, one of the charwomen, was already snoring gently. In the first cellar, however, they were still pushing furniture around. The old porter whose bed stood under the ventilator changed places with the young soldier: he could no longer face sleeping beneath the air shaft since the explosion, which had upset his sensitive stomach. It was not a bad bargain because his new neighbor, the waiter, although he bleated in his sleep like a herd of mountain goats pursued by wolves, was still offering his lucky right- and left-hand neighbors a little bacon at breakfast time.

Inter-bed conversation died down, the older people slipped slowly into the night. Even the explosions seemed to have become less frequent, and at times complete silence reigned in the cellar for a whole minute. In one of the longer pauses, however, an unexpected sound penetrated the cellar from the direction of the landing: the horse outside broke into a loud, sharp neigh.

Aunt Mari raised her head and put her hand behind her ear.

"Good Lord, he must be hungry!" cried the pregnant young woman, sitting up in bed with a jump—owing to her condition, she was allowed to occupy the bed alone.

Juli Sovany, who was cleaning the janitor's boots, clapped her hand to her mouth with a frightened gesture: some of the shoe cream settled on her nose and shined brightly. The widow Daniska crossed herself; Mr. Kovacs sneezed.

"He must be standing right outside the door asking to be let in," said the janitor.

The whole cellar listened with bated breath; after a few seconds of silence, the lonely, gentle neighing was heard again.

"He wants his dinner!" Juli cried, and, in her surprise, dropped the janitor's boot. The pregnant woman jumped out of bed in her bare feet; Mrs. Daniska also scrambled out from under her red and white checked eiderdown, and in a moment the whole cellar was up. His lips shiny, and his forehead puckered with annoyance, Councilor Pignitzky, the air-raid warden, emerged from his recess like a weather-cock.

"What's all the fuss about?" he demanded irritably. "Has the building collapsed?"

"The horse wants to come in, Councilor!" explained Aunt Mari excitedly.

"He probably wants to go to bed," the air-raid warden grumbled. "I knew there'd be trouble. Where are you going?"

"We must feed the poor thing," the old laundress said. "God knows when he last had a meal."

Pignitzky waved his hand; the thick shadow of his arm ran up the murky cellar wall as threateningly as Cain's fratricidal cudgel. A second later an ear-splitting explosion shook the red brick floor.

"He'll have to be slaughtered," said the Councilor when he regained the hearing of his temporarily deafened ear, and the spasm contracting his heart had eased. "We can't keep him here anyway."

"God forbid!" Aunt Mari cried threateningly. "We won't hear of it!" said the pregnant young woman, covering her eyes with her hands as if in self-defense. An old charwoman suddenly broke into loud sobs. In the meantime the men, too, had got out of bed, and the lame waiter, his face flushed, shook his stick menacingly at the shelter commander. "Not on your life!" he screeched in a thin voice overflowing with fury. "You won't stick your knife into an innocent animal that came here to seek shelter! We'll have something to say about that!"

The old porter, who was still smarting from the memory of his regurgitated dinner, nodded approvingly. "It would be a pity to kill such a valuable animal!" said the retired postman, starting out behind Mrs. Daniska's back toward the double wooden door of the cellar.

The horse was indeed in the lobby, but not alone. Beside him stood Uncle Janos, washing his wounds with a pail of lukewarm water in the light of the hurricane lamp that swung on a nail in the wall. The horse stood motionless, his head held proudly, looking with his gentle brown eyes straight into the eyes of the crowd that pressed through the door, stopped, startled, and then retreated a step.

"I bet he isn't blind," Aunt Mari said to herself while her reluctant nostrils took small sniffs of the raw smell of the humid, steaming animal hide.

"We should like to feed him," Mrs. Daniska announced in a loud voice.

The man did not answer; he was examining the horse's back. Only now did it become apparent how thoroughly he had rubbed down the horse.

"Don't you think he should be fed, Uncle Janos?" Mrs. Daniska asked shyly.

"You took your time," grumbled the man. "What have you brought?"

The animal's skin shone so youthfully and beautifully in the shaft of light cast by the hurricane lamp that Aunt Mari involuntarily closed her eyes.

"I brought him a slice of bread," she announced.

"Me too," said the retired postman.

"I brought a lump of sugar."

There was a silence. People looked at each other.

"That's a great help!" growled Uncle Janos.

A horse will eat neither bean soup nor bacon; nor honey either. The gray-moustached, tubercular barber's assistant offered the contents of one of his two straw mattresses; he was city-bred, and thus could not know that a horse will use straw only to lie on, not to eat.

"Has nobody a little maize?" asked the lad in the army blouse.

"I've got half a sackful," said one of the laundresses. "My son brought it from Torokbalint, but I couldn't find a goose to feed it to. It's upstairs."

By ten o'clock most of the Russian long-range guns had fallen silent; a calm, starlit night descended on the town. As the old laundress still did not have the courage to go upstairs, Uncle Janos climbed up himself.

He went up the back stairs, as that side of the building was more protected from the mines; when he reached the open corridor, he started to run, and ran all the way to the old woman's flat. However, he could not find the sack of maize under the bed despite his search; all he could find were a few stripped cobs in the corner of the larder.

The room had one opening overlooking a narrow side street of the Danube quay. If one leaned out, one could see the moonlit river and, across on the other bank, the dark Castle Hill crowded with cupolas. The cold, whistling wind ruffled the surface of the river into tiny, silvery waves, and its sudden gusts ruffled the torn, gold-flowered wallpaper. Like an arrow shot forth by the hill itself, the Church of St. Matthew strove darkly toward the moonlit sky; the houses beneath, in which all human consciousness had become extinct since the beginning of the siege, gazed at the deserted river with their dead eyes. The town grew and ran riot in the moonlight like an undisciplined monster from whose stammering only one sound emerged clearly: the rattle of a distant machine gun. From behind the Parliament building the river swept along in its reflection the red glow of a burning house, in the direction of the Chain Bridge.

The old man shivered, and retreated from the window. For a while he stood there, scratching his head and staring out into the night without moving.

He was overcome by the kind of tiredness one feels when one is trying to solve a riddle to which there is no solution. He looked around the dark room, then went up to the wall and, with an irritable movement, tore off a fluttering piece of wallpaper.

As he was leaving the flat, he met the old laundress at the

door. "I was frightened something had happened to you," said the latter, panting. "I couldn't think why you stayed away so long unless you got hurt on the way. That's why I came up—though I was so scared that I fell down on the second floor."

Fresh shots were heard from the direction of the Danube, and then came the jerky rattle of a machine gun.

"What's that?" asked the laundress, startled. "Are the Russians as close as that?"

The old man shrugged his shoulders. "Of course not," he replied moodily. "They're machine-gunning the Jews on the riverbank."

"Dear Lord, what a world we live in!" the old woman sighed.

The first bombers appeared over the Pest side early the next morning. Flying low over the rooftops, they machine-gunned the antiaircraft gun installed on top of the neighboring house, and now and again a bomb fell on the deserted houses like a coarse oath spat out by the cold winter dawn. At ten o'clock it was still impossible to get out to the yard for water.

In the stuffy cellar people lay listless, motionless and hungry in their beds. Sometimes a group would go out onto the landing to smoke a cigarette, but after fifteen minutes they would return, their fingers stiff with cold, to the stove. In the corridor, Mr. Kovacs was sawing up an uprooted tree that he and two others had dragged in on the janitor's sleigh on one of the calmer nights from Liberty Square; as they had to economize on both light and fuel, most of the cellar-dwellers assembled in the second cellar around the stove and a single oil lamp. The lad in the army blouse opened a free cobbler's shop in one corner, and, so far as his skill allowed, repaired the damaged shoes of the inhabitants one after the other. The retired postman sat patching his torn shirt, looking down at it through his steel-rimmed spectacled eyes; Aunt Mari thought of her husband with many a sigh.

From time to time, one of the old women would go out to the coal cellars to see whether the horse was still there. The animal stood, hanging its head in the pitch-dark corridor, and refused to lift it even when someone stroked his neck. His smooth, damp skin twitched as if he were shaking off a fly. Once, in the course of the morning, he neighed plaintively, but that was the only sign of life he gave.

It was midday before Uncle Janos and the lame waiter were able to start out for Liberty Square. They took a coal sack along with them; instead of a sickle, they had a long bread knife. The bombers had vacated the low, leaden, dripping sky, and for the time being the Russians were shelling the town from the direction of Buda only, so one could walk with relative safety on one side of the street. Here and there, bomb craters loomed darkly in the caved-in walls, splintered glass and rubble; in one place a burst water main had flooded the street ankle deep; a big china doll, its arms flung wide, floated on the dark, seething water. There were hardly any people about; an occasional soldier hurried past with lowered head, and sometimes a stray dog would scuttle into the ruins baring its teeth.

They had not reached Liberty Square when Juli Sovany overtook the two men. They were just skirting a tank trap, in the depths of which lay an overturned German truck and two dead soldiers with their faces in the mud beside it.

"What the hell are you following us for?" demanded the waiter.

The girl shrugged.

"Speak up, girl. Why did you come?" Uncle Janos urged her.

"I just came to help you," said Juli, "so that we get it done sooner."

"We don't need you. Go on home!" the waiter ordered. Juli did not answer, but bent her head and tramped silently on beside them. Her thin body, huddled in a big black shawl, huge cracked men's shoes on her feet, swayed to and fro in the icy wind like something in a fairy tale. The clouds, swollen with snow, sank so low that the street went utterly dark; one could hardly see more than ten steps ahead in the thick fog rolling up from the river.

"The Councilor wants to slaughter him!" the girl announced after a while. A second later she stumbled and would have fallen on her face had not Uncle Janos caught her arm.

"I've fixed that!" said the waiter in a superior tone of voice.

Juli shook her head violently. "You haven't fixed it," she replied nervously. "He said it again just after you'd gone. He said there was nothing to feed him with anyway, and he'd only starve to death."

The waiter stopped in his tracks. "That's none of his business," he grumbled. "Since when has he worried about someone else's food?"

In the meantime they had reached Liberty Square, where they went diligently to work. Cutting grass with the short-handled bread knife and the kitchen knife Juli had brought with her was a pretty clumsy business. Fortunately, the lawn had not been mown since the autumn so the grass was long enough, but the infantry and artillery crossing the square had trampled the wet, rusty grass-blades into the soil so that it was difficult to find a healthy, upstanding patch. The girl knelt down on the ground, and the two men followed her example. Their fingers soon grew stiff from the wet grass and the frozen clods. The guns from Buda opened up only intermittently, but one of the shells landed in the National Bank building behind them, leaving a ragged smoking hole in the wall.

Juli straightened up and stared at the house. "I hit him," she said suddenly. "I hit him," Juli repeated, her eyes filling with tears.

"Whom?"

"Councilor Pignitzky," the girl whispered.

The waiter stared at her as if he feared she had taken leave of her senses.

"Aunt Mari was so furious that she shouted at him," Juli continued, wiping a glistening tear from her protruding cheekbone with her fist. "And the other women started wailing, then Aunt Daniska pulled the Councilor's sleeve and screeched so loudly that I got nervous and hit Mr. Pignitzky. But it didn't hurt him because he didn't even turn around."

Uncle Janos stopped cutting grass, straightened up, and gave the girl a long, searching look from his small eyes. The lame waiter laughed so hard that he almost fell over.

"What is there to laugh at?" the girl asked, offended. "I know that we are born to do our duty, not to be happy. Still, that horse wasn't born to be slaughtered."

"And what about people?" asked Uncle Janos.

The fog had grown so dense that they tended to move away from each other without noticing it. It seemed to wrap them from head to foot in a thick gray layer of cotton wool. It was getting late, dusk merged with the earthly gloom, and it seemed advisable to return home. Uncle Janos lifted the half-filled sack onto his shoulder, and Juli took the lame waiter's arm to help him over the frozen slippery mounds of earth.

On the corner of Nador Street, they came to a sudden halt. Steps sounded from behind the curtain of fog, soft, squelching steps, as if a long, invisible procession were approaching through the sticky mud. First to emerge from the fog was the figure of a policeman, and behind him, in fours, came blurred swaying shapes with huge bundles on their bent backs or over stuffed sacks under their arms; one old woman was completely doubled up under the weight of a gigantic black traveling bag, which stretched her emaciated arm to breaking point; a man was staggering along pushing a pram, and two people, like rather denser portions of fog, carried bulky gray eiderdowns on their shoulders. As far as one could make out in the dim light, the procession consisted mainly of elderly men and women and small children who also carried bundles on their backs, and were walking with terror-stricken faces among the adults. Uniformed men with Arrow-Crosses on their armbands marched on both sides of the procession, their rifles covering it.

Juli Sovany pinched the waiter's arm in fright. "What's going on, Mr. Andrasi?" she whispered in the man's ear.

"What are you pinching me for?" the waiter cried irritably. "Can't you see it's the Jews?"

"Jews!" the girl repeated, horrified. "Where are they taking them?"

Receiving no answer, she drew her arm from under the waiter's, and clutched Uncle Janos's arm with both hands. "Where are they taking them?" she whispered, raising herself on tiptoe to reach the old man's ear.

"How the hell should I know?" he snapped. "Stop pulling my arm, do you hear?"

In places, the billowing fog penetrated so deeply between the columns that it would suddenly isolate an entire section of the procession. A gray-haired woman dragged herself past them, her hump bigger than her back; the wind blew her long hair steeply up into a halo of weakness. A long thin arm holding a stick, the end of which disappeared into the swirling vapor, reached out from another moving recess of the fog. Here and there, a lonely head would rise above it, further on a leg would sink into the billows which immediately swallowed it up together with the invisible trunk following it. When the smoky veil thinned out for a moment, one could glimpse the blazing house on the other side of the street, its flickering flames coloring the procession that wound its way below it a bright, burning red. The roof-beams crackled, pistol shots were heard from the end of the line.

A tall, skinny woman stumbled past them, dragging a little boy along behind her.

"Save my son!" she whispered hoarsely, turning her blood-less face toward Uncle Janos. The man turned away immediately.

"Look out!" he shouted to Juli, who had stepped forward. He pulled her back. "If they catch you they make you join the line!"

For a moment the fog around the tall woman dispersed, and her face, as it stared back at them, was as sharply outlined against the glare of the flames as a question at the confessional. Juli looked up to the sky. Clear before her eyes was the Angel of Death hovering in the rain of sparks above the woman's head. The shadow of the huge sword in its hand was falling across the woman's face.

Suddenly Juli let go of Uncle Janos's arm; holding her skirt down to her side with both hands, she ran up to the Arrow-Cross man who was walking at the head of the procession.

"Where are you taking them, sir?" she asked, in her clear, courageous voice. In the burning house, a beam crashed to the ground with an explosive thud, and was dully submerged in the soft sea of fog.

"Go to hell, or you'll find out for yourself!" the Arrow-Cross man growled.

Juli joined her hands entreatingly. "Please let them go, sir!" she begged, raising her tearstained little face to the uniformed man. The latter walked on in silence, his head bowed. The burning house was left behind, but Juli did not mind; she stumbled on with hurried little steps behind the Arrow-Cross man, and at times when she reached his side, raised her clasped hands to him in a gesture of supplication. Then someone took her by the scruff of her neck, spun her round, and planted a heavy boot so hard on her behind that she fell facedown in the mud.

By the time she got home to the air-raid shelter, the women were already busy preparing the evening meal. The card play-

ers' table shone in a fairy-like light; as the cellar had deprived
them of the common night-light, Mr. Kovac's had offered them
a huge, twisted pink candle from his own store for the evening
ceremony. Involuntarily, Juli stopped by the table and, bending
forward, sniffed the long pink stem and the golden petals vibrating above it; they had a devout, Christmas Eve-like scent.
For a while she sniffed it dreamily, then wiped her nose with
the back of her hand; then she ran into the second cellar, retreated into a corner and squatted down on a footstool.

The women were gay; here and there loud laughter rang
out below the high ceiling. Because of the fog, the guns had
been silent almost since noon, and planes did not come over; so
those in the mood could take a walk in the yard in the fresh air,
or go up to clean their flats, wash and do a bit of laundry; one of
the women even took time to bake a small white loaf from the
last of her flour. They returned to the shelter with their hearts
more at ease; perhaps, they thought, they would survive the
siege after all.

"They say the Russians have been driven back in Buda," re-
lated the janitor's wife who had even received a visitor that
afternoon.

"I wonder . . ." the old porter wagged his head.

"But on this side they're advancing into Rakosszentmihaly,"
said another woman who had paid a neighborly visit to the next
air-raid shelter in the afternoon. "I talked to the soldier son of
the Sabos family a while back; he's in the signal corps, you
know."

"I wish it was all over," sighed Aunt Mari.

The women did not dare imagine how it would end. The
two-fold wisdom of age and poverty did not inquire into de-
tails: they made do with the featherweight, wonderful hope that
they might stay alive and go on cleaning the rich families'
homes and laundering their dirty clothes. The most demanding
of them was the widow Daniska; she would have liked to see

her daughter once more before she died, but her daughter had married someone in Transylvania, and heaven alone knew whether she was still alive.

"It's easy for you, dear," she would say to Aunt Mari, "you have no one in the world to mourn if they were to perish!"

"Not even you, Mrs. Daniska?" Aunt Mari would ask, breaking into gentle laughter with the whole of her wrinkled old face.

The thick fog penetrated the lobby of the cellar from the courtyard; when they opened the door, a white rag of mist would slide into the cellar and draw into the air the shapes of the dangerous night. But inside, the accustomed landscape had become so intimately warm, familiar and safe that even the janitor's little boy, who was always whining, calmed down, and the other children virtually unsettled the whole cellar with their happy shouts and explosive giggles.

"Have you seen Juli?" the janitor's wife asked. "Where has that girl gone to now?"

"She ran out of the house at noon," someone said, "but I haven't seen her since."

"She may have slipped out to follow Uncle Janos to Liberty Square," a woman said. "Though he's been back for a long while."

"I hope nothing's happened to her!"

"A bad penny always turns up," said the janitor's wife, and sneezed.

Juli squatted motionless in the dark corner, making herself as small as possible, and listened zealously to the conversation. The retired postman's high, piled-up bed behind which she had sheltered hid her completely. But before evening fell they found her. It was Aunt Mari who discovered her with a severe flash of her inherited spectacles.

"So, you've been sitting here all the time," she said, lowering her voice involuntarily so as not to betray the girl. "Were you asleep, you poor little thing? Come now, help me fetch some water."

For a moment Juli did not answer, then she said loudly, "No!"

"Help me fetch some water!" repeated Aunt Mari more loudly.

"I won't help!" said Juli again, throwing back her head.

For a while, Aunt Mari looked at her thoughtfully, then she shrugged and turned away. The cellar calmed down. When even the lame waiter had stopped sneezing and they had put out the night-light, Juli slipped on tip-toe from the cellar, pulled the double wooden door carefully shut and, still on tip-toe, started out toward the coal cellar. It was pitch dark in the corridor, but the horse's warm smell guided her.

"Sh-h!" she said when, sensing her approach, the animal snorted nervously. She laid the palms of her hands on the horse's velvet-soft nose. "Be quiet!" she begged him, and gave his neck a reassuring pat. Then, squatting down on the thin layer of straw at the horse's feet, and leaning her back against the wall, she pulled the big black shawl closer to her breast. Dawn was breaking, an ashen gray light was creeping up the wall from the ventilator that opened onto the courtyard, when Councilor Pignitzky, on his way to the lavatory, turned into the corridor. Juli ran in silently up to him, and stabbed him in the heart with the bread knife she had brought back with her from Liberty Square.

Outside it was already much lighter. She roamed the streets all day, taking refuge in the nearest doorways against the infrequent raids, then stayed for a while with an old cook who had known her mother in her girlhood.

She was sitting on a pink cloud floating high up in the sky—this was what she dreamed as she sat on the narrow wooden bunk under the pink blanket—and the horse was standing beside her, holding its head up proudly, and happily shooing away the heavenly pink flies with its tail. The cloud swam away over Budapest, crossed the silvery Danube and hung suspended for a while over Mount Gellert. Wherever it passed, it was accompanied on earth, not by a shadow, but by a brilliant pink light that illuminated the streets and the steep roofs. Juli leaned comfortably back against the soft cumulus and folded her hands across her stomach. They were flying so high that her gaze could encompass half the country.

"Thank you for saving my life," said the horse. Its neck shone with a pink glow in the cloud's strong light.

Juli swung her legs above Mount Gellert. "I did what I could," she replied modestly, "otherwise they would have made you join the procession too, wouldn't they?"

"Certainly," said the horse.

The cloud started off again, but this time it flew toward Kobanya. By the time Juli returned to the wooden bunk, morning had come. She threw the shawl over her head and ran up the staircase. At the front door a soldier stopped her.

"Where are you running to, Miss?" he asked.

"To my mother," said Juli quickly, then she ran through the door, and flew like an arrow along the early morning street. At the first corner she stopped for a moment, turned her little snub nose, reddened with weeping, back in the direction from which she had come, then slipped into a side street. She was never seen again.

The Parcel

IN THE morning, when they opened the double door of the air-raid shelter, the draft that swept in from the direction of the yard stirred all the occupants of the cellar to an excitement like an exclamation. The bottles on the shelves clicked together, the blankets on the beds fluttered, dust rose up from the floor.

"Shut that door!" growled a man's voice. In the bed opposite the door, a girl stuck her tousled head up from her pillow, and blinked in amazement as she regarded the cloud of dust churning the air at the foot of the bed. Right and left people sat up abruptly or propped themselves up on their elbows.

"What's happening?" someone cried. Aunt Mari, the cobbler's widow, lit a candle and raised her arm, thus softly illuminating the face of the old woman next to her.

"Are you alive, Mrs. Daniska?" she asked.

"Why shouldn't I be alive?" the other mumbled indifferently. "What did you wake me up for?"

"Did I wake you?" Aunt Mari asked, amazed. "Didn't you hear the house cave in over our heads?"

"Well, what can I do about it?" grumbled the widow Daniska. "Do you expect me to stick it together again?"

The shelling seemed to have stopped; not a sound came from the yard. There was not even a crack on the low ceiling of the cellar, and the darkly sweating walls were unscathed. The herald of the event, the tall cloud of dust, crumbled suddenly and collapsed on the floor as if, on reaching its goal, it were disclaiming its own existence. People got out of bed and began to dress with quick, silent movements.

By the time Uncle Janos, the deputy air-raid warden, had pulled on his boots and put his Transylvanian fur cap on his head, his neighbor, Mr. Andrasi, the lame waiter, who always slept fully clothed and wearing his hat, had already returned from his reconnaissance. The yard side of the building had received a direct hit on the first floor, he announced; however, the damage was not serious, the shell had only knocked a small hole in the wall, and blown a piece out of the landing.

"But even that isn't too bad," he said, "because it hasn't torn off the whole of the landing, but only broken a piece out of it. So our nice little landing is now hanging from the house wall like skin from a sausage."

"How am I going to get into my flat, then?" asked the old seamstress.

The waiter shrugged his shoulders.

"What do you want to get in there for?" he grumbled. "Do you want to clean up again? Time enough for that when peace comes."

The women lit the stove, fetched water, made the beds, swept the floor; the men went out to the landing to smoke, or climbed up to the yard to look at the broken landing with appraising glances. The young man in the army blouse ran over to the baker's shop to see whether it was open. Half an hour later, as he was returning empty-handed, he ran into Aunt Mari on the stairway. The old woman flashed him a disapproving look through the spectacles she had inherited from her late husband.

"Why are you roaming the streets, child?" she asked reproachfully. "The Arrow-Cross men will catch you!"

"And why are you climbing up to the third floor?" replied the lad. "Do you want to catch birds?"

As he reached the dark, narrow, winding staircase that led down to the cellar, he picked the frightened old woman up in his arms, and, laughing loudly, ran down the steps with her.

"This way we get down quicker—true, Aunty?" he said, setting the small body carefully down on the floor next to the wall. "Coffee must be ready, I think—I can smell it."

Aunt Mari shook her head. "Oh dear," she said, "I can't eat now—I've seen a dead body."

"Where?"

"Right under my window!" the old woman sighed.

The lad stared at her. "Where?" he repeated. "Are you sure it was under your window? On our pavement?"

"You can look right down into the poor soul's face from my window," explained Aunt Mari.

The soldier emitted a long whistle. "That's bad," he said, "if he really is on the pavement."

After breakfast, the men filed onto the landing to discuss the day's joyless events. The Russian bombers droned harshly over the rooftops, their machine guns biting and chopping into the bare walls of the houses; the antiaircraft gun on the roof of the neighboring bank coughed unceasingly. When the gunfire died down for a moment they could hear from the yard above the slow, monotonous trickle of the thawing snow—a gentle reminder of the winter.

"It's a fact that he's lying on our pavement," the soldier reported, "right under Aunt Mari's window."

"A civilian?"

"A civilian."

Uncle Janos, the deputy air-raid warden, sucked the ends of his walrus moustache into the corners of his mouth and remained morosely silent.

"Well, if he really is a civilian, and is lying on our pavement, then we'll have to bury him," sighed the squat, pink-faced, white-haired janitor. He looked worried. "And, what's more, we'll have to ask some of the women to help—we can't manage on our own!"

The day before there had appeared a decree from the Mayor, according to which the tenants of each block were given twenty-four hours to bury any dead civilians found lying outside it, in the nearest public park. The nearest public park was Szabadsag Square, but heavy German tanks had moved in, and the Germans would not let anyone go close to it.

"Jozsef Square is full," said the retired postman. "We'll have to take him to Erzsebet Square."

How were they to carry the corpse to Erzsebet Square, which was a good twenty minutes away and in the line of fire of the Russian mortars? How were they to bury him when they could only muster two shovels between them, not a single pickax, and the ground was frozen hard? What were they to cover him with when the people in the cellar were so poor that one was lucky if one had a winding sheet for oneself?

By evening, however, man's cunning had solved even these painful questions. After dark, at the hour of the daily card battle, while the women, grouped around the stove, the evening light of the embers illuminating their faces, smoothed from their minds the wrinkles that had accumulated there during the day, the men stole out one by one from the shelter, and, led by Uncle Janos, marched along the front of the block. They walked in single file, close to the wall so as not to be seen, under Aunt Mari's window. The dead man lay close to the curb, his body straight, his black double-breasted winter coat molded to his body as if he had carefully arranged it beneath him before lying down; only his hat had rolled from his head, and his long gray hair hung down in disorder on the snow-caked paving stones. The moon shone straight into his face: his eyes were open.

The old men stood around him. The waiter took off his hat, then, sneezing violently, stuck it quickly back on his head. "Let's hurry," someone said. Although not a soul was in sight in the narrow, moonlit street, the pure, beautiful night could easily have enticed a bored cellar-dweller out into the street, or a Russian plane above it.

"Take his feet," Uncle Janos instructed Mr. Kovacs, the fat tailor whose flaming red face hovered like a lamp over the snow. "And you, Mr. Andrasi, help him. The rest of us will take his shoulders. Ready?"

The next corner of the block was not too far away, but the old men broke out into a sweat. The dead man was heavier than they had thought. The retired postman wiped his forehead with a red and white checked handkerchief. They put the body down so quickly that its head hit the pavement with a thud.

"Sh-h!" said the old postman, looking around nervously.

The lame waiter stepped back and took a careful look at the body. "Is it lying all right?" he asked. "Shouldn't we put it nearer the wall?"

"He was lying on the edge of the pavement at our place," said the soldier. "That's his natural position."

The lame waiter knelt down on the pavement and smoothed down the dead man's overcoat on both sides of his body. "Lift him up a bit in the middle, will you?" he grumbled. "I can't do it alone. You're right—let him lie the way he was."

It was a mild night; melting snow dripped from the rooftops. Some fell on the dead man's face.

"Shouldn't we move him a bit?" said the retired postman, crossing himself involuntarily.

"What for?"

The old man did not answer. The lad in the army blouse burst out laughing. "It will be quite a surprise," he said, and his white teeth flashed in the moonlight, "when they wake up in the morning and find a body to bury. God, won't that be an upheaval?"

"And they won't have to take too long about it, either," muttered Uncle Janos.

"Why not?" The waiter scrambled to his feet. "I get it," he said. "The weather has been very mild since yesterday."

"Lord, what a surprise!" repeated the soldier, pushing his cap to the back of his head expansively. "How these gentlemen will complain when they have to drag it all the way to Erzsebet Square. . . . What's the name of that pig-faced councilor who lives on the first floor here?"

At that, even the old porter could not help laughing. "And Director Lorincz," he whispered, poking a moonlit finger toward the flashing windows of the house, "and Mr. Finiasz, the lawyer . . . and Bor, the solicitor on the third floor, the one who used to make me take a parcel for him every week . . ."

"And now you're sending him one," said the retired postman.

Suddenly a cold wind rose from the Danube. A broken window on an upper floor flew open, and its cracked panes swept the pavement with their silvery reflection. A single shot was heard in the distance.

The tailor turned back. "They're coming," he growled, "be careful!"

There was a sound of light splashing behind them, as if the small puddles hiding in the dark had suddenly begun to talk. Two small, but denser, shadows detached themselves from the shadow at the foot of the wall that cut obliquely across the street, and, emerging into the moonlit part of the pavement, came two more shadows.

"Aunt Mari and old Mrs. Daniska," muttered the air-raid warden. "What ill wind blew these two here?"

The two old women teetered toward them holding tightly on to each other. "Have you moved my dead man?" Aunt Mari shouted from some distance away. "You see, they did move him—didn't I tell you so, Mrs. Daniska?"

"They moved him in front of the next house," the old laundress stammered, crossing herself.

Aunt Mari flashed her spectacles. "They were quite right to do so, Mrs. Daniska," she answered. "We'll have plenty to do, burying our own dead."

"Why are there so many old women?" said the lame waiter under his breath.

Aunt Mari bent over the dead man. "And this one isn't a boy any longer, either," she said. "Why didn't someone close his eyes?"

"Because it was impossible," the waiter growled. "I tried, but it was too late."

The dead man looked up at the sky through wide-open eyes as if he were watching the moonlight. Aunt Mari bent down lower, touched the woolly black winter coat, then straightened up, sighing. "Now I won't be able to eat my dinner either," she complained. "Every time I see a dead body I get heartburn."

"In that case, you'd better go home, lady."

"Will you leave the coat on him?" asked the old woman, taking Mrs. Daniska's arm. Then, holding her skirt down with her other hand, she set off homeward again.

The men looked at each other. Another muffled shot was heard from a long way off in the direction of the Danube. Suddenly Uncle Janos bowed his fur-capped head and turned slowly away. "Well!" gasped the soldier, raising his hand as if about to clap it to his brow; but his arm stopped halfway. The two old women had disappeared in the shadow of the house. Only their slow splashing was still audible in the night's quiet. The old porter wiped his sweating forehead with his red-checked handkerchief. "That thieving old witch ought to be burned!" he whispered, shaking his head.

At home, the two old women were already in bed by the time the men stole in one by one. Last to come was the lad in the army blouse, but he, too, came empty-handed. Aunt Mari, who had kept her eyes fixed on the door, raised her eyebrows disapprovingly, then, with a determined movement, she turned her back on the people assembled around the stove clattering plates and cutlery.

"So there you are," she sighed, turning her mild, bespectacled gaze toward the wrinkled face of old Mrs. Daniska who was lying next to her. "And poor Uncle Ruzicska doesn't have a decent rag to bless himself with. . . ."

The old laundress folded her hands contentedly under the blanket. "And still they didn't do it!" she said. "Yet Mr. Andrasi could certainly do with a better overcoat to replace that thin ragged coat he wears. But you see, dear, I've been doing the washing and ironing for the best families for forty-four years, and they put their laundry uncounted into my hands—I've never pinched so much as a dirty handkerchief."

"May God bless you for it," the cobbler's widow said.

A thin wail rose from one corner—the rebellious complaint of a ten-day-old child. Around the stove or squatting on the edge of their beds, rather like sparrows, the old people were noisily sipping the thick soup that had been distributed, while in a corner, by the light of a candle, a heavy, gray-haired woman, bending over a tub, was soaping her grandchild's pink bottom. Aunt Mari suddenly sat up in bed. "Why, have I ever taken anything?" she asked indignantly. "It's different if one person steals from someone else. But if a lot of poor people steal together, it's as if God himself were stealing!"

"Now don't take on so!" said the old laundress, lifting her hands defensively.

"And it's not as though they'd have been depriving anybody else!" continued Aunt Mari, her face flushing. "May God rest the poor soul, but he's just lying there on the pavement with nobody to mourn him and tomorrow they'll put him in a hole. If we take that overcoat off him it's no more than if we were taking the skin off an old dead sheep." Aunt Mari's spectacles flashed more and more severely. "You see, Mrs. Daniska," she continued, lowering her voice so as not to be overheard by the neighbors, "I couldn't even eat my supper—I get so upset when I see a dead body. But do you think those gentlemen next door will bury him with that good overcoat on? Either they pull it off him or we do. Or rather, they will, now."

The old laundress broke into unexpected laughter. "But at least they'll work for it," she giggled in her thin, old voice; in the dark, it sounded like a small cracked bell. "They were smart, those old fools, weren't they?"

Aunt Mari smiled. "They landed them with our property," she said, and with a quick movement she took off her spectacles and slipped them under her pillow. "Now they'll have to do some work. That poor old man! Well, good night, Mrs. Daniska."

She fell asleep quickly, but woke before dawn, and, resting her hand carefully on the side of the bed so as not to wake her neighbor, she sat up noiselessly. In the dim light of the night-lamp her eyes roamed over the cellar; the others were all asleep, their heavy snores jostled and entangled with each other under the low ceiling like an agitated curly-backed flock of sheep in a locked fold. Someone whimpered miserably in his sleep. From the next cellar one could hear the thin whistling snore of the retired postman. That's one we shall have to bury, thought Aunt Mari, lowering her feet carefully onto the cold stone floor. She pulled her spectacles out from under her pillow and dressed quickly. She longed for some fresh air before the early morning bombing began.

As the front door was still locked, she walked around the yard for a bit, and then went up to her own flat on the third floor. The gray light of dawn had not yet suffused the coherent world outside, but when, a little later, she glanced out of the window to look up and down the street, she could distinguish clearly the hoarfrost-covered pavement with the outline of the dead body that had regained its original position under her window. Frightened, Aunt Mari clapped her hand to her mouth. They've put it back! she thought, her heart beating. Upon my life, they've put it back!

Gathering her skirts in both hands, she ran at breakneck speed down the stairs. In the air-raid shelter, people were beginning to wake up. Some were clearing their throats. Uncle Janos, his fur-capped head bent low, was pulling on his boots. At the creaking of the wooden door, every head turned toward the flushed and panting old woman who stood there in the open doorway. "They've put it back!" she cried breathlessly. "May Christ be my witness, they've put it back!"

"What?" asked the lame waiter, alarmed.

"The old gentleman."

"What?" stammered the old porter. "I don't understand."

"They must have noticed, the scoundrels, and put it back during the night!" Aunt Mari cried angrily.

The entire cellar crowded around the excited old woman, the children screamed and jumped up on the benches. "They've put it back! . . . they've put it back!" screeched the janitor's six-year-old son, shaking his rattle. Suddenly a sharp explosion shook the open door.

"Come in!" grumbled old Aunt Focher, a charwoman who was deaf in both ears. "Keep away from the door, he can't get in that way!" But who it was that could not get in she did not vouchsafe.

As the gunfire increased in intensity, going out into the street to inspect the situation was out of the question. The more loudly the women wailed, the more stubbornly silent the old men, outwitted, became; only the lame waiter seethed with indignation, and threatened the dark and oozing ceiling with his cane. The old porter stole out unnoticed from the shelter, and tramped up to Aunt Mari's flat.

The dead man, in his double-breasted overcoat, lay right under the window on the very edge of the pavement, in the exact spot from which they had dragged him the previous evening. The solicitor has returned my parcel, thought the old porter, and such bitterness welled up in him that he would have liked nothing better than to burst into tears. He leaned far out of the window, and stared at the next house.

"You'll pay for this, don't you worry!" he shouted angrily, shaking his old fist at the house. A flock of pigeons rose with a flurry of beating wings from the roof next door, and, seconds later, in a cloud of smoke and dust, a shell slammed into the shuttered window of the corner grocery.

Aunt Anna

ABOUT SEVEN o'clock in the morning, both doors of the air-raid shelter flew silently open, and a heavy-framed old woman appeared on the threshold in the milky light. Her gray hair fluttered; she swung a small bundle in one hand, and the other hand she held pressed to her belly.

"Wake up!" she cried in her deep, booming voice, like waves shifting pebbles on a beach. "Wake up! The Flood's upon us!"

A night-light stood on a shelf fixed to the wall, its flame swaying in the draft, casting a tiny yellow spot of radiance on the wall, no bigger than a rose petal; however, it left dark the huge, low-ceilinged cellar that connected with an even darker room at its farthest corner. The people snoring on beds, chairs, or divans, huddled close together, gradually stirred; here and there someone heaved himself half upright on one elbow, someone else yawned mightily, like a cat.

"Wake up!" cried the old woman, as she stood on the threshold, stretching her arm toward the sleeping people. "May the Lord kick you out of your last resting place! How much longer are you going to idle away this black day?"

"What's happened?" screamed a woman.

A young girl sat up in bed and raised both hands to her head. Several people sneezed. Mr. Andrasi, the lame waiter, reached for his stick, and, flushing scarlet, brandished it at the ceiling. Aunt Mari, the cobbler's widow, produced the spectacles inherited from her husband from under her pillow and put them on her nose; then, bending over the widow Daniska, who lay sleeping beside her, began gently to coax her awake.

"What is it now?" Mrs. Daniska murmured. "Have you been dreaming about that horse again?"

"The Flood's upon us!" whispered Aunt Mari, bending over the other widow's wrinkled face.

"Upon us?" the latter asked, still half asleep. She drew her hand along her body, shook her head in negation, and turned onto her other side.

In the first cellar someone lit a candle. The tiny yellow waves of light were quick to interpret the unfolding outside world. Half-clothed figures swayed in the semi-obscurity, wrapped in shawls or dressed in trousers and shirts.

"What's happened? Who is she?" asked Mr. Polesz, an old cabby who had only recently moved in after being bombed out of his flat, pointing a finger at the massive, gray-haired old woman at the door.

"That's Aunt Anna," replied his brother, the retired postman. "She lives on the second floor."

"I've never seen her down here before," grumbled the old cabby.

"Well, she wouldn't leave her flat," the postman explained. "She says she isn't a rat, so why should she live in a cellar."

"So why has she come down now?"

"What's happened?" quavered the woman who had screamed.

"Jesus Christ, the Russians are here!" screeched another.

In a second the whole cellar was on its feet. The women thronged with pale faces around the old woman who, pressing one hand to her belly and swinging her tiny bundle in the other, stood motionless facing the excited crowd. Her black crocheted shawl had slipped off her head, and the draft stirred up the thick, iron-gray locks like a cloud of dust. The age-old layers of the big-boned, powerful face below remained unmoved.

"Well, have you left your nests, my chickens?" she cried, leaning her shoulder up against the door frame. "Damn and blast this lazy populace, snoring so loudly on Judgment Day that it can't even hear the Angel's trumpet! Get a move on, slaves, fetch water!"

"Is the house on fire, Aunt Anna?" yelled the pregnant young woman in alarm, raising her hand defensively in front of her body.

"Of course it isn't on fire, child," said the old woman, her face expressionless. "I want a cup of coffee!"

Then she threw her bundle down on the floor, bent forward like a naughty little girl with her hands, palms downwards, on her knees, and broke into loud, mocking laughter in her strong, masculine voice. Her big, bony frame swayed backward and forward, the dry, clay layers of her face threatened to crumble in this explosion of mirth; her eyes sparkled.

"No, the house isn't on fire, girl," she shouted, "but I want my coffee! Now—before the spring!" she added, in one of her rare good moods, slapping her thigh with her hand. "Mrs. Daniska, I hear your potatoes have sprouted!"

"I haven't got a single potato, Aunt Anna," she replied startled.

"I thought you had," murmured the old woman mockingly. "No matter, you'll have enough next year if you live that long!"

"God forgive you, Aunt Anna, but didn't you say the Russians were here?" the old postman asked plaintively.

"I didn't," the old woman shook her head.

"Then why did you come down?"

"Because they shot me out of my flat, daddy," Aunt Anna replied. "The ceiling caved in on me—it's a miracle it didn't crush me. But let's get a move on, my little birds. Stop preening yourselves and build a fire in that stove as if you were building it on Mount Sinai!"

"The ceiling caved in?" Aunt Mari, the cobbler's widow repeated in a shaky voice. "Heavens, you might have been killed, Aunt Anna!"

"So what?" said Aunt Anna in her thunderous voice. She picked up her ridiculously small bundle from the floor, and set off with creaking steps toward the stove in the inner cellar. "An electric furnace once exploded right beside me at the factory, and nothing happened to me. . . . Whose bed am I going to sleep in?"

The two cellars were connected by a short narrow passage; just before one turned into the passage, there was a small recess opening out from the first cellar in which the most distinguished inhabitants of the house, the widow and children of Councilor Pignitzky, nursed their delicate orphanhood amidst the rough waves of the poor population surrounding them. There was also a small stove in the recess for the exclusive use of the Pignitzkys; the meals shared by the rest of the cellar-dwellers were prepared by the women on the large stove that stood in a corner of the inner cellar. Apart from the Pignitzkys, only the janitor and his wife lived on their own cooking—it was customary for her to throw their meals together in their own ground-floor kitchen during lulls, long or short, in the bombardment.

Aunt Anna stopped in front of the recess and pushed aside the curtain that doubled as a door. "Good morning," she said in a loud voice, her sharp gray eyes slowly scrutinizing the dim recess. "Well, there's enough room here. I can sleep on the couch with one child, and the other can share the bed with its mother."

"What does this woman want?" Mrs. Pignitzky cried, raising herself on one elbow, an alarmed expression on her face.

Aunt Anna threw up her head and bent slightly forward. "What does this woman want?" she repeated quietly. "Only what is every woman's right before childbirth and death: a bed."

"Do you want to have a child here?" asked Mrs. Pignitzky, startled.

Aunt Anna gazed at her and nodded her head twice, emphatically. But before the other woman, lying in bed, could open her mouth again, she released the curtain, turned her back on the inhabitants of the recess, and went abruptly back into the passage.

"Do even rats give themselves airs?" she cried, tramping noisily down between the two rows of beds toward the stove where an old laundress was chopping firewood with the shelter axe. "Do the big rats still call the tune for the small rats to dance to before they all fry together in the fires of hell? Are there still big shots and small fry among the rats?"

"Hush, Aunt Anna," said a tiny old woman who, trotting up behind her, grasped her arm. "Leave her alone. She lost her husband less than a week ago."

Aunt Anna stopped in her tracks, then, in slow motion like a lion, she turned around to face the diminutive charwoman who took an involuntary step backward.

"What? . . . She lost her husband?" she asked in her booming voice. "So, is there a single woman in this dump who hasn't lost her husband or won't lose her husband before she herself crawls under the ground? I raised four children myself without a husband . . . and here's one of them!"

She pointed to a lad aged about twenty wearing an army blouse, who was crouching on the edge of a bed munching a piece of dry bread.

"All right, ma, cease fire," he said quietly. "You don't have to eat the poor woman alive!"

"Shut up, you pipsqueak!" said the old woman, turning her massive gray head toward her son. "Did you ever see anything to beat that?" she growled indignantly. "Have you ever seen a rat getting up on its hind legs and holding out its forepaws to be kissed? And have you ever seen another rat crawling close and kissing them for it? Why don't you look after your mother, you heartless creature, instead of hiding behind your girl's skirts all day?"

The quiet cellar, with its peaceful herd of elderly men and women, telling their beads, was brusquely catapulted out of its normal rhythm by Aunt Anna's appearance. The gentle, inward order of resignation, hitherto disturbed only by the brutal outside events of the siege, disintegrated into its wild, thorny elements and revealed its concealed fires. And as if the world outside had only been waiting for this moment, it seized the cellar, crouching in its fright, like a naughty child its broken toy and hammered it.

An hour after Aunt Anna had moved in, a retreating German machine-gun unit settled in one of the more protected areas of the house opening on to the courtyard—a little tailor's shop—and one of their trucks backed into the front door, blocking it so completely that one could reach the street only by crawling out between the wheels and the wall. The truck was loaded with cases of ammunition, and if a shell or a bomb had fallen near at hand, the explosion would have blown the house up, and buried the cellar-dwellers beneath its ruins.

During the morning, rumors began to circulate that the Germans had no intention of vacating the tailor's shop, but that, on the contrary, they were setting up a machine-gun nest on a first floor balcony and, in case of close-range fighting, would defend the building to their last bullet. The members of a Romanian labor detachment had been busy for a week digging tank traps at the corner of the street to defend the line of retreat toward the Danube—this, too, confirmed the rumors. But what was to happen to the inhabitants? Would the Germans evacuate the cellar?

The two old widows, Aunt Mari and Mrs. Daniska, were shelling beans for dinner, sitting on the edge of their beds with a white tea-towel spread across their knees. Mrs. Daniska's hands were shaking so much that the beans jumped from her fingers like fleas.

"Where are they going to put us then?" she complained. "The cellars in the other houses round about are so crowded already that there isn't room for another person in them. And where am I to put my bed where I've slept for forty years to save it from being blown up?"

Aunt Mari nodded seriously; her spectacles slipped down the ridge of her nose. "Perhaps they won't evacuate us," she said. "They can't chase so many people out into the streets, can they?"

"I've heard," went on Mrs. Daniska, "about a house in the Ferenc district where the German's didn't evacuate the inhabitants, but just settled down with them in the cellar, and the Russians threw grenades down the air shafts. Just imagine a grenade like that falling on my bed!"

"It may not fall on yours, dear. . . ." Aunt Mari comforted her. "Who told you this? Was it Mr. Polisz?"

"It was."

"He should know better than to go making people nervous," Aunt Mari grumbled. "Where has that soft-witted old porter got to?"

As the old porter was the only one in the cellar who spoke some German, they sent him in deputation to the occupying forces to find out what they intended to do with the house, the fatherland and their lives. In the interests of greater emphasis, prestige and appearance, Mr. Andrasi, the lame waiter, and the shelter commander accompanied him. A whole hour went by, and there was still no sign of them.

"Come nearer, dear," Mrs. Daniska signaled to the other widow. "I want to tell you something."

In the eight years since fate had thrown them together in their one room and kitchen flat on the third floor, the two women had become so familiar with each other that each knew the other's reaction to situations in advance: like the shadow of a familiar object before a known source of light. Once again, Aunt Mari knew exactly what her co-tenant wanted to talk about.

"Aunt Anna?" she asked, nodding her head.

"It's that old witch who's brought the Germans down on us!" whispered the widow Daniska.

The other woman looked up, startled. "What do you mean?"

"I don't know," said the laundress, "but you'll see, she'll bring misfortune to the whole cellar. The moment she came in the world went dark round me . . . and this is a bad sign, a hunch that has never let me down yet."

"But you were asleep, Mrs. Daniska!" Aunt Mari cried indignantly. "I could hardly shake you awake!"

The old laundress ignored this piece of evidence. "She picks a quarrel with everybody," she whispered, and her mild face flushed with anger. "She sets everybody at everybody else's throat. There's no order in her. She loves neither God nor man."

"Who is her son's girl, do you know?" Aunt Mari enquired.

"I know."

Aunt Mari awaited a continuation of this reply in silence. As it was not forthcoming, she reached up and tied the kerchief around her head. "I wonder why there's been no raid today?" she said tactfully.

"And that's another bad sign," Mrs. Daniska replied. "They save it all up and then come down on us like a cloud of wasps."

Suddenly, both fell silent. Arriving back from the courtyard, the delegation entered the cellar, and at the same moment, like a musical accompaniment, a succession of mighty explosions crashed in through the entrance, surrounding the delegation with an aureole, and increasing its stature.

"Nothing doing," announced the old porter, scratching his nose. "We can't get a word out of them. They say we're just to keep calm, and they'll warn us in time if we have to evacuate the cellar. They'll give us at least two hours."

"Good God, two hours!" cried the pregnant young woman, throwing up her hands. "How are we to get ready in two hours

with the children and food and things? And where do they in-
tend to move us to?"

"Oh, my bed!" sighed Mrs. Daniska.

"They're whacked," the old porter continued, "so whacked
that they just threw themselves down on the floor—they didn't
even eat their rations. Their officer comes from Berlin."

A long shadow appeared on the wall; the small group was
suddenly plunged in darkness. Someone had stepped in front of
the night-light.

"Don't make yourself so important, you wrinkled old busy-
body!" grumbled Aunt Anna who had been asleep on one of the
bunks, quiet and motionless, ever since she moved down to
the cellar in the morning, and now suddenly came to life at the
sound of gunfire. "Who wants to know where your officer
comes from?"

Abashed, the old porter fell silent.

"We'll have to move out in two hours, Aunt Anna, and I
don't know where to," the lame waiter told her.

"So what?" boomed the old woman. "I moved out of my flat
in ten minutes. That's how long it took me to crawl out from
under the rubble."

"Anna dear, perhaps you could go up and talk to the commander," the widow suggested slyly. "Say that this place is full of
old people and invalids, so perhaps they'd better move next
door."

"Damn you!" yelled the old woman furiously. Then she
burst out laughing; she laughed happily, boisterously, like a
child, her gray locks shaking around her massive head. "You're
a one, Mrs. Daniska, you are. . . !" she shouted, with a flash of
her big yellow teeth. "You want me to go up and ask them, do
you? Do you know, my little pigeon, when I last asked a favor
from anyone? Forty years ago, when I asked my mother to give
me a clean nightgown for my wedding night! And never since,

even though I brought four children into the world and buried two of them."

She was silent for a second and passed her gaunt, bony fist over her forehead. "That they should get out of here because the house is full of old people and invalids?" she repeated after a while. "Should I send them to the young and healthy, Mrs. Daniska, my dove, so that they can disable them, too? No, my little birds! If we had to make war, we must perish ourselves!"

"I didn't make this war!" cried Mrs. Daniska indignantly.

"So what did you do?" replied Aunt Anna indifferently, switching her sharp, gray eyes from one wrinkled face to the other. "Was there just one single woman in this saintly herd who forbade her husband or son to go off soldiering? If we women had shut up shop, the men couldn't have made war— not on their lives! Now, of course, that they have shot both our husbands and our sons from our beds it's no use moaning. Too late for that, my little birds. But my son won't go to war as long as I live."

About four o'clock in the afternoon, the Germans moved out with their ammunition trucks. But no sooner had the excitement stirred up in their hearts by this unexpected pleasure settled down again—and their joy was so immoderate that Mr. Polesz, the cabby from the Ferenc district, had jumped into the middle of the cellar where he proceeded to do a dance, snapping his fingers, while in the corner, an old laundress retched convulsively over a pail—no sooner had the fun and games calmed down, that another alarming rumor came to upset their short-lived peace. About six o'clock the janitor returned from the street with the news that an Arrow-Cross unit consisting of eight or ten men had taken up quarters in the next house, armed to the teeth with Tommy guns, rifles and hand grenades.

Just as flies buzz more loudly and sting more venomously in

the autumn, before they die—as if quarrelling with death—so did the Arrow-Cross men roam the martyred town in the last weeks of the siege, hitting out even more and destroying their opponents with increasing barbarity. During the day they hunted for deserters, and at night they murdered the Jews; in the mornings, the flagstones on the bank of the Danube, especially near the bridge-heads, shone black with the blood of the victims. As soon as it was dark, and the besieging guns fell silent, the stillness of the deserted streets began to resound with the rattle of machine guns.

"There's a raid on next door," the janitor announced, twirling his thick gray moustache nervously. "Then we can obviously expect them, as they haven't been here yet."

There were no Jews in the house, but there was a deserter. Aunt Anna's son had been sitting in the cellar for eight days now with a forged furlough pass. He had shed his army blouse when the Germans came—the old postman took it and lent the lad his old jacket instead. But what would have been protection enough against the Germans would obviously not satisfy the Arrow-Cross men.

"Give me a piece of bread, Ma," the lad said, "I'll disappear for a while."

"Where are you going to hide, child?" asked Mrs. Daniska in a shaky voice.

"What do you want to know that for?" growled Aunt Anna, taking her last piece of bread from her little bundle. "Why should everybody be in on the secret? I don't know either, but you don't hear me asking!"

The lad put his face close to the widow Daniska's ear, whispered something, then he laughed, turned round and ran out of the shelter. The old woman stared after him, horrified.

"Even at a time like this he can crack jokes," she whispered.

Mr. Andrasi, the lame waiter, went out to stand watch at the street door. But when, half an hour later he came back in, chilled to the bone, he had no fresh news about the raiding party, which was still busy in the next building.

"It's no use standing out there," said Aunt Mari, "time enough to find out when they're here!"

"Let them come!" said an elderly charwoman whom the cellar—since she spent the whole day warm in her bed—had almost completely cured of her chronic rheumatism, "Let them come, there are no Jews here!"

They had a thick soup for dinner and some lentils left over from noon. People gathered around the stove, sitting on bunks and on the edges of beds, but the food went down no more easily than it had at noon while the Germans were still in the house: nobody asked for a second helping. Nor did anyone feel like going to bed: what was the use of falling asleep if the raid would wake them up anyway? Only Aunt Anna retired immediately after dinner. The pregnant young woman, who had been sleeping in a bed by herself because of her condition, moved over and made room for her. The old woman's sleep was as quiet as her body was big; she slept deeply and without moving, like a child, and there was a good chance that she would not disturb her hostess. Her old, brown, furrowed face rested peacefully in the delicate light of the candle, like bread wrapped in a cloth.

Toward midnight, however, by the time the Arrow-Cross men marched into the cellar, everybody was asleep, and the startled faces, slowly shedding the bark of sleep, stared like livid masks into the zigzagging beams of the flashlights. The wind came whistling through the open door; a man next to the wall broke into low sobs.

"Light a candle!" shouted one of the Arrow-Cross men in a hoarse, thin treble.

There were three of them; an elderly, mustachioed man wearing a green hunting hat with a feather, and two short, pale, dark-haired boys. All three wore Arrow-Cross armbands and carried a number of red-handled hand grenades in their belts. They looked like children going to the playground with their tutor.

"Are there any Jews here?" screeched one in a penetrating voice. "Out of bed and have your papers ready!"

The light of the candle flickered in the second cellar. Aunt Mari bent over the widow Daniska and tugged at her pink flannel nightgown.

"Wake up," she said in a low voice so as not to alarm the old woman. "We have guests!"

"What's up, now? Why are you bothering me?" the laundress murmured. "Can't you see I'm shelling my beans?"

Before she could turn over onto her other side, Aunt Mari pulled the blanket off her. "Stop cooking!" she said angrily. "Where are your papers?"

Mrs. Daniska sat up in bed. "Tell me, dear," she said, her voice shaking with indignation, "are you determined not to let me sleep? The whole cellar is my witness that you wake me night after night on some pretext or other. . . ."

One of the Arrow-Cross men blocked the door with a Tommy gun in his hand, the elderly man in the hunting cap sat down at the small table near the entrance, and the third walked slowly along between the beds shining his flashlight into the faces of the men and women as they hurriedly dressed. The silence was so absolute that the janitor's little daughter woke up and started crying.

The shelter commander and the janitor stood in front of the table. "Total?"

"Forty-seven."

"Jews?"

"No, sir," replied the porter.

The elderly man drew his hand across his forehead with a tired gesture.

"If we do find a deserter or a foreign national, we'll take

you both," he said in a low voice. "You can still change your mind."

"There aren't any, sir," repeated the porter. "Only poor people live in this house."

The man who had examined both cellars with a torch returned to the table. "Forty-three," he reported.

"Four missing."

"Have you been in the recess as well?" asked Uncle Janos, the shelter commander.

The short, dark Arrow-Cross man departed and came back a moment later. "One woman and two children," he announced in high pitched shrill voice. "Forty-three and three, in fact."

"That's still one short."

"There's a soldier who is at the front," said the janitor.

The elderly man closed his eyes as if yielding to sudden exhaustion. "Why have you still got him on your list?" he asked after a while in an ever lower voice. "If he doesn't live here, strike him off your list."

"He used to stay here with his mother," the janitor said.

The elderly man made a note on the sheet of paper lying in front of him.

"Any other premises here?"

"No."

"You're lying!" the elderly man said, quietly. "I saw seven or eight doors at the end of the corridor. Coal cellars?"

"Yes," said the janitor, flushing.

"Those are counted as premises, too," the Arrow-Cross man explained. "Now, send me in first the women, then the men, one by one, with their papers."

The short young man with the effeminate voice went to the back of the cellar. One by one the women presented themselves at the table; the pale, dark-haired girl who slept in the bed opposite the door turned faint with excitement, and had to sit down on a chair. When Aunt Anna announced her name, the elderly man mused for a while, his head bent, fiddling with his pencil. He had a thick gold pencil.

"Are you that soldier's mother?" he asked.

The old woman seemed to shrink, her booming voice became soft and melodious, her face gentle and sweet. "Yes, sir," she replied, "I have a soldier son."

"Where is he?"

"If only I knew!" the old woman sighed. "Last week I had a postcard from him, but it didn't tell me where he was. If only I knew whether he is still alive!"

The elderly man nodded approvingly as if he were satisfied with her answer. "Toddle over to the wall, aunty," he said. "Over there near the door, not with the others."

The old woman's face twitched almost imperceptibly. "Yes, sir," she said. The pale, dark-haired girl pressed her hand to her mouth and gave a low moan. The elderly man turned his head in her direction, looked her over carefully, and then bent over his papers. He questioned two more women and then turned back to the girl.

"You go and stand by the wall, too," he said quietly. "There, next to the old woman. And be quick about it!"

Half an hour later, when he had finished with the men, he motioned to the young Arrow-Cross man standing at the back of the cellar, to join him. They talked in low voices so that nobody could catch a word of what they were saying. The young Arrow-Cross man went out through the door. The elderly man leaned back in his chair, stretched his legs out, took his gun from its holster and put it down on the table. He sat quite still, his head thrown back, until the Arrow-Cross man returned, accompanied by another one; in front of them they pushed Aunt Anna's soldier son. The lad's hands were tied behind his back, and his face and hands were covered in a thick layer of coal dust.

The pregnant young woman hid her face in her hands and screamed.

"Be quiet! I don't want to hear a peep out of you!" screeched the shrill-voiced, short Arrow-Cross man. The janitor's face suddenly went livid and he took an involuntary step backward.

"Where is that furlough pass?" asked the elderly man.

"In my pocket," the lad replied in a low voice.

"Take it out for him!"

The short Arrow-Cross man reached into the soldier's breast-pocket and pulled out a folded sheet of paper. The elderly man took a look at it and then tore it up with deliberate movements. "It's faked," he said wearily.

The soldier did not answer. The Arrow-Cross man standing next to him prodded him in the ribs with the butt of his Tommy gun. "Can't you answer?"

"What can I say?" the soldier growled. "It isn't faked."

"Is that why you hid out there in the coal?" the elderly man asked him.

"I hid so you shouldn't arrest me," the soldier said. "And so you shouldn't tear up my furlough pass."

The dark-haired girl standing by the wall burst into loud sobs. The candle in the second cellar went out.

"Why have you put out that candle, you bunch of bastards!" the Arrow-Cross man by the door yelled. "Light it, or I'll let you have it!"

"It's burnt out!" cried a shaky, old, female voice. "Will you please wait until I light another?"

"It's burnt out. . . ." said the elderly man thoughtfully. "Send me that little old man there." He raised his arm, and slowly pointed to the retired postman squatting on one of the beds at the back of the cellar between Mr. Andrasi, the lame waiter, and the old porter. The postman immediately rose and walked up to the table.

"Where did you get that army blouse?" the elderly man asked him.

"From him," the old man muttered.

"Did you swap?"

"We swapped."

"Why?" the elderly man asked, looking into the postman's face from under half-closed eyes.

"Why?" the postman shouted. "Because I've had enough of this war!"

For a moment there was silence.

"Don't!" the elderly man said to the short, shrill-voiced Arrow-Cross man who had raised his arm to hit the old man. "What did you say?"

"I said, with no disrespect to you intended," the postman answered, flushing, "that this snotnose had better not touch me or I'll kick his guts out as surely as my name is Karoly Csukas."

The two Arrow-Cross men standing by the table laughed loudly. But not a muscle moved in the elderly man's face.

"We won't lay a finger on you," he said. His voice sounded more and more tired. "We won't touch you, but we will execute you. Go and stand by the wall."

Before the old man could move, Aunt Anna, who had been standing with her back up against the wall motionless, watching her son with eyes which contracted like a cat's, took two long strides toward the table. She bent her massive torso forward, and stared into the elderly man's face.

"Are you going to shoot my son, too?" she asked in her deep voice.

"Draw your horns in," the elderly man murmured, while the two Arrow-Cross men pulled the old woman back by her arms. "What's happened? Have you grown? A moment ago you looked a lot smaller."

"Even the corn on my toe is bigger than you, you bastard!" the old woman said.

The dark-haired, pale young girl by the wall began to slide slowly down until she was sitting on the ground.

"What's getting you all worked up, Aunty?" asked the elderly man. "We won't shoot you—you're only the mother!"

When the two Arrow-Cross men took the soldier and the postman between them, and began to herd them toward the door, Aunt Anna sprang after them. She kicked one in the leg, and turned the other one toward her by the shoulder to rake his face with her long, bony fingers. "Run!" she cried hoarsely. A gun went off behind them. The soldier jumped through the door.

The Arrow-Cross man whom Aunt Anna had kicked lay on the ground on his belly, while the other fingered, whining, his bleeding eyes and face. Aunt Anna slipped slowly sideways, then fell heavily to the ground. More shots were heard from the lobby, and then from the yard. In the second cellar, someone groaned.

TOWARD MORNING, before she died, the old woman regained consciousness for an hour.

"My little birds," she said, "you're about as brave as dry goat's droppings. Yet it doesn't become the old to be cowardly. The young still hope for happiness, but what have we, the old, got to lose? We've been deserted by God and man, we are alone with our unwanted love, our hopes have fallen by the wayside, so why not show some dignity before we breathe out our souls? We have lived in ignominy ever since we first opened our eyes, those of us who possess anything stole it, those who don't lick bottoms in order to gain; we never gave nor received any gift on this stinking earth except a child in our wombs or a rope around our necks. And now, when you were offered this cheap opportunity, because you were standing on the brink of your graves, anyway, you missed even that, my little birds. He who has kept his eyes on profit all his life, and cannot pull himself together even at the last moment to bring his blurry eye back into focus, deserves the hell he has invented for himself. You'll die as uselessly as you lived. I've spent half a lifetime in this house and if, during that time, I had found only one person who stood up on his hind legs—and that only once, I'd say: 'All right, I forgive you for having been born.' But even the best among you claim salvation on the grounds that you have neither cheated nor stolen. The good were good because they arranged a pillow under someone's head, the brave were brave because they held out their other cheek to be slapped, the loyal were loyal because they didn't bite their mothers' ankle when she turned her back on them—but that's all there was to your virtue. Everyone here lay low quietly in the warm dung so as not to catch cold. Yet the poor have duties to perform. I'll say it out loud so you can hear me! Because only the poor know what misery is, it is up to them to protect the others from it. Because the poor alone need God, let them reject him! Because their lives aren't worth a fig, let them give them away! Because the poor hear no other music than the rattling of their chains, let them rattle those chains until their unborn children's eardrums burst with it! Do you think, my little birds, that because you cover each other up, share your rations, and put up with each other's bad smell, you have paid creation even that one measly onion it claims in taxes?"

Fear

THE RIVER Lethe does not run past the front doors of the houses on Nador Street. Descending the double spiral staircase to the cellar-underworld of the apartment building, the widow Daniska carried on her sandals the live dust of the street. The terrestrial dust brought the underworld alive and turned it into hell. Ceaselessly, memory sent down its sulfurous flashes of lightning.

The widow Daniska looked around blinking in hell.

"Are you asleep, Aunt Mari?" she asked after a while.

"Why should I be asleep?" the woman addressed replied. "Why should I be asleep in broad daylight when I can't even sleep at night?"

The two widows had moved together about a week before from the air-raid shelter of their tottering house to the cellar of the neighboring Nador Street building. Apart from their memories, they had saved only their bedding and two red saucepans from among the smoking ruins that had buried the eight years of their common past. Fortunately they had landed in a more or less familiar environment. Mrs. Daniska had been going out to wash and iron and Aunt Mari to clean the well-to-do homes of the neighborhood, and thus they were not short of high-class acquaintances. Mr. Finiasz, the Council Secretary, and his family gave the two old women a little cold food in the evenings. Lawyer Bor's wife offered them white bread with caraway seeds and an occasional cup of tea, not to speak of other good-hearted cellar-dwellers. . . .

"If you are not asleep, Aunt Mari," the widow Daniska went on, "then tell me who that man standing at the door is. He never takes his eyes off me!"

The tiny old woman turned her eyes toward the gaunt, bearded young man standing at the door, but her wrinkled, mild face, like a dim mirror, remained unaffected by the sight.

"I don't know him," she mumbled. But if I look more closely," she added slipping her spectacles down to the point of her nose and scanning the young man at the door once more with her naked blue gaze, "if I look more closely, it seems to me as if I've seen him before."

"I never have," declared Mrs. Daniska, "but as far as I can see in this Godforsaken darkness, he seems to be waving to me."

"Or to me," the cobbler's widow opined. "Shall we go and look?"

"If you want to."

"Well, why doesn't he come here if he wants to talk to me?" murmured Aunt Mari with sudden suspicion and her clear, old face darkened.

From the corner of her eye, she threw a quick glance at the long-necked, fur-coated woman sitting on the bed next to hers, who stared motionless in front of her, her hands resting in her lap. Every time the dull, hissing sound of an exploding bomb penetrated from the landing, a nervous twitch rippled over her thin, big-eyed bird's face, like a small wave over the surface of water. Since eight in the morning, when the air raid began, she had never for a moment lifted her straight glance from the vision of death. "In a quarter of an hour they'll shut off the water in No. 12, dear lady," an elderly man next to her said. "If they don't stop by then we won't be cooking lunch today."

The widow Daniska suddenly rose and set out toward the door to the landing.

"Come along, Aunt Mari," she called back.

They had to make their tortuous way between two rows of beds to get to the door. The huge cellar, propped up in all its length by thick posts, was illuminated by a single small nightlight; the oblique shadows of the posts divided the uncertain semi-obscurity into wavering sections in which the figures, squatting motionless side by side seemed like the letters of an obituary. Whenever the door leading into the neighboring cellar was opened, the coats hanging at the feet of the beds fluttered in the draft and chased the fleeing shadow of a line across the huge room.

"Come out to the landing, Mrs. Daniska," the bearded young man at the door said when the two widows reached him and, without waiting for their reply, he turned and walked out through the door.

The landing was deserted but somewhat lighter than the cellar; a little sunshine seeped in from the stairs leading to the yard.

"Don't start moaning," said the young man hoarsely, "and, what is more important still, don't call me by my name. Are there any Arrow-Cross men in the cellar?"

"No," replied Aunt Mari in a shaky voice. The widow Daniska crossed herself.

"Take me someplace where we can be alone," the young man murmured. "And hurry up, I want to sit down."

"You want to sit down?" Mrs. Daniska repeated, surprised.

"Let's go," the young man said. Aunt Mari led the way. A narrow, low-ceilinged corridor opened from the landing and ran along the private coal cellars with their locked iron doors and ended at the central heating furnace, which was surrounded by a wooden fence. The young man switched on his flashlight. In the corridor, the boom of the guns was louder and one could clearly distinguish the nervous clatter of the fighter planes' machine guns.

"I've had bad luck with the coal once already," the young man murmured, sweeping the beam of his flashlight across the furnace room; the billowing coal-mounds sparkled black in the rays of the electric light. "The Arrow-Cross pulled me out of one coal cellar. Aren't there any here?"

He threw himself down on the coal.

"Don't people come in here?" he asked stretching out his legs. "If this place is safe I could stay here until nightfall."

The widow Daniska broke into loud sobs. The young man immediately put out his flashlight.

"Shut up, or I'm on my way," he growled. "I haven't slept for three days. When did your house collapse?"

"A week ago today," Aunt Mari replied. "It was hit by a big bomb in the morning and another one at noon."

"The day after your mother's death. . . ." sighed the widow Daniska wiping her eyes.

"Is my mother dead?" the young man asked.

"She is, child," Aunt Mari answered.

The coal began to roll from under the young man's boots, a few lumps jumped with a thud against the iron wall of the furnace. "Jesus Christ!" he swore, "can't you keep quiet?"

He bent forward, the muscles of his face tensed, his chin jutting forward; but his ear caught no alarming sound. His eyes had become used to the darkness, to his right and left the swaying shadows of the two old women emerged undulating from the denser darkness of the coal.

"How did she die?" he asked curtly.

"The Arrow-Cross men shot her dead," Aunt Mari replied, "the moment you jumped through the door."

"I heard the shots," the young man growled. "I thought they were firing at me."

Aunt Mari shook her head.

"There were two shots, weren't there?"

"Two."

Another lump of coal slid out from under the young man's boot, but this time he didn't notice.

"Then I heard right," he said after a little while. "I heard two shots, almost simultaneously. I thought they were shooting at me. . . . Are there no Arrow-Cross men here?"

"No, there aren't, child," said Aunt Mari.

"Are you sure?"

"They wouldn't recognize you anyway," the widow Daniska whispered in a barely audible voice, "even we, ourselves, didn't recognize you at first. We both wondered, Aunt Mari and I, whether it was to us the strange, bearded young man was waving."

"Don't chatter, Mrs. Daniska," the young man said. "I didn't ask you whether they would recognize me or not, but whether there are any of them here or not. Can't you give me a straight answer?"

"There aren't any," the old woman replied patiently.

The young man sighed. Aunt Mari stared silently in front of her in the thick coal-dusty darkness, her knees shaking.

"Wouldn't you like to eat something, child?" she asked, pressing her hand to her breast.

"I wouldn't mind," the young man said absentmindedly. "I haven't eaten for three days except for a few raw carrots. What is there to eat?"

In quick succession two ear-splitting explosions penetrated the cellar from the direction of the yard; the air was filled with thick coal-dust.

"That one was next door," the young man said, coughing. "They are strafing this neighborhood. I was almost hit by one last night."

"Where?" the widow asked.

"On the corner, among the ruins," the young man coughed again. "That's where I hide out nights but I can't sleep for the cold. If I could stay here tonight . . . I haven't slept for three nights. . . ."

The two old women were silent.

"So my mother is dead," the young man said after a while. "One could say that she died in my place, couldn't one? I was the deserter and she was shot dead. How old was she?"

"Sixty-four," Aunt Mari said. "When were you born?"

The young man made no reply, he was obviously thinking. The widow Daniska shifted her weight from one leg to the other, the crumbling coal crackled beneath her feet. From afar, toward the other end of the corridor, they heard the creak of an iron door being opened.

"When were you born?" Aunt Mari asked in a louder voice.

For a while they waited for the answer, then both turned carefully around and, on tiptoe, groping, their arms outstretched, they set out toward the corridor. They were followed by slow, even snores. Mrs. Daniska shuddered.

"He fell asleep," she told herself aloud and shook her head in amazement. "He fell asleep, Aunt Mari!"

Reaching the lighter corridor, both stopped.

"The janitor's assistant belongs to the Arrow-Cross," Aunt Mari said. "He must not know or he would denounce him."

"Mr. Finiasz, the Council Secretary is also an Arrow-Cross man," replied the widow Daniska.

When they came to the bend in the corridor they stopped again. Aunt Mari leaned her back against the wall.

"Dr. Bor, the lawyer, is one of them, too," she declared.

"What's the name of that long-necked woman sitting beside you?" Mrs. Daniska asked.

"Mrs. Milos," Aunt Mari murmured. "She belongs to them too.

"The janitor is also an Arrow-Cross man," the widow Daniska said and burst out crying afresh.

Reaching the landing, the two old women stopped again. Aunt Mari waited patiently until her friend's emotion had abated, then she took her own handkerchief and tenderly wiped away the tears from around the old laundress's nose.

"The assistant janitor steals coal from the furnace room," she said. "I saw him yesterday, he was taking away two pailfuls."

"Then he will find the boy," Mrs. Daniska cried.

Another falling bomb shook the walls. Inside, a piece of plaster dropped from the ceiling and fell on the head of the lawyer's little daughter, scratching her forehead. For a while, the company assembled around the lawyer's bed remained silent, only the frightened sobs of the child were audible in the corner.

"They've reached Andrassy Avenue already," said the lawyer. "The Pest side is finished."

"Karoly, I beg you, let's cross over to Buda before it is too late!" whispered his wife, a powerfully built, round-faced woman with flashing white teeth and bushy brows meeting at the root of her nose. "We'd all be comfortable in my mother's house."

"I'm not going," said the lawyer.

Mr. Finiasz, the Council Secretary who, having no bed, slept in a green leather armchair between his wife's divan and the lawyer's bed, sniggered.

"I'd go if I were you," he grumbled. "We'll have nothing to laugh about when the Russians get here."

"If they get here!"

"Two more days at most," the lawyer said and his putty-colored face twitched.

"Are you going to try your luck, my dear colleague?"

The lawyer shrugged.

"Karoly, I beg you . . ."

"Either it comes off or it doesn't," her husband said, looking around blinking. "For they'd catch up with us not only in Buda but in Germany as well, my good Finiasz. What are you hoping for?"

Someone from the next cellar threw open the connecting wooden door, stopped for a moment on the threshold, looked around and, reassured, retreated.

"It didn't drop here," announced a retired colonel three beds further off, who, though he was hard of hearing, accompanied all ballistic events with pronouncements that allowed no appeal. Tiny pieces of plaster fell from the ceiling onto the beds.

"God almighty!" screamed a female voice in a remote corner of the cellar, "I can't stand it any longer!"

Nobody moved. A bespectacled old woman broke into low sobs.

"Damn that bitch!" said Mrs. Finiasz, a short, dark, mouse-faced woman. "She has a ton of potatoes in the cellar, but she wouldn't let anyone have even a single one."

The Red Cross nurse of the cellar rose reluctantly, her face stormy, from the edge of her bed and revived the unconscious woman with some vinegar. But less than fifteen minutes later, the swan-necked Mrs. Milos was also in need of the vinegar sponge.

Mrs. Milos sat next to the lawyer on a low stool between the two beds, wrapped in her fur coat, her head bent, listening motionless to the conversation that sped back and forth above her. When, at times, she raised her eyes from the gray concrete floor where she searched for the never-to-be dreams of a different world, her shining, metallic glance crept up to Mr. Finiasz's angular, sanguine face, alighted on it for a second, then returned hurriedly to her underworld visions. It seemed at such times as if her body changed its tone, it tensed, her neck flushed, her beautiful, pearly teeth flashed ecstatically between her lusty, painted lips. The town clerk turned his face away.

"Either it comes off or it doesn't. For they'd catch up with us not only in Buda but in Germany as well, my good Finiasz. What are you still hoping for?"—he heard the lawyer's voice.

Mrs. Milos threw back her head, her eyes rested for a second on the town clerk's face, her knees parted a little. Her lips moved but her words remained inaudible because the sudden explosion and the screams of the woman in the corner suppressed all other sounds.

"She has a ton of potatoes in the cellar but she wouldn't give anyone even one," repeated Mrs. Finiasz who, with her gray, mousy face and skinny body was as unsuited to her powerfully built husband as the fragrance of hay is unlikely to fill the stomach of a hungry ox. Mrs. Milos shook her head mechanically. The damp air of the cellar grew even heavier from the smell of vinegar.

"God almighty, I can't stand any more of this!" screamed the woman in the corner, "It is driving me mad!"

Mrs. Milos raised her head again.

"What do you think," she asked the lawyer, "do I have to vacate my flat if the Russians come in?"

"Was it a Jewish flat?"

The woman nodded silently.

"Probably," the lawyer said, "though it obviously depends also on whether or not the former owner returns."

"I don't even know them."

The Council Secretary laughed.

"You'll get acquainted when they return."

"And if they don't?" asked the woman, turning away her head and addressing her words to the lawyer as if she had not heard the Council Secretary's malicious laughter.

"Why shouldn't they return?" the lawyer grumbled irritably. "As soon as we leave they'll break out of the ghetto like wild animals. Unless . . ."

"Unless the ghetto gets blown up first?" asked the woman hoarsely. "Isn't that so?"

"And if it does get blown up," said the Council Secretary after a while, "one specimen of the breed is certain to survive and he, my dear lady, will make you pay for all seven of Christ's wounds!"

Mrs. Milos raised her bird's face, suddenly it was burning, her dim glance assumed a new sparkle.

"Me?" she cried raspingly, "Why, what harm did I do them? Did I send them to the ghetto? I moved into an empty flat allotted to me by the authorities. Is it my fault if . . ."

"Calm yourself!" the lawyer said.

But Mrs. Milos paid no heed to the warning. She pulled herself slowly up from the stool and, smoothing down her narrow hips with her two palms, spreading her feet wide and bending her waist slightly forward, she turned with her entire body toward the Council Secretary.

"What do you have against me?" she asked, almost humbly. "Why do you torment me?"

"What do you mean?" asked the man flushing, and threw a quick glance at his wife.

Mrs. Milos closed her eyes.

"Will they put me out of the flat?"

"Stop fretting, Ilonka," said the lawyer with increasing irritation. "Just at present we don't even know whether there'll be any flat left . . . or if you'll ever enter it alive. If they go on like this we shall all burn to cinders in this hell."

This time the bomb must have hit the house itself: the ground rose beneath their feet, dust exuded from the walls, a glass rolled with a loud clatter from the table. The lawyer's wife grasped the edge of the bed with both hands.

"So I shall be put out of my flat," repeated Mrs. Milos. "And who will pay me back what I spent on having it cleaned and redecorated? You, who allotted it to me?"

"I?" asked the Council Secretary aghast.

Suddenly the woman clapped both hands to her face and threw herself full length down on the bed. In a second, the storm of weeping dissolved the severe discipline of her narrow body, her limbs jerked wildly, the way a tree whips in a whirlwind, her belly rose immodestly above her loins, her neck writhed as if it wanted to tear itself from her body, one unlaced shoe flew off her foot. The shadow of unconsciousness painted her face dark. It took more than half an hour before the fit passed and her wild yells, which upset the whole cellar, abated. From her fainting spell she slid without transition into deep sleep.

By then, the cannonade had ceased; the cellar emptied quickly, only the children remained underground—watched over by a few women—and an old woman in mourning, who spoke with a German accent, and her son who had moved in from one of the neighboring houses. The ventilating shaft was opened, the women began to sweep. The fresh, soaked wood crackled loudly in the large stove. The assistant janitor brought two pails of water from the next house where the water supply had been turned on for an hour because of the morning air raid.

"Is that all?" asked the lawyer's wife, air-raid warden of the building, when she saw the man placing the two pails near the stove and getting ready to chop wood.

The man shrugged.

"Why, this isn't even enough for the cooking," the woman said. "We need two more pails in the lavatory."

"I won't get to the tap again," the assistant janitor grumbled, "half the street is out there and at twelve sharp they are cutting it off."

"Don't answer back!" the woman said sharply.

By the time the man returned with the two pails of water, Mrs. Bor was no longer in the cellar. The man slammed down the two pails, swearing; half the water splashed out. His face was bathed in perspiration.

"That sort wants shutting up in a ghetto, too," he said, his back bent, his narrow eyes above the wide cheekbones burning with hatred. "They are no better than the Jews when it comes to exploiting us, God damn them!"

The widow Daniska who was on her knees, busy wiping up the spilled water, turned her mild, reddened face to the man.

"You must not swear, Uncle Peter," she said kindly. "It'll make you neither wiser nor fatter."

"But he is right," put in one of the sweeping women. "Because it wouldn't hurt Her Ladyship to do a hard day's work."

"She might lose weight," said another woman.

The assistant janitor, who had been standing motionless near the stove, his back bent, his eyes glaring at the floor, turned suddenly around and set out toward the door, swinging his shoulders. At the wooden door he looked back.

"I'm going to have my lunch," he said ironically, twirling his colorless moustache, "but let me tell you, women, it's a rotten world in which one is compelled to steal."

The women picked up the thread he had dropped and fell to imagining in a wealth of capricious detail the endless variety of relationships between master and servant. They stuck their sniffing, pointed noses into the gentry's full larders, made an inventory of the never seen and yet precisely known stock, weighed the material and aesthetic difference between a thin soup and smoked gammon and then, returning from the adventure with a melancholy, patriotic sigh, began with strong hands and long-suffering souls to translate the soup into reality. Meanwhile the widow Daniska and Aunt Mari drew back into a corner and started a low but excited conversation.

"Did you hear what he said?" asked Mrs. Daniska. "He's compelled to steal! Do you think he is gone to the furnace room for coal?"

"It was around this time that I saw him coming out of it yesterday."

"Sh . . . sh!" whispered the widow Daniska.

Aunt Mari turned her head and threw a quick glance at the old woman in mourning, dozing in an armchair placed against the wall, and her son sitting by her.

"Nothing to fear from them," she said, "they are Jews. . . ."

"Jews?" Mrs. Daniska exclaimed in alarm. "What did you say? . . . Jews?"

"They have some kind of American passport," Aunt Mari informed her, "that's why they haven't been deported yet. Do have a look in the furnace room, Mrs. Daniska!"

"What am I to tell him if he finds me there?" asked the old woman, walking with heavy, anxious steps toward the door.

The widow of Dr. Karoly Veress, the old lady in mourning who spoke with a German accent, woke in her armchair at exactly five o'clock every morning. As it would have embarrassed her to wake her neighbors and, as with her somewhat uncertain, eighty-year-old legs and eyes, she dared not embark alone on the journey—these tiny, furtive adventures frightened her more than the bombing—she had to wait until the whole cellar woke around seven, and her son, with a dripping candle in one hand and the old lady's three handbags, her shawl and umbrella

in the other, accompanied her to the little woodshed at the far
end of the corridor where, among the sour-smelling oak logs,
holding on with one hand to the wall, she could, with a low but
angry rumbling, relax the morning tension of her bowels.

"If you only knew what torture it is to wait so long," she
told her son every morning, words and intonation unchanged,
while, carefully tapping the uneven flagstones of the corridor,
she strove eagerly but with great circumspection toward her
goal, pushing forward her head wrapped in a thick white shawl,
extending her left arm and tilting her body after it, a living example of passionate motion, its rhythm disciplined only by a
lifetime of fateful experience.

The time between five and seven was usually spent in pon-
dering those experiences. Fixing her tired eyes on the flickering
oil lamp that hung on the opposite wall of the cellar—which,
like the fire of a distant lighthouse, gave warning but no light—
the old lady carefully scrutinized the diverse phases of her life.
One by one, memories of mineral rigidity came to life dragging
their giant, swaying shadow-bodies through the dark cellar,
which readily fell in with the wiles of the unreal and, like a re-
volving stage, took the rapidly changing scenes on its lap.

"If only I knew what time it is!" said the old lady now and
again after one scene or another, whipping the floor with her
cane whenever her body reminded her with a rude gesture of
the passing of time. "Are you going to sleep forever, apes?"

During the day as well there was plenty of time for the
weighing of memories. As the inhabitants of the cellar (she had
only known them for a week) drew away from her because of
her San Salvadoran citizenship—her last living relative had sent
that from Switzerland—and her son sat beside her in silence,
his head bent. Mrs. Veress had sufficient leisure not only to
revive her past but also to engage in a loftier occupation: she
recited poetry, murmuring verses in a low voice, with wide-
open, ecstatic eyes. Like the earth which catches and preserves

its prehistory in its deeper layers while the changes taking place on its surface are blown away by the wind within hours, the old lady's memory retained the pliocene events of her life that had withstood every crisis, petrified and unmarred. She carried with her toward her grave all that she had learned at the age of seventeen: poems by Goethe and Byron, entire scenes from Shakespeare's dramas, Klopstock's odes and Lessing's epigrams without a single gap, in all their full pomp, unaltered in form, like a collection of minerals; while she dusted away all recent events and often forgot that she was living in a strange house among strangers and that only a miracle had saved her from being shot dead.

"*Heraus in eure Schatten, rege Gipfel!*" she declaimed, sitting in her armchair at dawn when her bladder was giving her too much trouble, wagging her head, and throwing disapproving, indignant glances at her neighbors as they snored unsuspectingly, in cheerful unison under heavy blankets in the seesawing, weak light of the oil lamp.

"Did you hear, Tamas, they say we are Jews!" she whispered to her son when the widow Daniska and Aunt Mari passed her armchair on their way to the landing. "I wonder how they know?"

"Don't pay any attention to them, mother!" said her son.

"How could I not pay attention," the old woman grumbled. "Crazy as people are today, they may denounce us!"

Two strange men came in from the landing accompanied by the assistant janitor. For a few seconds they remained standing at the entrance, surveying the cellar, then walked straight to the old lady's armchair. One of the men lifted his hat.

"Mrs. Karoly Veress, widow?"

Her son rose.

"Yes, my mother."

"Your mother," the man repeated. "Tamas Veress?"

"Yes, that is my name."

"State police investigator," the man said, "take your papers and come with us."

The old lady who had, in the meantime, begun her daily gymnastic exercises—she performed every day before breakfast four hundred arm, wrist, leg, knee and ankle exercises in a precisely determined order and distribution—threw both her arms up horizontally toward the detective.

"I am sorry," she said, "but I shall have to ask you to wait because I cannot go now." With a graceful gesture of her hand she pointed to the nearby bed. "Please, take a seat. I shall be ready in half an hour and then I am at your disposal."

"What?" the detective asked.

The old lady flung her arms up again.

"I am indeed sorry to have to ask you to wait, gentlemen," she said panting a little, "but I cannot interrupt my exercises. True, they won't take long, but afterward I shall have to rest for half an hour as I am usually a bit overheated from the exertion. Now I must not speak."

The women who had remained in the cellar had come to stand around the small group. Tamas Veress, who had, in the meantime, drawn the other detective aside, had succeeded, after a little bargaining, in getting permission to leave his eighty-year-old mother—of whose escape there was little danger—in the cellar, while he accompanied the detectives to Police Headquarters. He was released an hour later after he had presented their San Salvadoran citizenship papers, their permit of residence in Hungary and the letter of the Swiss consul that entitled them to live in a Christian house. He did not go back home. Taking a roundabout way, so as to make certain he was not followed, he entered a house in the Istvan Tisza street.

He rang the doorbell of a studio apartment. He had to ring five times.

"You are late," said the man who opened the door.

Veress did not reply at once. He sat down on a kitchen stool and opened his overcoat.

"Here are the papers," he said. "A birth certificate from Nagyvárad, and one from Kolozsvár, two marriage certificates from the same places, a Catholic certificate of baptism from Nagybánya. Three Swedish safe conducts. Two and two is four, five, eight. All right?"

He buttoned his overcoat.

"I was almost caught," he said hoarsely. "They took me to Police Headquarters with these papers in my pocket. Fortunately, I wasn't searched."

"Where did they get you?" the man asked.

"In the air-raid shelter."

"You were denounced?"

"Yes."

"In that case you had better move," the man advised. "The Arrow-Cross boys might show up in the evening."

"You know of a place?" Veress asked.

The man shook his head.

"And nothing in sight?"

"No."

"Give me a cigarette!" Veress said. "Couldn't we stay with you for one night?"

"Impossible," the man growled. "Nobody can come here."

The young man rose and walked toward the door. When he reached it he turned back once more.

"I shouldn't like my mother to be shot and thrown into the Danube," he said. "Take her in for one night. I know you've had others sleeping here."

The man shook his head again. "Impossible," he said, "I am very sorry. Come back tomorrow or the day after in the late afternoon, perhaps I can find something by then."

His wife, a gray-haired, fat woman with a pink complexion

who had been kneading bread in a blue basin at the kitchen table during their conversation, suddenly turned back.

"What's the use of his coming here?" she said nervously. "We can't find him a place anyway. If he had come two days earlier . . ."

"You're out of luck," said the man yawning. He opened the door.

Dull explosions were heard from far away, like the noise of a distant poolroom. It was pouring with rain. By the time Veress reached home, the majority of the tenants had come down from the flats, the cellar was humming with lively talk. His mother was sitting in her armchair with her eyes closed. Her bony face with its carved chin and big, straight nose, was hard as an epitaph. Although she was a little deaf in both ears she recognized her son's steps from afar: her cheeks filled out suddenly, her eyes opened, grew larger, and sparkled.

"Well," she said.

"Everything's all right, mother," her son said. "They wanted to see our papers. I had to wait for a long time, there were many before me."

The old woman nodded.

"I thought so," she said. "It took a long time. Help me get up."

"What for?"

"What for?" the old lady whispered angrily, "I want to go out there again. I haven't been out there since seven o'clock this morning. How long, do you think, I can stand it? *Quo usque tandem abutere Catilina patientia nostra*, your father always used to say."

On the way back they stopped at the staircase leading into the yard.

"I got rid of them quickly, didn't I?" she asked. "I told them off, didn't I? Expecting me to go to Headquarters and present my papers. As if they couldn't have looked at those papers right here. They were scared of me, weren't they?"

"They certainly were, mother," her son nodded.

The old lady burst out laughing.

"You should have seen his face!" she said while bringing out her fine cambric handkerchief from the pocket of her winter coat and wiping her lips. "He stared at me in such a way I was afraid he'd have a stroke. What I should have really liked to do was to ask him: My good sir, don't you know what physical culture is?"

The noise of planes penetrated from the yard.

"Air raid?" the old lady asked. "Good thing you are back. If you hadn't come until two o'clock I'd have run after you."

Tamas laughed.

"To Police Headquarters?"

"I have already arranged that with Aunt Mari, she was going to accompany me," the old lady informed him. "We shall wait until two, I told her when she sat down next to me to comfort me, if he doesn't come by then, we shall go and fetch him. . . . Couldn't we go up to the yard for a little walk?"

"Not now, mother."

The old lady's face turned suddenly poppy-red with fury. "How much longer am I to wait?!" she cried, hitting the stone floor with her stick. "Yesterday, you said that the Russians were already at the Eastern Railway Station. Twenty-two years ago, in 1922, when we got back from Savanyukut and there were neither streetcars nor taxis, old as I was, I walked from the Eastern Station to Arpad Street in three quarters of an hour. These people have been on the way for a whole day now. . . ."

Above them, footsteps descended the stairs. The old lady fell silent.

"Who is that coming?" she cried, throwing back her head. "The lawyer's wife?"

"In person, dear Mrs. Veress," replied Mrs. Bor when she reached the bottom of the stairs. Her husband, coming down behind her, lifted his hat and walked on without a word.

"So here's your boy," the woman said, smiling; her huge, red face with the pointed teeth in it shone in the tired air of the cellar as if a god had molded it from the substance of summer. "Didn't I tell you, dear Mrs. Veress, that your son was all right but he'd certainly got a long wait. . . ."

She took the old lady's arm.

"Let's go in," she said, "there's an air raid coming. . . . So they let you go at Headquarters, Mr. Veress. . . ."

"As you see, Mrs. Bor."

"They gave you back your papers, of course."

The young man made no reply. He waited until his mother had entered the shelter from the landing and advanced along the narrow path between the beds with a loud tapping of her stick.

"Just a moment," he said to the lawyer's wife who was about to follow her. "Was it you who denounced us to the police?"

The woman turned slowly around.

"What gives you that idea?" she asked calmly, but her face turned a shade paler.

"The detective told me."

"The detective lied," the woman said. "I did not denounce you. I was at the police station and I asked them whether I was allowed to keep foreign citizens in the house, but I did not denounce you. I am block-warden, Mr. Veress, I have my responsibilities."

"Did you ask the Arrow-Cross Party as well?" the young man asked.

"What do I care about the Arrow-Cross Party?!" the woman cried. The light of the storm-lamp illuminated her white animal teeth, the black hair piled up on her head sparkled with electricity. "You know very well that I don't belong to them!"

The young man nodded.

"I don't know it," he said dryly, "but if you don't, then it is a pity you denounced us, Mrs. Bor. Because if someone from the police puts the Arrow-Cross people on us, then we won't be the only ones taken away from here tonight."

The afternoon passed in relative calm, even the expected air raid did not materialize. Rumor had it that the Germans were attempting a breakthrough in the Székesfehérvár area, and the Russians had obviously concentrated their air force in that region. The ordered schedule of the cellar disintegrated, hardly ten or fifteen people loitered in the two large rooms and even these were either sleeping or lying on their beds, their nerves relaxed. The women had scattered in the various flats and the majority of the men stood around in the yard smoking or looking out from the front door at the devastated street and the fast darkening winter sky, the low clouds of which were, at times, illuminated by the flash of a distant gun. Now and again a fierce gust of wind would sweep the street from the direction of the Danube.

Mrs. Milos stood smoking in one of the recesses of the lobby, opposite the spiral stairs. When Council Secretary Finiasz, coming in from the yard, turned into the narrow corridor leading to the shelter, she threw away her cigarette.

In spite of the darkness, she noticed that the Council Secretary was startled by her presence, and instead of stopping took another step toward the shelter. Only then did he turn back.

"Why are you spying on me?" he asked nervously.

The woman did not reply to the question.

"We go in the back way," she said. "I have to talk to you."

"What is there to talk about?!" the man growled. "Talk . . . always talk . . ."

The small recesses opening on both sides of the corridor had been furnished by the more well-to-do tenants with divans, armchairs, curtains, as private sitting rooms; some had even put a stove in and spent their nights there. Mrs. Milos's private cellar was at the end of the corridor, next to the furnace room. The Council Secretary stopped at the door.

"I am not going in," he said when he heard the woman rummaging among her keys.

She did not answer. The door opened with a creak.

"Didn't you hear me? I am not going in."

"Are you afraid of me?" the woman asked.

The ceiling here was so low that the man bent his head involuntarily so as not to hurt it in the dense darkness.

"What is the point in my going in?" the man murmured. "If you only want to talk, we can talk here."

He heard her striking a match inside.

"I want to see your face," the woman said. The pale light of the candle fell like a translucent, yellow veil on her slender, supple neck and lent a brightness to the heavy, red lips protruding from her thin bird's face. Behind her back, a picture of Christ hung on the board-wall in a yellow puddle of light.

"Come in, Lajos, don't be afraid of me," the woman said. With one smooth movement she stood before the Council Secretary and put both arms around his neck. The man drew back.

"Stop that!" he said irritably.

The woman immediately dropped her arms.

"Lajos, what have I done to you?" she whispered. Her eyes filled with tears, her face turned gray like a deserted street.

"Is that all we have to worry about, damn it?" the man swore, striking the thin board-wall with his fist. The dull sound answered, as though in echo, by a thunderous explosion from the direction of the yard. The death rattle of the world above made the candle flame flutter and the shadows leapt about like wild goats in the narrow recess lined with red carpets and curtains. The effects of the blast had not yet settled when a new explosion whizzed along the corridor shaking the walls.

"Were these hits?" asked the woman.

"What else?" the man replied ironically. Suppressed fury drove the blood to his head.

"Could you do me a favor and not throw yourself at me in

front of my wife?" he growled pushing forward his mighty, square chin. "Do you think people are blind? God damn it to hell, don't you have any shame left in you?"

"No," replied the woman simply.

"Well, as far as I'm concerned, I've had enough!" the Council Secretary burst out with such anger that his knees began to shake. "Enough, I say. . . ."

"Of me?"

"Of you, too."

"Then why aren't you going?"

The man lowered his eyes, his lips twitched almost imperceptibly. For a few seconds he stood there, silent, then, lifting his hand in an uncertain movement to the back of his head, he turned away slowly. But before he had finished turning, the woman stepped up to him and took his arm.

"Lajos," she said entreatingly, "what have I done?"

"Nothing."

"Calm yourself, I beg you!" The woman placed her cool hand on the man's neck.

The explosions now followed each other uninterruptedly, the narrow cubicle danced, trembling, on the sound waves. The picture of Christ, hanging near the edge of the red wall-carpet swung backward and forward in the blast which was throwing the furniture about—the red plush divan, the bowlegged table and the two velvet chairs—as if it had suddenly sucked them clean of weight.

"You didn't do anything," the Council Secretary said gnashing his teeth. "You didn't pull up your skirt in front of my wife, did you? Only almost. Don't you understand? I've had enough of you!"

"Obviously you have other things to worry about," the woman said enunciating every word clearly and emphatically.

"I beg your pardon?"

"You're afraid for your skin, aren't you?" She bent forward, her eyes contracted like those of a cat before it jumps, and she pressed both fists to her groin.

"Are you threatening me? Careful, you might burn your fingers!"

"You can still escape to Buda," the woman whispered. "Go on, get away, go over to Buda before it is too late. Very soon, we'll live in a world where anyone who has a single enemy should start digging his grave today!"

"Will you denounce me?"

The woman nodded without a word. The floor beneath their feet rose again, and dust blew in through the cracks in the door. Both sat down involuntarily on the red plush divan.

"Why not?" the woman said after a while, dispassionately. "You have ruined me, so why shouldn't I ruin you as well? They'll take away my flat. . . ."

"How did I ruin you?"

"You don't love me!"

"Jesus Christ! Is this the time for loving?" the man had to shout to be heard above the successive explosions. The candle went out.

"The candle's gone out," he said surprised, lowering his voice involuntarily. "What do you want from me?"

The divan creaked.

"Lajos," he heard the woman's voice in the dark. "Why do we have to hurt each other?"

"Light the candle," the Council Secretary said.

Instead of answering, the woman drew closer and touched him with a lewd gesture. He drew back. For a moment there was silence.

"There you are!" the woman whispered, panting. "I knew that you no longer loved me. And now go! I never want to see you again as long as I live!"

She waited until the pocket flashlight with its swinging beam of light had disappeared behind the turn in the corridor, then she locked the door and lay down on the divan. Council Secretary Finiasz went straight to the air-raid shelter, which had, in the meantime, filled up again. The Bor couple were not yet in their place but his wife had already gone to bed and supervised the child's dinner. He had a large piece of bread and dripping, and a beautiful, red apple. Two beds away, a blond, skinny lad, brother of the assistant janitor's wife, was sitting with his back to the wall watching the listlessly eating child with bulging eyes. His lips moved in time with the lazy chewing. The Council Secretary sat down in the armchair.

"Where have you been?" his wife asked. "What's the matter with you?" she added, alarmed, when she noticed that big drops of sweat covered the man's large, sanguine face, the corners of his nose, his forehead.

He glanced at the child and shook his head silently.

"You can speak," the woman said in a low voice. "He isn't listening."

"I talked to her," the Council Secretary said quickly.

"Well?"

"I broke with her."

"For good?" the woman asked in a low voice, bending closer.

The man nodded. "It's a pity, though," he whispered. "We were in too much of a hurry. She threatened me."

"What with?"

"She said she'd denounce me. I won't get away with it. You could have waited a little longer."

The tiny, mouse-faced woman picked up the plate lying on her lap with a big, dripping piece of bread, and flung it with all her strength to the floor. The fragments scattered wide on the cement and the child, lying next to her, winced as if she had slapped him.

"What's going on here, are you bombing us too?" said Mrs. Bor who had just reached the bed with a loaded tray in her hand. "Keep cool, children, here's your dinner! Lajos, would you take the teapot off the tray?"

"Where did you make the tea?" the man asked.

"At the assistant janitor's. They're having a fine old time up there, my children," she reported while putting down the tray on the bed and placing plates around it. Her round face under the wealth of piled-up black hair bent over the golden-yellow silk counterpane like Ceres's face once upon a time when she inspected the rich wheat fields of Greece. "Half a dozen armed Arrow-Cross men are sitting in the kitchen, bottles of wine are lined up on the table, and on the floor, at their feet, stands a huge laundry basket full of silk shirts, new shoes, damask tablecloths and God knows what else. I saw two gold watches on the table."

"They won't enjoy it for much longer," the Council Secretary said.

"Quite possibly," said the woman curtly. "By the way, did you know that the police let the Jew go?"

"Good for them!" cried Mrs. Finiasz so loudly that some of her neighbors turned around questioningly.

The lawyer's wife sat down on a footstool between the two beds and poured out the tea.

"How I've begged Karoly," she said quietly, "to move to Buda to my mother's villa. In a week people will hang here side by side like sausages in the loft."

"We too?" asked Mrs. Finiasz throwing a quick glance at her husband.

"We too."

"Where will we hang, mommy?" asked the child who had, in the meantime, finished his beautiful red apple and thrown the core at the head of the assistant janitor's brother-in-law. The lad wiped his face with the back of his hand and turned away. In the corner, the widow Daniska and Aunt Mari squatted on two kitchen chairs weaving the black cloth of their shared troubles with burning cheeks and excited whispers.

"Did you know that the assistant janitor is entertaining Arrow-Cross men?" the widow Daniska asked.

"I've just come from there," the bootmaker's widow said. "I've even spoken to them."

"What do they say?"

"They are crazy!" Aunt Mari replied, frightened. "They've brought a laundry basket full of gold, diamonds, boots and now they're sharing them. And the assistant janitor is standing there watching them coldly, and he says he doesn't want any of it because they'll have to give it all back, anyway."

"Give it back?" the widow Daniska asked, scared.

"Sure!" Aunt Mari nodded and the spectacles inherited from her husband flashed severely in the soft light of the candle. "Haven't you heard that Mrs. Milos will have to give back the flat?"

The old laundress made no reply.

"Now they're sharing the loot and at night they'll go raiding," the bootmaker's widow went on. "To taste blood, before they're all hanged, they say. Have they all gone mad?"

"Before they're all hanged?" the widow Daniska repeated.

Aunt Mari nodded.

"Look! What is the matter with Mr. Finiasz?" she asked, pushing her spectacles up her nose and inspecting the Council Secretary sitting three beds away. "Look! His teeth are chattering and he is as pale as death!"

"His forehead is covered in sweat," the widow Daniska stated.

"He must be ill," Aunt Mari opined. She threw another glance at the Council Secretary, who sat with his head lowered, a small tea cup in his hand, motionless, staring at the floor, then she jumped up from her chair. "I'm going out to the back," she whispered, "to send the lad away. They might start their raiding right here!"

"God help me!" the widow Daniska whispered back.

"What's the matter?"

"I'm coming with you," the old laundress said getting off her chair.

They set out one behind the other along the narrow path between the beds that led through the board-door and the other cellar toward the lobby. Most of the cellar-dwellers were already in bed, some of them asleep. In the second cellar, opposite the exit, in a cubicle between two pillars that was illuminated by a separate candle which closed itself in, withholding even its light, a few men were playing cards, their purple faces bent over the table.

"God help me!" the widow Daniska whispered again when they reached the cold lobby.

"What's the matter with you?"

The night was clear, silent. From the darkness of the sky pouring down over the spiral stairs and circulating in the deeper darkness below as blood circulates in the body, a spark of hope would flash at times into this dim underworld. The two old women stopped and stared silently for a moment. They heard a hoarse, drunken yell from above, a revolver shot, singing.

The widow Daniska extricated a small parcel from her voluminous bosom and with trembling fingers, undid the tissue paper. It contained a small silver cross without a chain.

"Aunt Mari, do I have to give this back?" the old woman asked and her eyes filled with tears. "I found it last night on the staircase but I know whose it is."

"If you know, then give it back," Aunt Mari said. "The devil take this miserable world!"

The two widows set out together toward the furnace room. As they had no lamp, they advanced in the blind darkness cautiously, with hands groping on the wall, and seeking feet, and they struck a match only when, after the second turning they had to find the board-door of the furnace room. The deserter lay in the corner, behind a pile of coal, his legs widespread, his cheek on the ground.

For a while they called him in vain, he didn't wake up. Aunt Mari squatted down next to him, shook his shoulder, pinched his ear, spoke to him in desperate whispers, but the lad was so deeply asleep that he didn't even raise his hand to protest. And when, finally, both widows went to work on him and, joining forces, turned him over on his back, he opened his eyes for a brief second.

"Get up, child," the widow Daniska whispered in his ear, "you must go, there are Arrow-Cross men in the building!"

"Where?" asked the lad and closed his eyes to shut out the light of the match, which cut like a knife.

"In the house!" Mrs. Daniska whispered.

"In the house," the young man repeated after her. He sat up, shook his head, lay back again. No warning, no argument could induce him to continue the conversation, even less to rise and leave that ill-omened place. The moment Aunt Mari stopped shaking his shoulder, he immediately began to snore.

After a while, the two widows gave up the vain attempt and, in astounded silence, left the furnace room. The sleeper, however, was awakened by the very silence. When they reached the board-door, a few pieces of coal came rolling down noisily, as if someone had directed an angry kick at the pile.

"I'm not going," they heard a hoarse voice behind them in the darkness. "Not even if I have to rot here!"

"God help you, child, get a hold on yourself!" said Aunt Mari, frightened. But they got no reply. Old Mrs. Daniska's knees shook so that she had to be supported, and when they got back to the lobby she flopped down on the lowest step of the spiral stairs, regardless of the ice-cold, misty air blowing in from the yard. Snatches of drunken singing could be heard from the assistant janitor's flat.

In the cellar the people had retired to bed. The majority were lying down fully clothed; some hadn't even taken their shoes off; raised on one elbow, they gazed into the dull semi-

obscurity, or pulled their hats over their eyes to protect themselves against the blinding light of awareness. There was hardly
any conversation going on. At moments, the silence was so
complete that one could discern the chattering of Council Secretary Finiasz's teeth. Soft moans rose here and there, but only
a fourteen-year-old girl who had recently lost her father in an
air raid had the courage to cry aloud.

About eight o'clock the assistant janitor had been down in
the cellar. He had stayed only a few minutes, pretended that he
was looking for something among his belongings, and had put a
small iron pan under his arm.

"There'll be a raid soon," he remarked offhandedly. "You'd
better get your papers ready."

He repeated the warning in the second cellar as well, looking pointedly at Tamas Veress and his mother, who were sitting
quietly in their usual place.

"Come here, man, come here!" the old lady called to him
raising her head alertly on the lookout for an entertaining conversation. "Come here! What were you winking for?"

"I didn't wink," said the assistant janitor, stopping for a moment by the old lady's chair. "I was only looking to see whether
you were asleep."

"But you also said something," the old lady insisted. "What
did you say?"

There came no reply.

"You must forgive me, my good man," the old lady excused
herself with a charming smile, "but I am hard of hearing, and
like most deaf people, apt to imagine things. I thought you had
said something. Well, then, God bless you, my good man, have
a good rest tonight, you need it."

She smiled, nodded, the assistant janitor raised his hat
and left. The women pulled their handbags closer, the men patted their wallets. The widow Daniska felt that the last of her
strength was seeping out of her, she lay down flat on her bed

and closed her eyes. Outside, the night was calm, the besiegers were quiet, not a single shot went off, so everyone could wrap themselves in their own silence which let them straight down to hell on the silk thread of imagination. The darkness was unbearable. Mrs. Bor rose and lit another candle. Even through the closed cellar door they could hear the drunken shouting and revolver shots coming from the yard.

Aunt Mari picked up her little footstool and went out into the lobby. No one asked her where she was going. She put the footstool down next to the spiral stairs, sat down, folded her hands in her lap and began her vigil. After a while, young Veress joined her. He lit a cigarette but stayed out there even after it was smoked. Outside, a dense fog must have descended on the town because the spiral staircase seemed to be wrapped in steam and even the singing, overflowing from the assistant janitor's flat, sounded duller.

Aunt Mari's watchful eyes followed the young man as he walked with long strides up and down the lobby.

"Why aren't you running away, young man?" she asked when, deep in thought, Tamas stopped near her.

"I am not going to leave my mother."

The old woman hummed.

"And why don't you take the old lady as well?"

"The front door is locked," Veress replied. "Besides, my mother wouldn't be able to take ten steps in this darkness."

They fell silent. Up in the yard a door was flung open, a medley of thick voices streamed out and was cut off suddenly by another banging of the door. The noise of uncertain, heavy steps sounded from the yard.

"He is alone," the old woman said. "Taking the air."

Veress listened without a word.

"Why don't you hide in one of the flats?" Aunt Mari asked. "If I had one, I'd give you the key. But there must be someone . . ."

"There isn't," Veress said.

"Have you tried?"

"I have."

"Try again," the old woman advised. "If they catch you when they are in a bad mood they'll take you down to the Danube and shoot both of you. In the house where I lived they caught a deserter, his mother was shot dead, same as him. Where have you tried?"

Veress did not reply at once.

"I tried Council Secretary Finiasz," he said after a while. "He is coming toward the cellar stairs, can you hear him?"

"There's nothing to fear as long as he's alone," the old woman mumbled.

The steps, splashing in snow water, were now more clearly discernible; they stopped, then started again. A moment later they stopped for good near the cellar stairs. Thick, retching sounds were heard, then disjointed gargling. Aunt Mari laughed softly.

"He's vomiting," she whispered. "The pig! Isn't he ashamed of himself?!"

"And this pig will shoot me," said Veress.

The bootmaker's widow shook her head.

"Being drunk is not a crime," she said quietly. "Everyone has a right to some fun even if someone else has to pay the price. Why did the gentry drag the poor people into this war? That's where they learned to kill."

Veress made no reply. The cellar door creaked open, the teenage brother of the assistant janitor's wife stuck out his head and addressed the young man.

"The old lady is asking for you," he said with lowered eyes. "Go in, sir, I'll stay out here until you return."

Old Mrs. Veress was sitting bolt upright in her armchair, resting her hand on the knob of her stick. Her two patent leather bags stood on the floor at her feet, her umbrella hung from the back of the chair, her head, wrapped in her black lace shawl, was supported by a tiny, pale green silk cushion. "I am glad you are here," she said when she heard her son's steps, and she tapped the floor twice with her stick.

"You wish to go out to the back, mother?" the young man asked.

The old lady shrugged irritably.

"Do you think that's all I ever want you for?" she grumbled. "Sit down by me. I hear that there are Arrow-Cross men in the house."

"Yes, mother, but they are here as guests."

"Fine," the old lady said. "Everyone here is expecting a raid. Take the money, your father's gold watch and ring, from my patent leather bag and try to get out of the building. I hear the front door is locked. Give the gold watch to the janitor if he lets you out. If he doesn't, try to get out through the pub or by a window in a ground floor flat."

"I wouldn't even think of it."

The old lady's face turned suddenly white, then, without transition, blood-red, under the double pressure of love and anger.

"Don't argue!" she shouted, hitting the floor furiously with her stick. "What help is it to me if you get shot, too! And if they leave us alone, we meet here tomorrow morning. Off you go!"

The young man burst out laughing.

"Don't shout, mother, as if you were alone," he said catching the old lady's peremptory index finger in his hand with a pacifying gesture. "Everyone is asleep."

"Nobody is asleep," the old lady said. "Half of them are afraid of the Arrow-Cross people, the other half of the Russians. I've been hearing for two days that they are at the Eastern Station. They certainly are a lazy crowd, even I would have got here by this time. Now, as I said, off you go!"

Before her son could answer, she rose from her armchair,

put both arms round the young man's neck, gave his bottom an affectionate pat with her stick and kissed him passionately on the mouth with her wrinkled lips.

"God be with you," she murmured. "We may never see each other again."

At that moment the noise of movement, frightened exclamations, were heard from the next cellar. The connecting door flew open and the brother of the assistant janitor's wife jumped into the vibrating light of the night-lamp, his thin neck tensing forward, his two arms raised.

"They are coming!" he cried.

"I don't know what to do," Mrs. Bor whispered to her husband and her large, healthy face turned ashy gray under the thick, black crown of hair. They had to decide at once, she told her husband. He lit a cigarette in his excitement even though smoking was prohibited in the cellar; however, in the general pandemonium, no one noticed. The whole cellar was humming with excitement, but the emotion was cold, not daring to show itself, it turned in on itself. Everyone pretended indifference. Latent in each slow, sluggish movement, was the speed of a fleeing fawn. Those who were lying down got up and put on their shoes, those who had been sitting up lay down again as if, by changing their position, they could change their dangerous situation. Body and soul were so completely attuned that— when emotion changed its rhythm—feet, hands, eyelashes and the pores of the skin immediately adjusted themselves to it, concealing the inner upheaval; no one was misled by another's apparent indifference; on the contrary, it quickened one's sensibilities.

In a corner, someone blew out a candle to make it darker, and at the same moment, in another corner, someone lit another candle, to make it lighter. There were a good many families in the house who were members of the Arrow-Cross Party, or at least sympathized with it, but now they were just as fidgety as their neutral fellows or those few stubborn burghers who dug their heels in and opposed the stream, perhaps neither in word nor in deed, but out of fastidiousness. At a glance, one could hardly notice the difference between the various layers. The lawyer Bor and his wife had, for long, been members of the Arrow-Cross Party, but they were as pale as Tamas Veress, the citizen of San Salvador. They were balanced on the razor's edge. The woman was block-warden, it was part of her job to know that tropical citizenships always covered Jews and she should have reported it to the Party long ago; if she did not warn these raiding Arrow-Cross men now, they might well bring her to look for hiding Jews. In addition, the approaching company was dead drunk—their confused shouting could already be heard from the lobby and then who knew what shape that calling to account would take. If, on the other hand, she did tell them, a thing that could hardly be kept secret, and Veress and his mother were as a result taken away and executed, in a week's time, when the Russians arrived, she would be denounced and the journey to the scaffold or lamppost would not be any longer than the Jews' journey from Nador Street to the Danube.

"How I begged you to move to Buda, to my mother's!" she said to her husband who sat staring in front of him, chewing his moustache, his face chalk white.

"It won't take a week . . . they'll be here in three days!" whispered Council Secretary Finiasz who was sitting in a green leather armchair opposite, pressing a white silk handkerchief to his mouth to stop the intolerable chattering of his teeth. The lawyer's wife threw him a hate-filled glance.

"Now, what's the matter with you?" she said contemptuously. "How can someone who calls himself a man be such a coward?"

"You shut your trap!" the Council Secretary growled. "Mind your own business."

Outside it had begun to rain. Through the ventilator which was left open, they could hear the monotonous, gentle drumming of the raindrops that, like an old song from an old, half-forgotten age, smuggled into the cellar the merciful memories of free winter nights. A sudden gust of wind swept the smell of snow as well into the faded air of the cellar which, revived, began to whirl. Mrs. Milos, who had returned to the shelter half an hour before, got up from her bed, stepped to the wall, rearranged the holy picture that had swung to one side during the morning's air raid, then sat back silently on her bed, directing her dim, rigid glance at the face of the Council Secretary sitting opposite her.

In the meantime, the noise from the lobby had quieted down, the Arrow-Cross men were obviously searching the private cellars along the corridor. The widow Daniska and Aunt Mari squatted trembling on the edge of their bed. The bootmaker's widow was so nervous that she took her spectacles off and hid them under her pillow. Mrs. Daniska was sweating with fear to such an extent that the cold perspiration had dried onto her skin and her entire body was itching. It was evident that if the Arrow-Cross men searched the whole cellar they would inevitably find the deserter concealed in the furnace room. Time passed slowly; it spread before them like the infinite, shoreless sea before a shipwreck; when the heightened moment lifted them up like the back of a wave, even from up there they could see only the thunderous desert of time reaching to the edge of the horizon. In people's souls, fear grew in geometrical progression. Man is conscious of time only when there is too little or too much of it, that is, when it increases beyond bounds or suddenly runs out; on such occasions, its place is imperceptibly taken by another medium: anxiety, in whose stream the soul loses its sense of proportion, its sense of direction, its everyday weight, and founders in it as helplessly as a body falling unexpectedly from the air into the mud of a swamp, or the water of a river. To Mrs.

Daniska, it seemed as if she had been waiting for the entrance of the Arrow-Cross men, not ten minutes but ten days, and as every coming minute would use up at least one full day of her life force, her vitality, it can be said that she was living not in time but in fear, and that time only exists when it doesn't exist.

Not even ten minutes had gone by since the Arrow-Cross men had left the lobby when quick, hard steps were heard in the oppressive silence, from the direction of the second cellar, the door flew open, and the deserter appeared in the lamplight. His clothes glistened black from the coal dust, his face and hands were also smeared with it. In a second his eyes had found the two petrified old women and immediately he set out toward them. The noise made by the Arrow-Cross men had awakened him in time and he had fled along the other branch of the corridor. He hoped that the air-raid shelter itself had already weathered the raid and he could hide there until the Arrow-Cross men had left the house. As soon as he learned from Aunt Mari that they had not been in the shelter yet, he turned around and left the cellar at a run. The two old women hadn't had time to recover from their fright nor had Mrs. Bor, busy with her own troubles, been able to ask what this stranger was doing in the house in the middle of the night, when the now familiar quick, hard steps were heard again and the deserter appeared again in the door. His teeth sparkled crystal white in his blackened face and his eyes shone glassily with fright. The front door was locked, he couldn't get out of the house. The key was in the pocket of the janitor who, together with the assistant janitor, was trailing along with the Arrow-Cross men. Without finishing his sentence, the fugitive turned his back on the two old women and ran out of the cellar.

The figure of a fleeing man will, in a second, grow to such proportions from the weight of his emotions that, before our very eyes, he sheds the ordinary measurements of man and enters the mirror of our senses as a towering giant. His feet, hands, features and movements run through us multiplied manifold and leave giant footprints in the soft soil of memory. Fear transforms not only time at its own pleasure, but also space; the running figure of the deserter—although the time for observation was short—penetrated through the nervous systems of the people with as much emotional weight as if a Titan had run out of the cellar in front of their eyes. His coal-dusty suit, white teeth, wet, blond hair, and long, waving arms created, in a second, as many involved and definite memories as if they had watched him for hours. They all recognized themselves in the fleeing figure and paled under the confrontation.

Council Secretary Finiasz jumped up from his armchair and started, involuntarily, toward the door. Someone moaned loudly and in a corner an old woman clapped her hands together and began to wail. Mrs. Milos bent forward and put her hand on the arm of the Council Secretary.

"Stay," she said in a loud voice.

A new wave of noise washed in through the door. A thick voice, surrounded by a spray of thin voices, and behind them a formless, monotonous humming. In the next cellar someone overturned a chair.

"Where are the two Veresses?" Mrs. Milos asked.

Silence fell in the low room, one could hear the sibilant sputtering of the candle.

"Where have the Jews gone to?" Mrs. Milos repeated.

Everyone turned around; the old lady's armchair and the white kitchen chair next to it were empty.

"What Jews?" asked Mrs. Bor.

"Don't pretend," cried Mrs. Milos and her slender neck above the fur coat flushed.

"I saw them here a moment ago," said the lawyer.

"You know as well as I that they are Jews," cried Mrs. Milos, turning to the lawyer's wife. The latter made no reply. The noise seeping in from the lobby became more stratified, more involved; shouts, even snatches of words, could be distinguished. Mrs. Milos rose and stepped before the Council Secretary.

"Did you hide them?" she asked in a loud voice.

"What is she saying?" a surprised, thick voice asked in the corner. "Did she say he hid them?"

The Council Secretary stood motionless beside a bed, his right hand pressing the silk handkerchief to his lips.

"Where did you hide them?"

"Calm down, Ilonka," Dr. Bor said irritably. "What has got into you?"

"What has got into me? I'll tell you. He is providing himself with an alibi so's they won't hang him next week."

The Council Secretary still didn't answer. The lawyer's wife rose and stepped beside Mrs. Milos.

"He won't get away with that!" Mrs. Milos said in a low voice but with such suppressed emotion that every breath she took could be clearly heard even in the farthest corner of the cellar.

The lawyer's wife took hold of her arm.

"Have you gone out of your mind?"

"Why don't you say something?!" Dr. Bor said to the Council Secretary. "They'll be here in a moment!"

"Sure, they'll be here in a moment!" Mrs. Milos's lusterless eyes gleamed triumphantly. "So where did you hide them?"

It grew a shade darker in the cellar; one of the candles had burnt itself out, the wick bent, the flame died. Pressing her two hands to her hips, Mrs. Milos bent forward and her rigid glance rested on the Council Secretary's face. "Either you bring them back," she said with the shadow of the dead candle in her voice, "or I'll report you to the Arrow-Cross for hiding Jews!"

"You're mad!" the lawyer's wife screamed. "You want them to kill me too?"

The Council Secretary reached into his pocket, brought out a revolver and fired two bullets into the heart of the woman standing in front of him. Mrs. Milos collapsed without a sound and stretched out on the ground. A few minutes later, when they had lifted her onto the bed and the first-aid nurse established that she was dead, old Mrs. Veress appeared in the connecting door leaning with one hand on her stick, the other on her son's arm. The women standing around the bed blocked her view of the body.

"Where have you been?" asked Mrs. Bor, her face ashen.

Old Mrs. Veress sat down in her armchair with a little groan, hung her stick on the arm of the chair and pulled her new Scottish plaid onto her knees.

"Out to the back," she said jerking her head toward the wood-cellars. "*Naturalia non sunt turpia*, don't you know," she added smiling. "Besides, I did not wish to cause my son trouble in the middle of the raid."

"You were in the lavatory?" the lawyer's wife asked, pressing both hands on her stomach.

Old Mrs. Veress, who did not hear the question, wiped her forehead and lips with a tiny black lace handkerchief.

"By the way, the Arrow-Cross men have gone," she informed them. "When we reached the lobby on our way back, they were all hurrying toward the stairs. I can easily do without their company," she added tactfully, "for they were rather intoxicated."

LEARNING THAT the Germans were evacuating Budapest and were going to blow up the bridges in an hour, the Arrow-Cross men fled from the house in a panic. By the time Dr. Bor reached the top of the spiral stairs, there was not a soul in sight. The assistant janitor's windows were dark, the street door stood wide open. A few steps from the door, on the corner of the street leading to the Danube, a man stood in the middle of the road in his jacket, his head uncovered, staring motionless toward the Buda mountains.

"Is that you, janitor?" the lawyer asked when he reached him.

The man turned his head toward him. In the dense winter night, the white of his eyes winked like a marsh-fire. In the great silence one could hear the chattering of his teeth.

"What a bloody cold wind!" he said.

"Where is your assistant?" the lawyer asked.

"Gone with them."

For a while both kept silent.

"Good for him," the lawyer said. "He has no children."

The janitor turned the whites of his eyes toward the lawyer.

"Good for him," he repeated slowly. "For if he hadn't gone I'd have kicked that Arrow-Cross bastard out of here so fast . . ."

The lawyer did not immediately grasp the other's meaning. Involuntarily he lifted his hand, but fortunately the movement merged with the darkness. He had to watch his breathing as well, it was liable to rasp in his excitement. A cold wind blew from the Danube, he began to shiver.

"I'm glad we got rid of him at last," said the man next to him with ponderous, peasant calm. But his teeth continued to chatter. The sound of a rifle shot reached them from the direction of Buda like a greeting from afar. "Those who have something to fear did well to go, isn't it so, Dr. Bor?"

Below, in the shelter, all were sitting on their beds, fully dressed in the wavering shadow-cages thrown by two rows of pillars. The door to the lobby was wide open and this time a candle was burning in the lobby as well. At the foot of one of the beds, an old woman prayed on her knees, her head bent; her two black shoes, standing on their toes, could be seen under her skirt, tapping rhythmically on the floor.

Dr. Bor sat down on the bed next to his wife.

"Is it true?" the woman asked.

"Yes."

"Did you go outside?"

"To the corner."

The lawyer glanced at the next bed with Mrs. Milos's sheet-covered body lying on it. The toes of her shoes and, at the other end, her nose protruded sharply from the sheet.

"The janitor has already changed over," he said ironically, and his teeth began to chatter again. "He has a quicker mind than I have. He almost got me."

The woman turned her large, pale face toward him questioningly. Her thick, dark brows met above her nose, and her white teeth seemed to have concentrated all the light in her mouth.

"He was cursing the Arrow-Cross," said the lawyer, wrinkling his nose.

His wife clapped her hands over her mouth.

"But he is a Party member!"

"Perhaps only his son," the man replied hoarsely. "And he has run away."

"Look!" whispered the woman, jerking her head in the direction of the opposite corner.

In the entire cellar only one person was asleep: Mrs. Karoly Veress. Resting her wrapped-up head on the green silk traveling cushion, she was breathing softly in the oblique candle-light; her straight, sharp-edged nose threw a small rectangular shadow on her left cheek. One of her hands lay on the shoulder of her son, who was eating a slice of bread at her feet.

"His appetite's come back," the lawyer said through chattering teeth. "The bridges were blown up after midnight."

Council Secretary Finiasz, who had been sitting beside his wife with his head lowered, his arms hanging, without a word, came suddenly to life. "What was that?" he asked raising his head.

"They have blown up the bridges!" cried the lawyer at the top of his voice. His large, pale face flushed blood-red with fury and malice.

The door of the lobby flew open and shut with a bang.

"We're finished," said the Council Secretary. He rose from his chair, then quickly sat down again.

"The Russians'll be here by morning," cried the lawyer's wife, hitting the bed with her fist. "We shall be free again, Mr. Council Secretary!"

The explosions came rolling down into the cellar in uninterrupted succession, crushed the fluttering candlelight and absorbed every latent sound. The door of the lobby flew open.

"Free again," repeated the Council Secretary in a soundless moment between two explosions. He gave the woman a long, curious glance. "I see," he said. "I understand, dear comrade."

The deserter, who had come back to the cellar after the departure of the Arrow-Cross and who was now lying on the widow Daniska's bed, turned to Aunt Mari. "What did she say about the Russians?" he asked.

The two widows were sitting on the edge of the bed, each watching the other's anxious face.

"They'll be here by morning, child," Aunt Mari informed him.

"Of course they will," said the lad. "What time is it?"

"It must be after midnight," the widow Daniska opined.

"Daybreak cannot be very far," said Aunt Mari musingly.

The deserter shook his head laughing. With the two large coal-dust patches on his cheekbones, his coal-pointed nose and russet hair, he looked like a black-painted clown in the court of the underworld.

"You whisper like bushes in the breeze," he said. "One cannot get a straight word out of you. Perhaps midnight . . . perhaps dawn . . . I asked you what time it was!"

"We don't know, child," said Aunt Mari.

"Don't know . . . don't know . . ." grumbled the lad. "It doesn't matter. I'm going back into the coal. For now it's the Russians who will arrest me, isn't it so, auntie?"

"Is that what you are afraid of?" asked Aunt Mari.

The widow Daniska folded her hands in prayer and stared before her with tear-filled eyes. The explosions had ceased and the silence, like a wall above the river, had cut the town in two.

"You can see for yourself," the lad said, "that this will never end. Now they'll shoot at us from the other side. Now from one side, now from the other. Wherever you run, they shoot at you."

The two widows remained silent. Aunt Mari twiddled her fingers.

"That's how it is in the world," she said severely after a while. "The poor man is always there where there's shooting. He's only got himself to blame, why doesn't he change it?"

"We'll change it, never fear," murmured the young man. "Is it certain that my mother is dead?"

The two old women nodded.

"They shot her twice?"

"Twice."

"Then I heard right," said the lad. "I heard two shots, almost simultaneously. I thought they were firing after me. Both shots were for her?"

"Both."

"Of course," the young man murmured. "Did it take her long to die?"

"An hour."

The deserter rose and stretched.

"Let me have a piece of bread, I'm going back into the coal," he said. He smoothed down his tousled, fair hair and pulled up his trousers. "For once one begins to shoot," he said moodily, "one never stops as long as one lives."

It was getting light when the first Russian soldier appeared in the cellar. His fur cap sat obliquely on his head and he held his machine gun in his arms as if it were a baby. Although they lighted several candles in his honor, one could not distinguish his features under the soot and filth. His eyes wandered slowly around the cellar.

"Germanski?" he asked in a deep, throaty voice.

He had laughing, blue eyes. He walked around the cellar in his soundless boots and gazed into every face. He stopped before a little boy of six with an army cap on his head. He said something in Russian that no one understood. For a while, he gazed at the child shaking his head, then, with two fingers, he carefully lifted the cap from his head and flung it into a corner. He laughed at the child, looked round once more, then, with soundless steps, he ran from the cellar.

"Strike me dead!" cried Aunt Mari, swearing for the first time in her entire life, and big tears of joy ran down her cheeks from under the spectacles inherited from her husband. "The war is over, so help me, Jesus! The war is over, to hell with whoever invented it!"

"Come and have some breakfast, God damn it!" said the widow Daniska with tears in her eyes. "I'm starving, the devil take this miserable world!" She took Aunt Mari's arm and dragged her toward the shelf on which the cellar-dwellers stored their food. "Where's that bloody footstool?" she grumbled. "Hold me, Aunt Mari, I'm afraid I'll trip, to hell with this blessed foot of mine!"

"I'm holding you!" shouted Aunt Mari. "God damn my weak hands!"

The widow hopped onto the footstool like a grasshopper. "I can't see my basket," she murmured and wiped her eyes. "The devil take whoever invented darkness!"

"What are you looking for, blast it?!" said Aunt Mari. "Tell me!"

The widow Daniska climbed off the footstool with a basket in her hand. "I've got a little bread and honey left," she said. "Let's finish it before it goes to the dogs!"

Translated by Kathleen Szasz

PHILEMON AND BAUCIS

THE OLD couple were resting peacefully on the narrow garden bench, enjoying the autumn sun as it cast the shadow of a nearly barren walnut tree over them. The stillness of the usually quiet garden on the outskirts of the town was disturbed only by the occasional distant clatter of the express. A lonely yellow leaf fluttered to the ground. The old woman was knitting a gray sock, while the old man by her side would have fallen into a pleasant slumber had the clicking of the knitting needles not jolted him repeatedly awake.

"Old Tímár's gone," he said heavy eyed. He had meant to tell her the news earlier in the day, but it had skipped his mind.

"What?" the old woman asked. She was a little hard of hearing.

"Old man Tímár. He's dead," he said again, more loudly than before.

"What was the matter with him?" the old woman asked.

"He killed himself," the old man said.

"Well, he was well on in years," the old woman said.

"Just two years older than me," the old man added.

"What's that?" his wife said.

"He wasn't that old," the old man said diplomatically.

"Old enough."

The sun was comfortably warm. The old man was preoccupied with his thoughts. "He drank," he said.

"What was that?" his wife chided. "Can't you speak up?"

"He drank away his pension every month," the old man shouted, leaning closer to his wife's ear. "He drank it away. To the last penny."

Another parched leaf fluttered from the walnut tree. The old woman followed its slow descent with her eyes.

"The sun is so nice and cozy today."

"I'm going for a walk," the old man said and stood up. "Don't catch cold. Would you like your shawl?"

"No thank you, dear. You're off again?"

The old man checked the temperature with the back of his outstretched hand.

"I'll bring it out anyway," he said. "The October sun can be treacherous. You'll catch cold before you know it. And please check on the dog."

By the time the old man returned from his walk, it was late afternoon, and the sky was overcast. He'd brought his wife a present for her birthday, a hearing aid he'd planned to give her over dinner. It lay hidden under his coat, inside a bouquet of Michaelmas daisies. He'd given up cigarettes a year before in order to afford it. But now, as he silently tiptoed into the parlor, his heart was heavy, and he was gripped by doubt. What if his wife was mortified? She didn't know she was hard of hearing. Just the other day she'd looked up in response to a not-too-distant burst of gunfire, cast her eye at the door, and said, "Come in!"

The old man entered the kitchen.

"I'm back. What's for dinner?"

"What kept you?" his wife asked.

"It was such a lovely walk," the old man said.

"You're probably up to something again," his wife commented. "We're having fresh roast."

The old man smacked his lips. "It's been a long time since we've had meat."

"I hope you're not going to annoy me with a birthday present again," his wife chided. "We have no money, and the pension isn't due for another week."

"We'll manage," the old man said.

"What?" his wife said. "Don't blather. Set the table while I get dinner ready."

Outside, it began to rain. The heavy drops of rain clattered loudly against the windowpane. The old man set the table. Since it was for a birthday dinner, they were going to eat in the parlor. As he went about his business, the rain continued to pound against the windowpane. But now the sound was suppressed by another, more distant sound which ceased, then started up again. The old man walked up to the window and listened. The wind was up, and he could hear the cracking of the walnut branches. Then all at once, the two yellow patches of light stretching along the cement in front of the house across the way disappeared. Someone had turned out the light inside. The old man quickly closed the shutters, then went out to the hall and secured the front door. The fighting had not reached the outskirts before, but now, it seemed, it was coming closer. Even through the wooden shutters, the old man could hear the rat-tat-tat of machine guns. He went to the kitchen where the air was permeated by the smell of fat, garlic, and roast meat. Luckily, the sizzling and sputtering deadened the sounds from outside. Thank God I haven't given her the hearing aid yet, the old man thought.

"What are you up to?" his wife asked. "Why did you bolt the door?"

"It's raining cats and dogs outside."

"So what?"

"The wind will sweep the rain inside," the old man said.

"Still. Did you have to bolt it? The kitchen is full of steam. Cat's got your tongue?"

"It's windy," the old man said. "The door's loose and the wind'll break it, driving in the rain. We'll be wiping it up all night."

"You're imagining things again," his wife said. "I can't hear any wind."

The rat-a-tat of the machine guns was closer all the time. There were sporadic bursts, but mostly the volleys came in series, or right on top of each other without a break. They could be heard more and more distinctly all the time.

The old man went out to the hall again. The front door faced the street. It was easier to tell how the fighting was progressing from there. As he crossed the parlor, he snatched up the bouquet of Michaelmas daisies with the hearing aid from his wife's plate, a surprise, and hid it under the sofa cushion. The fighting had reached their street by then, and was approaching the house. Luckily, the kitchen door and window faced the small garden in the back. The old man walked back to the parlor, gathered up the silverware, the plates and the tablecloth, placed them on a tray, and took them out to the kitchen.

"What are you up to?" his wife asked. "Haven't you set the table yet? Why are we eating in the kitchen?"

"Why not?" the old man asked.

His wife turned to face him. "Have you forgotten, dear?"

"Forgotten?" the old man asked.

"It's my birthday," his wife said with a gentle smile, but her brow was flushed. "On my birthday, we always eat in the parlor."

Now it was the old man's turn to blush. "I forgot," he said, and his wrinkles reddened. He put the tray down on the kitchen table because his hands trembled so. "I wonder how it slipped my mind."

"Never mind, dear," his wife said. "At least the parlor won't smell of food. Go to the hall. There's someone at the door."

"At this time of night?" the old man said.

"What did you say?" his wife asked.

"Nobody comes at this time of night," the old man shouted, leaning closer to his wife.

"I hear knocking, I tell you," his wife said.

The old man shuffled out to the hall. He pressed his ear against the door. It seemed to him that the gunshot he'd heard just now came from the street, just across from the garden gate. He crouched down, thinking a stray bullet might hit the door. The whistling of the wind and the wild whiplash of the walnut branches lay like a deadening blanket over the other sounds of the street. It was like the jamming of the radio broadcasts. Yet even as the bullets bit relentlessly into the dark stones outside, the old man thought he could hear the thud of heavy-booted feet. Then came another round of gunfire.

His wife called to him from the kitchen. "Dinner's ready, dear!"

"Be right with you," the old man said.

"Is anybody there?" his wife asked.

"No," the old man said, louder this time.

"I can't hear you," his wife scolded.

"I said there's nobody here," the old man said. His body, tall and gaunt, hadn't perspired in years. But now his palm was moist and his forehead was beaded in sweat.

"What's keeping you?" his wife called from the kitchen. "The food's getting cold."

"I'll be right there," the old man said. "I'll just check on the dog to see if she's in pain."

The dog lay quietly in her basket, sequestered in a dark recess of the hall. The old man stroked her head, then turned back to the door. During the irregular intervals when the wind was still, he could hear solitary bursts of machine-gun fire, but they came muted now, overpowered by the still louder broadcasts of nature. And then, the gunfire passed the house.

"Why don't you come to the table?" his wife asked again. "Your dinner will get spoiled."

"I'm coming, I'm coming," the old man shouted, "you can start serving."

He went back to the recess where he'd hidden a bottle of red wine for the birthday dinner, then took his dark jacket out of the wardrobe and slipped it on. In his haste he threw his everyday jacket on the sofa.

"What's keeping you?" his wife chided from the kitchen. "Are you feeling all right?"

"I'm fine," the old man shouted, "I'm all right."

He went out to the hall once again, pressed his ear against the door, and listened. In his agitation he inadvertently flicked on the light switch. The light flooded the hall, and he had to turn around to switch it off. While he was at it, he switched off the parlor light as well. When he opened the kitchen door, in the brightly lit, clean room so close to his heart, he caught a glimpse, as on a picture postcard, of his silver-haired wife, an old woman with a serene smile sitting by the laden table in her threadbare but clean mourning dress, oblivious to his presence, with two long, flashing knitting needles in her hands, and a gray sock dangling into her lap. The old man was so touched, he tripped over the brightly polished brass threshold. This time a knock came clear and unmistakable from the direction of the front door.

"You're here at last," the old woman said. "Why don't you come to the table."

The pounding at the front door was repeated. The dog, too, barked in her recess, but did not leave her basket.

"What's that you're hiding behind your back," the old woman said. "You're up to your old tricks again, I bet."

"Someone's knocking at the door," the old man shouted.

The old woman smiled. The old man felt a shiver run down his spine. His wife's self-assured smile, the sickening cleanliness of the bright kitchen and the full table suddenly repulsed him.

The banging at the front door came again, more insistent than before.

"Can you hear it now," the old man asked softly. He turned around and crossed the parlor, leaving the door ajar, and went out to the hall. The front door was double locked. He opened it. A young man, a stranger, crossed the threshold, his hands pressed to his loins. His face was smeared with blood.

"Lock the door," he said urgently. "And turn off the light!"

"What do you want, son?" the old woman asked through the kitchen door.

"I think they got my balls," the young man said.

"What did he say?" the old woman asked, "I can't hear. What does he want?"

"He's wounded," the old man shouted.

"Don't shout," the young man said, "they might still be lurking out there."

"What did he say?" the old woman said. "Why can't you speak clearly? And that goes for both of you!"

The old man turned toward the kitchen door. "He says there's a bullet lodged in his thigh."

"What?" the old woman asked again.

"His thigh," the old man said, "there's a bullet in his thigh."

The old woman smiled at the stranger. "Sit down in that chair, son, there, in the corner, and wait," she ordered.

"What will you do with him?" she asked the old man after they'd gone to the parlor and she had cautiously closed the kitchen door. "You want to keep him here?"

The old man made no answer.

"Well, he can't stay," the old woman said. "His clothes are covered in blood. He'll bleed all over the sofa. Besides, where would I put him?"

"I don't know," the old man said.

"I have an idea," his wife said. "Take him over to the Molnárs. They have three rooms."

"But no empty beds," the old man said.

"Why don't you put that bottle down?" his wife said. "Take him over to old man Tímár's then. They have an empty bed now."

"He's not buried yet," the old man reminded his wife, "he hasn't been taken out of the house."

Her smile gone, his wife gazed at him from under her silvery crown of hair.

"He can't stay," she said. "Which thigh?"

"I don't know," the old man said.

"He'll bleed all over the sofa, and I won't have it. He's got to go!"

"You can't stay here, son," the old woman said, turning to the young man who was sitting in the hallway, his hand still pressed to his loin. "For your information, three of my sons have died in the war. Two were killed in action, the third was murdered by the fascists. I've had enough. Leave us in peace, son. Go away. I have nothing against you, but go away. This house can take only two more corpses, son. Just two!"

The young man did not budge.

"Didn't you hear me?" the old woman said. "We don't have room! My husband will help you over to our neighbor's house."

A quarter of an hour later, the old man was back. His wife was sitting by the full kitchen table again, knitting. Two pots were steaming on the stove, over a low flame. The old man went to the hall, hung his coat on a hook, picked up the bottle of wine he'd left there, went to the kitchen, and placed it in the center of the table.

"Come here," his wife said, "you've got blood all over you."

"Where?" the old man asked, looking at his clothes.

There was blood on his shirt and his collar, his short, gray moustache, and the corner of his lip.

"You've had a nosebleed, dear," the old woman said. "Let's go into the parlor and lie down."

"Never mind," the old man said, "I'll just sit on a chair and lean back my head."

But when he reached the parlor, his steps faltered. Since his wife realized that she couldn't support his heavy-boned frame to the bed, she laid him on the wide, grass-green sofa close to the kitchen door, took his handkerchief out of his pocket—it was also soaked in blood—and pressed it against his nose. Then in order to make sure that he was lying perfectly flat, she pulled the heavy cushion from under him.

The bouquet of Michaelmas daisies with the hearing aid rolled to the floor. The old woman picked it up and put it on the table by the sofa. She remembered that she had a small wad of cotton wool in the linen closet to stop the bleeding. She applied a cold compress to the back of the old man's head, untied his shoes, pulled them off his feet, and covered him with a worn blanket. But the old man was bleeding so profusely that in a matter of minutes the cotton under his nose was soaked through. The grass-green sofa was also stained with blood. Thank God the old man hadn't noticed, his wife thought. She pulled back the shutters and opened the window. The old man could hear the renewed rat-a-tat-tat of machine guns again.

"Turn off the light," he said.

His wife did as she was told.

"Does the fresh air feel good?" she asked.

"Yes," he said. "Did you find it?"

"Yes," she said.

"Have you looked?"

"Not yet," she said. "Don't talk, you'll tire yourself out."

"Can you forgive me, Rozi," the old man said, "but I thought you'd get good use out of it."

"I hear perfectly well without that thing," she said. "It must have cost a fortune."

"Can you hear the guns?" he asked.

"Yes," she said. "Just lie still."

"Can you hear better in the dark?" he asked.

"Yes," she said. "Are you still bleeding, dear?"

"I can't tell," the old man said. "It may have stopped."

There was no more cotton wool in the house, and the cold compress didn't seem to help. The blood came in torrents from the old man's nose.

The old woman did not take her coat from the wardrobe; she didn't want her husband to know that she was going for the doctor.

"Where are you going, Rozi?" the old man asked when the kitchen door opened and a yellow patch of light hit the floor.

"I'll be right back," his wife said. "I think there's more cotton wool in the shed."

She stood in the kitchen door and listened. Love had sharpened her hearing. Muted by the soft patter of the rain, the gunshots came from close by at scattered intervals. Covering her head with a kerchief, the old woman ran across the yard and through the Molnárs' garden, and from there, out into the street.

The street was dark. The lamps had all been shattered by stray bullets. Puddles splashed beneath her feet, muddying her clean black mourning dress. All around, the shutters had been closed, or the lights had been switched off. Only the shots, sometimes sporadic, sometimes issuing in line like the links in a chain, indicated that there were people on the street. The old woman continued running in the dark, but her lips trembled in fear. The dark was even more terrifying than the guns, for it tasted of what would follow after the gunfire had ceased.

As she continued running down the street, the old woman kept glancing at the sky. But the sky, too, was uniformly black. Even the crimson glow that usually came from the direction of Pest was gone. The old woman was not praying, she was just terribly frightened. When she turned the corner, the next street was pitch dark, too. The old woman's eyes had adjusted to the dark, but only enough to allow her to distinguish the non-physical space from the physical objects that, in their present shapelessness, were more terrifying than the former.

The old woman ran out into the road, where there were fewer objects. Up until now, she managed not to fall. If only there were no people hovering under cover of the dark, she might even die happy, she thought. But the people, she was afraid of the people.

In order to reach the doctor's house, she had to pass along a narrow street with the upper end conjoining Marx Square. This street was pitch dark as well, lit only by a solitary lamp at the lower end that had somehow escaped destruction. As she turned the corner, the old woman spotted a man crouching and running in the muted sheen of the pearly rain, dimly lit by that one solitary lamp. As far as she could tell, the square itself was also under cover of darkness. But it reverberated with the fire of machine guns. The district council building was under siege. The doctor lived immediately behind it, and from one of the upper windows, blasts of machine-gun fire sprayed the darkness with regular semicircles of light. Just a couple of feet from the doctor's door, the old woman fell, her face turned up to the sky. She did not close her eyes. She felt no pain. For a moment, she felt almost happy, for she had no more accounts to settle in this world. Later, as she lost more blood, her fear returned. But this time, it wasn't of people.

Lying on the sofa, the old man had lost a lot of blood himself, and the loss of blood had made him fall into a deep slumber. When he woke up, he shivered and drew the worn blanket up to his chin. He'd have liked someone to close the window because the cold autumn wind swept in straight to his bed.

He called his wife, but she did not answer. Through the open kitchen door, he could still hear the bubbling of the two pots. "Rozi," he called again. I'm glad I bought that hearing air for her, he thought after a while, and he glanced at the small black gadget on the table. He would have liked someone to come and close the window, but his wife did not come. He was afraid to stand up, lest his nose started bleeding again. The wind swept in the rain through the open window. The old man was happy. He was more convinced now than ever that he'd done the right thing when he purchased the hearing aid.

When the dog began whining in the hallway, the old man got up. By the time he'd pulled up a small stool and sat down by her side, the first of the puppies with its disproportionately long, wormy tail and pink paws was already squirming in the basket. The folds of the blanket under it were filled with amniotic fluid. The recess was lit only by the light filtering in from further down the hallway. The house was quiet, and so was the dog, who was mustering her strength, laboring in silence. Only the rasping sound of her tongue as she licked the slime off the black fur of her newborn puppy broke the perfect stillness. For a moment another spasm made her stop, but as soon as the pain subsided, she turned her attention back to her firstborn, and with her red tongue, continued to lick it clean. From time to time, the open window in the parlor made a creaking sound.

The old man heaved a sigh. His stomach quivered with excitement. Under its glassy caul, the second puppy was also black. Except for the bubbling pots in the kitchen, the house continued still. Outside, on the street, the shooting had stopped. Even though he no longer needed the cotton wool, the old man could not bring himself to leave the basket and call his wife in from the shed. With the palm of his hand he was helping to support the dog, who had propped herself up on her foreleg, arching her back, trembling with every muscle, straining her body. As she littered her third puppy, the first found a nipple and began to suck. The second puppy squealed like a rusty door. The dog took turns licking her two puppies. As she bit off the umbilical cord of the third, the blood trickled onto the blanket.

The old man got up, went to the parlor, and closed the window. He didn't want the puppies to catch cold from the draft. He felt sorry for them, but resented them just a little bit, too. When he sat down on the low stool again, resting his gray head in his hands, the dog turned on her side, opened her mouth, and let her tongue hang out. Her big black eyes spoke of happiness. The old man stroked her. He had no idea how long he'd been sitting in the silent house attending to the untiring, rasping sound of the dog's tongue, but he felt no fatigue, and a strange sort of joy crept into his heart. He was so preoccupied with his thoughts, he did not realize that his wife had not come back from the shed. And then the dog's tail stiffened again, and she was in the throes of yet another spasm of pain.

Translated by Judith Sollosy

B E H I N D   T H E
B R I C K   W A L L

COMRADE BODI left Karoly Brock Street, which led to the main gate of the factory, turned into the first side street, and a few minutes later came out onto the bank of the Danube. He still had half an hour until the relief of the night shift. He had time to take a stroll and enjoy the early spring sunshine. He had a headache.

Across the Danube, in Pest, he could see the long row of dust-colored warehouses and, farther off, the bridge, above which seagulls slowly wheeled. The wind blew strongly from the west, ruffling the river and chasing the garbage along the water's edge. When the gusts became more violent, yellow clouds of dust suddenly rose into the air, darkening the sun. The river's edge, left derelict, was littered with rubbish. Some way off, beside the water, a stray dog, shaggy and emaciated, sniffed at some dried-up filth and watched uneasily as the man approached.

There the high, red brick wall that surrounded the factory broke the force of the wind a little. Garbage was strewed on the ground beneath the wall, but at least a man's eyes and mouth were not filled with grit and sand when the wind blew too hard. Comrade Bodi stopped a moment, his back to the wind. He leaned against the wall, turning to the sun his thin face with its day's growth of beard. Just as he was about to set off again, he noticed a brand-new piece of leather at his feet, partly covered with sand brought by the last gust of wind. It was twelve or fifteen inches long. Comrade Bodi picked it up, studied it carefully, then went on his way with the thick piece of leather in his hand.

He had hardly gone a few steps when another piece of strap fell in front of him, almost grazing his cap, and coming from the other side of the brick wall. A third and fourth followed, curving in a great arc over the wall. Comrade Bodi examined them for a few moments and then continued on his way. On the other side of the wall there was a low storeroom attached to the workshops.

Bodi made his way straight to the locker room. Every morning he slipped on a pair of oil-stained overalls to save his clothes.

"What's this?" asked a machinist, sitting on a bench nearby.

"What?"

The man had pulled off his shoe. His big toe, yellow and crooked, poked through a hole in his sock. Carefully, he removed the sock and held it up between two fingers.

"What's this?"

Comrade Bodi averted his head slightly. "Are you talking to me?" he asked.

"Yes, what's this?" the worker repeated, waving the sock in front of Bodi's face.

Bodi turned his head even more. "Take it away," he said quietly.

"Don't you know what it is?" asked the worker. "It's the 'sock of the new Man.'"

The night shift was already leaving. Some of the workers greeted Bodi. Others did not. Some had known Bodi for twenty years, ever since he had come to the factory, yet they passed without a word. Bodi crossed the yard, the wind lashing at his face once more. Here the air seemed denser, more solid, because of the litter suspended in it. In another part of the plant, employees arrived one by one at the main office. Comrade Bodi reached the office in his turn.

Behind the desk sat a corpulent man with a face marked by illness, flesh yellow and puffy beneath the eyes, jowls flabby and wrinkled. Bodi greeted him. The man nodded curtly, then asked, "What's wrong now?"

"They're stealing the leather now."

The fat man said nothing.

"I saw it with my own eyes."

"Where?"

"Shop Number Four," said Bodi. "They're throwing the belting over the wall. I was walking at the back of the factory."

The two men stared at each other without speaking.

"Makes leather to mend their shoes," said the fat man, the corners of his mouth twisted in a faintly sarcastic grimace.

An old man wearing eyeglasses, tall and stooping, came into the office. He gave a humble greeting and then, as if expecting a kick in the ass, fled precipitately into the next room. Two workers followed him; one, a slight girl with dimples, had a face as fresh as the peonies she had been picking that morning in her garden before leaving for the plant. Comrade Bodi waited until the door was shut, then rested his hand on the desk. The flesh of the hand was blue-white, the nails trimmed close.

"It can't go on like this," he said. "No, not like this. God! Not any more."

"I'll see about it," said the fat man. He spoke with a tired air, staring vacantly at the door through which the peony-girl had disappeared.

Outside again, Bodi had the wind behind him. An empty oil drum began to roll before the force of the wind; it clanged to a stop against the wall of the gasoline depot. The wind was fresh, a fine spring wind. The workshop windows rattled so much that he could hardly make out the din of the mechanical hammers.

IN THE workshop, someone was waiting for Bodi. He worked in a corner of the assembly shop, in a glassed-in cubicle through the door of which so much soot and dust blew that at night the shift had coal-black faces and hair gritty with metal dust. The place was full of people waiting or jostling. The foreman stood by the window, lost in some document, his glasses pushed up onto his forehead. The man waiting for Bodi stood with his head bent; he slouched against the wall and did not look up until Bodi took his place behind the desk.

"Hello, Ferenc," said Bodi.

The man took a step forward.

"What's up?"

"Do you know what's going on?"

Comrade Bodi looked at the production schedule the man held out to him.

"You know," the man went on. "You're responsible. What the hell does it mean?"

Comrade Bodi examined the sheet more closely. "Don't get excited, Ferenc," he said.

The paper continued to shake.

"Where do you get this crap?" the man went on, speaking in a low, desperate voice. "Ninety seconds per piece! What kind of a norm is that? You want me to live on love?"

"Don't get excited, Ferenc."

The man put the paper on the desk. "Where do you get a crazy norm like this?" he said, his voice still low. "Just tell me how. If you can show me how, all right. I'll go back to my bench. But show me."

"In the morning, from now on," Bodi said, "you won't have

to wait until the materials arrive. You gain half an hour from
that alone."

"You think so?" said the man, ironically. "What next?"

Bodi avoided his eyes. "You know it's necessary, Ferenc," he
said. "Production costs are too high. We're eating into re-
serves. Expenses are so heavy that . . ."

"Is that so?"

Bodi looked at him out of the corner of his eye, to see if he
was being sarcastic. "That is so," he replied. "Don't be funny."

"Funny?" said the man.

There was silence. Comrade Bodi turned to the door,
which had opened; no doubt it was a visitor for him. He folded
the paper on the desk.

"How much do I take home?" the man asked. "Don't give
me that paper back. Work it out. See what I get deducted. See
what I'll take home to the wife and kids. Work it out!"

"Put your back into it, Ferenc," said Bodi. "You'll make it
up in a month." He got no reply; he raised his eyes. Ferenc was
looking him in the eyes for the first time since the beginning of
the interview. Comrade Bodi turned away his head. The man
turned on his heels and left the cubicle without a word.

"There's a man who hasn't got any love for you," said the
typist near Bodi.

A few minutes later Bodi walked through the workshop
again—the manager had just sent for him—and noticed that
Ferenc's bench was empty. The violent wind snatched the
workshop door from his grasp and sailed his cap toward a puddle of oily water that had lain in a hollow of the clay-like soil
since last week's rain. Two young apprentices sniggered when
they saw the cap blowing along toward the puddle. A third,
coming toward Bodi, could have put out his foot to stop it, but
seeing Bodi running he looked the other way. The two apprentices guffawed. The cap fell in the greasy water. Bodi shook it
out and went on slowly. He felt their eyes on his back.

On his way from the manager's office he skirted the administration building. Behind the metal shop, in a narrow alleyway between the red brick wall and the workshop, he let himself slowly down to the ground, his back against the wall. No one ever came here. His head was splitting. The world seemed dark around him. His eyes throbbed, misted over with tears of pain. His forehead ran with sweat.

Usually these attacks came in the evening, between eight and ten o'clock. Sometimes he suffered during the day, but the worst pains did not come until evening, at supper or after. For two years now he had not gone out after work nor after his evening meal, except on the days when he had a Party meeting. On Sundays he stayed in bed; on that day the pain never left him. He tried all kinds of analgesics: aspirin, pills, sedatives— the whole range of cures. What helped most was to lie down with his head hanging off the bed.

Here, beyond the workshop where no one came, he told himself he could rest for just a quarter of an hour. He stretched himself at full length. He was at the foot of the wall, sheltered from the wind that crept into the alley, sometimes raising dense clouds of dust. He rested his neck on a brick and tilted his head backward. Above him long, boat-shaped clouds sped so quickly across the blue sky that they made him dizzy. "I'll shut my eyes," he said to himself. As he shut his eyes, the wind whistled in his ears. Go back again to the doctor? What for? For two years he had trailed from one hospital to another. At first the doctors had suspected a tumor on the brain: they examined the back of his eyes, x-rayed his skull and brain. Then they had sent him to a nerve specialist. Then to the general section. Six months before, they had done a cisternal puncture. "Undress and don't worry. I am going to insert a needle in the nape of your neck. It won't hurt. Don't move, or the prick could cause a fatal lesion. It will only hurt for a moment. Don't be afraid. Be calm." He had not felt much pain, but when the thick needle had plunged into his neck he had felt something he would never forget. It was worse than anything until then.

BACK IN the cubicle, the foreman asked: "What did the old man want?" He pushed his glasses back on his forehead.

Bodi shrugged.

"Production costs?"

"He talked about that."

"What else?"

"The thefts."

"Our fault, I suppose?"

"Well," said Bodi, "I'm a member of the council for discipline."

"That's a big leg up."

"He's right," Bodi said. "I'm not active enough. I lack vigilance, enthusiasm. He's right."

"You think so?"

"Yes," said Bodi. "I think he's right."

"What are you shutting your eyes for?" asked the foreman. "Are you sick? What's the matter?"

"Nothing's wrong. Nothing at all."

The foreman stepped toward Bodi. "You look like a corpse."

Comrade Bodi began to laugh. "No, I'm fine. By the way, yesterday was Karcsi Olajos's trial."

"The fool! What did he get?"

"Six months."

The foreman looked at Bodi without a word. His round Magyar face, with its little stiff moustache, had gone white with rage.

"That's a hell of a story to take around," he said. "Six months! What an article for the wall newspaper. Christ! Six months for a few yards of copper wire. How many yards?"

"Four or five," said Comrade Bodi.

"Goddamn fool!" said the foreman. "He gets himself six months for five yards of copper wire. No appeal?"

"No appeal."

The foreman looked out of the window. Outside, men were pushing along a wheelbarrow full of scrap. "Nothing will stop them," he muttered. "What a fool. What did he want the copper wire for?"

"To hang out his washing," Bodi said. "Copper doesn't leave rust marks on the washing."

THE NEXT day, they arrested two of the men who had stolen the leather—a lathe operator of about forty and his accomplice, an old man who worked in the factory stockroom. They had been cutting the straps and hiding them under their coats. The Party organization called a meeting in the main workshop. The manager and Party secretary were there. Three or four hundred men gathered around a big drawing table in the middle of the workshop.

The two culprits stood on the table. The lathe operator, motionless, his face chalk-white, arms dangling, looked down at the sheet of rusty tin plate that covered the table. Beside him the old man stood gawking at the silent crowd. Now and again he smiled: he did not understand what had happened to him. He wore a canary-colored beret which he kept pushing back and forth on his bald head. He seemed tired from working all night. He shifted his weight to each foot in turn, moving his old, lined face to right and left, as if begging for help. Above his head the factory loudspeaker bellowed happy marching tunes.

Comrade Bodi's speech only took a few minutes. The sullen-faced workers listened without moving. When Bodi paused between his slowly spoken sentences, they could hear the scraping of the old man's iron heels on the metal tabletop.

Other workmen arrived from nearby shops, and the crowd around the table grew. Above the table the arm of a crane had stopped in mid-transit. Five or six men stood in the idle bucket, just above the two thieves. The lathe operator stood motionless; sweat ran down his face. The old man continued to rock from one foot to the other, smiling emptily.

Just before the end of the meeting, the canary-yellow beret slipped from the old man's head and fell to the floor. An old workman bent down to pick it up and put it on the table. In his confusion the old man rolled it up and stuffed it in his pocket. He left his hand there, and as the meeting ended one might have thought he was listening to Comrade Bodi's speech, smiling jauntily, not caring at all. The men standing near the table saw that he had wet his pants.

Before the morning shift ended, the word went around that the lathe operator had committed suicide. He had hanged himself in the washroom. He had made a noose of brass wire, climbed on a toilet seat. Then, with his head in the noose, he had stepped off into space. When they found him, his body was already cold.

"WELL, WHAT did you say at the meeting?" Mrs. Bodi asked when he got home that night.

Comrade Bodi was stretched out on the couch, his head hanging over the edge. He had his usual migraine but seemed calm. The large room was lit only by a little lamp with a pink shade on the bedside table.

"What could I say?"

The pale little woman paced up and down the room, wringing her hands. "My God, my God! The Lord will punish us," she wailed. "They'll all say it's your fault. What did you say?"

"I made a speech," said Bodi.

"Saying what?"

"What I had to say."

The little pale woman went on wringing her hands and wept.

"Don't get upset," said Bodi.

"What?"

"Don't get upset. Sit down. You make me dizzy."

She sat down near him and put a cold, bony hand on his forehead.

"What did you say?"

"I said what I had to say."

"The Lord will punish us. Why did it have to be you?"

"The manager picked me."

"But why did it have to be you?"

Bodi did not answer.

"God will punish us. Why did it have to be you?"

The man tilted his head still farther back, just above the floor, which glowed under the red light of the lamp. "I'm a member of the council for discipline," he said, looking at the pallid face of his wife. "It was up to me to speak. I couldn't get out of it."

"What did you say?"

"Stop moving around like that," said Bodi. "You make me dizzy. Sit down on the couch."

The woman sat down again on the couch, at her husband's feet. "The good Lord will punish us," she said. "It was no job for you. You're too good. You'll make yourself ill. How did you speak?"

"With great care," said Bodi, looking up at his wife's face. "I said what I could in his favor."

"What?"

"That he was a first-class skilled worker."

"God will punish us," the woman repeated. "What else did you say?"

"I said that he had worked in the factory for fourteen years. I said that he never missed a single day, that he was a good timekeeper, dependable in his work."

"God will punish us, anyway," she said. "What else did you say?"

The man held his head between his hands. "I said that he had been a Party member since 1945, that he had fulfilled all the tasks that the Party set him, but that for some time he had done his political work grudgingly. I said that Communists must set an example . . . that they must always be first . . ."

"Yes," said the woman. "You would say that."

". . . that they must set an example in production and also in discipline."

"Naturally," said the woman. "You said that."

Comrade Bodi looked at his wife's face. It was red in the lamplight. "That's what I said. And I said that when a Communist harms the State and does not respect Socialist property, he is twice a criminal and has no place alongside honest workers."

"God will punish us," said the woman. "He stole because he wasn't earning enough."

Slowly the man lifted his head onto the couch. "That's what they all say."

"Poor man! Look at your own shoes," said his wife. "When will you have the money to buy yourself another pair?"

Comrade Bodi did not look at his shoes. He stared at his wife's face which had aged so much in recent years. Their godchild, who was married and lived in Miskolc, had hardly recognized her when she visited Budapest last winter.

"Go to bed," he said. "I'll sleep on the couch. Turn out the light."

"Did anyone else speak?"

"Yes."

"How many?"

"Two."

"What did they say?"

"They didn't say anything," muttered Bodi. "Go to bed.

Put out the light. It was all decided in advance. None of the workers spoke."

"Because they all steal," said the woman. "Poor men. We are poor people, too. When will the poor have a little peace ?"

THREE DAYS after the suicide, at lunchtime, Comrade Bodi walked down the narrow alley between the metal shop and the red brick wall. He stretched himself out at the base of the wall, his head resting on a brick. He had a headache. A strong wind blew. From time to time a cloud of dust and litter rose and, when the lull in the wind came, fell back to the ground like a veil. The sun went in and out behind the swift clouds. Comrade Bodi stretched out for a moment, then got up, dusted his trousers and went toward the shop. At the end of the alley he saw a man with his back turned toward him, carrying a bulky package under his arm. When the man saw Bodi, he began to run. Bodi continued slowly on his way.

The man turned back. "All right, Bodi!" he said. "You bastard, tell them."

Bodi walked on.

"You saw me, you bastard," the man shouted. "Tell them. Do you think it matters? I'm not afraid to die."

"I won't denounce you," said Bodi.

"You're lying, you louse. I know your kind. I won't run away from you. Come on. Go to the police. Here's the proof for the bastards."

"Get the hell out of here," said Bodi.

The next day Comrade Bodi did not go to the factory. He spent the whole day at home. He fixed the leaky kitchen faucet; he fixed the washer and packed it with caulking; then he went to see about some plumbing fixtures. He knew the owner of a neighborhood workshop. He worked until late in the afternoon. Then he fixed the kitchen table and polished the stove.

The next day he bought two cans of white paint and painted all the kitchen furniture. He put two coats on the garbage can because the first was rough. He stayed home a week, until the end of the month.

Arriving early, he left Karoly Brock Street, which led to the main gate of the factory, turned into the first side street, and a few minutes later came out onto the bank of the Danube. He still had half an hour before him until the night shift.

The spring sunshine was warm and clear. The light was like crystal over the wide river. On the far bank—Pest—the long row of dust-colored warehouses was framed by sky, shimmering in the crystal air. Behind them smokestacks rose black, as far as the horizon, in a sky empty of birds. The Danube flowed silently. No ripple disturbed its surface. If it had not been for the sharp stench of ammonia from the factories and the piles of garbage scattered on the sand, he would have stretched out on the ground at the water's edge.

The red brick wall glowed in the sun. In an angle of the wall, well beyond the stockroom, Bodi saw a piece of leather. He walked on his way. A pleasant breeze blew in from the river. Every now and then it drove away the stink from across the brick wall.

"Hello," said the foreman. "Are you better?"

"All right."

"Flu?"

"That's it."

The foreman rummaged around in his desk. "Me too—every year around this time."

The foreman stood up, pushed his steel-rimmed glasses down onto his nose, and went toward the door. He gave Bodi a pat on the back.

"Don't worry, Bodi," he said. "All right?"

"Of course," said Bodi.

"And the wife?"

"Not too bad."

"That's good," said the foreman. He left the cubicle.

A young girl came into the dimly lit place with a little dance step, laughing. She had a face as fresh as the peonies she had been picking that very morning in her garden at Budafok before setting off for the factory.

Comrade Bodi stared vacantly at her for a moment, then, without knowing, sighed and sat down again behind his desk.

In the evening, his wife set the table in front of the open window. The window looked out onto the island where the shipyards lay.

"Do you like it?" she asked.

Comrade Bodi liked noodles and cabbage. "Good."

The woman poured out a glass of water for him and cut a piece of bread.

"A headache?"

"No."

"No pain during the day, either?"

Bodi thought for a moment. "No. None."

"It makes me laugh," said the woman a little later. "You always have to have a piece of bread with your noodles and cabbage. For eighteen years. You eat bread with everything—soup, vegetables, noodles, even cake."

The man looked at his wife's face, waiting to see what she would say next.

"You told me eighteen years ago, when I gave you your first meal. 'Listen,' you said, 'I'm an eater of bread. I even eat it with noodles. Bread always on the table, always a piece beside my plate.'"

Comrade Bodi continued to look at his wife.

"For eighteen years now I've been cutting bread for you."

Bodi nodded his head. "That's true."

"Of course, it's true," said the woman, laughing. "Eighteen years now. But you don't eat what I cut."

Comrade Bodi looked at the piece of bread lying untouched beside his plate. At his side his wife was laughing so much that her thin, faded face was suddenly filled with a youth that effaced its lines.

"For years now. You sit down to the table, you look to see if there's bread by your plate, then you go after the noodles with a spoon. The bread, that stays where it is."

"It's true."

The woman laughed again. "You're getting old, Bodi."

"I must be," admitted the man.

"You're no longer an eater of bread."

The woman looked out of the window at the Danube, which shone with a dark brilliance.

"You didn't have a headache yesterday, either. Did you? You didn't lie on the couch, and you didn't ask me for medicine."

"Didn't I?"

"No. It must be at least four or five days since you asked for medicine. Unless you bought some yourself."

Staring in front of him, he shook his head. "No, I didn't buy any," he said. "Four or five days?"

"Thank God!" said the woman with a sigh. "Thank God. May the Lord be praised! Perhaps you won't need any tomorrow, either."

"Maybe," said Bodi.

He grew suddenly gloomy, stood up and went to the window.

"Maybe," he repeated, morosely, as if to himself.

Translated by Kathleen Szasz

L O V E

THE CELL door opened and the guard tossed something in.

"Grab it," he said.

A sack with a number painted on it fell to the floor in front of the prisoner. B. stood up, took a deep breath and stared at the guard.

"Your stuff," said the guard. "Put it on. They're going to shave you."

In the sack were the clothes and shoes he had taken off seven years ago. The clothes were creased and limp, and the shoes moldy. He smoothed out the shirt, which was also moldy. When he had dressed, the prison barber came in and shaved him.

An hour later they took him to the small office of the prison. Some eight or ten prisoners were standing around in the corridor all wearing their own clothes, but they called him in first—almost as soon as he reached the office door.

A sergeant sat at the desk, another stood beside him, and a captain paced slowly up and down the small room.

"Come 'ere," said the sergeant at the desk. "Name?" . . . "Mother's name?" . . . . . . "Destination?". . . . .

"I don't know," said B.

"What d'yer mean?" asked the sergeant. "Don't yer know your destination?"

"No," said B. "I don't know where they'll take me."

The sergeant made a wry face. "They ain't takin' yer no-where," he said. "You can go home to the old lady for dinner, and tonight you can have a piece in bed. Get it?"

The prisoner did not answer.

"Destination?"

"No. 17, Szilfa Street."

"Which district in Budapest?"

"Second," said B. "Why are they letting me out?"

"D'yer understand?" growled the sergeant. "They're letting yer out. Period! Aren't yer glad to get out of this place?"

His personal possessions were brought in from the next room: a cheap wristwatch, a fountain pen, and a worn greenish-black wallet that had been his father's. The wallet was empty.

"Sign here," said the sergeant.

It was a receipt for the wristwatch, the pen, and the wallet.

"This one, too."

This was another receipt for a hundred and forty-six forints in wages. They counted the money for him on the table.

"Put it away," said the sergeant.

B. took out his wallet and stuffed in the paper money and the change. A musty smell clung to the wallet as well. The last thing he was handed was his letter of discharge. The dotted line marked "reason for arrest" was left blank.

He stood around in the corridor for about an hour. Then they escorted him, together with three other prisoners, to the main gate. Just before they reached the gate a sergeant came running out and stopped them. He picked out one of the four and marched him back to prison, between two guards with Tommy guns. The man's newly shaven face turned a sudden yellow. His eyes became glassy.

The three went on to the gate.

"There's the tram, get going," said the guard to B. when he had searched him and returned his letter of discharge.

B. stood there, staring at the ground.

"What are you waiting for?" asked the guard.

B. was still standing, surveying the ground at his feet.

"Get the hell out," said the guard. "What are you hanging around for?"

"I'm going," said B. "You mean I can go?"

The sentry did not answer. B. pocketed his letter of discharge and walked through the gate. After a few steps, he wanted to look back, but he checked himself and went on. He listened, but there were no steps behind him. If I make it to the tram, he thought, and no one grabs my shoulder or calls out my name from behind, then, presumably, I'm a free man. Or am I?

When he reached the tram stop, he turned suddenly: nobody was following him. He poked around in his pocket for a handkerchief to wipe the sweat off his forehead, but couldn't find one. He boarded the tram that came screeching along. A prison guard with a pockmarked face was getting off the second car and, in passing B. on the first car, his small piggy eyes looked him up and down. B. did not salute. The tram started.

At that moment—from that split second onward, when he did not salute the guard and the tram started—just then, the world broke into sound. Much as in the cinema, when something had gone wrong with the projector and the film had been running silent for a time and, suddenly, right in the middle of a sentence or a word, the sound blasts out of the gaping mouth of the actor. Then the theater, a deaf-mute space, in which the very public seemed deprived of its third dimension, on an instant impulse is rocked to the rafters with vibrant song, music and dialogue. All about him the colors started exploding. The tram coming from the opposite direction was yellower than any yellow B. had ever seen, and it raced by at such speed past a low, shimmering gray house, that B. thought it would never get under control again. Across the street, two horses, red as poppies, galloped in front of an empty cart. The enchantment of its rattle made the fairy clouds dance in a mackerel sky. A tiny garden, bottle-green, with two sparking glass globes and an open kitchen window undulated past. Millions of people milled about the pavements, all in civilian clothes, no two of them alike and each one lovelier than the other. Many were amazingly small, only knee-high, and some had to be carried. And the women!

Since B. felt that his eyes were swimming, he went inside the tram. The woman conductor's voice was sonorous and very tender. B. bought a ticket and sat down on the first seat at the end of the car. He shut off his senses. If they remained open, he would lose all control. At one moment he saw out of his window on the pavement opposite by the brewery gate, a man caressing the cheek of a young woman. He felt again in his trouser pocket for a handkerchief, but there just wasn't one to wipe the fresh beads of sweat from his forehead. A worker sat down on the empty seat across from B., with a half-dozen bottles of beer in his open briefcase.

The conductor laughed.

"Won't it be a bit too much?"

"I'm a married man, sister," said the worker. "My wife likes to watch her old man have a few."

The conductor laughed.

"Just watch?"

"Sure."

"Is it dark beer?"

"Right."

"But light beer is nicer."

"But my wife likes dark to look at."

Again the conductor laughed.

"Why don't you leave me a bottle?"

"Dark?"

"All right, dark."

"What for?"

"I'd take it home for my husband."

"What good is dark to him if he likes 'em fair?"

The conductor laughed. They came to a stop. B. got off and hailed a taxi. The taxi driver clanked down the tin flag.

"Where to, please?" he said after a while, since his fare said nothing.

"To Buda," said B.

The taxi driver turned and eyed his passenger.

"By which bridge?"

B. looked straight ahead. Which bridge, indeed.

"You a stranger here?" asked the taxi driver.

"By the Margit Bridge," said B.

The cab started. B. sat erect, not leaning back. The sunlit street's smell of dust and petrol, the clanging bells of the street-cars rushed through the open cab windows. The sun blazed down freely on both pavements and the shadows of the pedestrians, streaking by their feet, seemed to double the volume of traffic. The awnings of a sweet shop had orange stripes that shed russet light on a young woman who sat smoking. Further on at the corner, a small chestnut tree was budding, gathering underneath it a minute patch of lacy, exhilarating shade.

"If you could stop for some cigarettes somewhere . . ." said B. to the taxi driver.

They stopped at the third door. B. looked out of the window: they were directly opposite the open door of a small shop with bundles of red radishes, mounds of green lettuce and red apples in a heap. Beside the shop was the narrow doorway of a tobacconist's.

"I'll get 'em for you," the cab driver said, turning around. "What brand?"

B. was looking at the radishes. His hands trembled.

"Would it be Kossuths?"

"Yes," said B. "And a box of matches."

The taxi driver got out. "Don't bother," he said, "we'll put it on the fare. One pack?"

"Yes, please," said B.

The driver returned. "Won't you have one now? My brother-in-law was also in for two years. First thing he did was pick up some cigarettes. Smoked two Kossuths, one after the other, before he went home."

"Can you tell?" asked B. after a while.

"Well, maybe a little," said the driver. "My brother-in-law also had such a sick-lookin' color. Of course, you might come from the hospital, but they don't crease your clothes like that. How long y'been in?"

"Seven years," said B.

The driver whistled. "Political?"

"Yes," said B. "A year and a half in the condemned cell."

"And now they let y'out?"

"Looks like it," said B. "Does it show a lot?"

The driver shrugged up both shoulders and let them fall again. "Seven years!" he repeated. "No wonder."

B. got out of the taxi at the funicular railway station, and walked the rest of the way. He wanted to get used to moving about easily, before he met his wife. The taxi driver refused to accept a tip.

"You'll need your money, comrade," he said. "Don't spend it on anything except your health! Get yourself some meat every day, and half a bottle of good wine. That'll put you on your feet in no time."

"Good-bye," said B.

Sideways across the street he saw a narrow mirror in the window of a clothes shop. He stood in front of it for a while, then he continued on his way. Since the Pasarét Road was full of people, he took a footpath up the hillside, past a tennis court, to Hermann Otto Road. But there was too much open space all around him here, with empty lots facing the range of hills opposite. He grew dizzy and sat down on the grass. His wife wasn't expecting him, anyway, he thought, so he had time to sit on the grass for half an hour. Facing him was a fence, and behind it stood an apple tree in full bloom. B. looked at it for a while, then went over to the fence. The waxy, shining white flowers were so thick on the boughs that looking up from below into the snow-white dome, one could hardly see the stark blue plane of the vibrant sky. Each flower held at the center of its large round petals a tinge of pink—a tender touch of color for its bridal splendor. So many bees buzzed in and out of the petals that the tree seemed to have a veil over it blowing in the wind. B. stood listening to the tree. He found two boughs through which he could look into the sky, while far away a downy cloud looked like yet another apple tree in bloom. He gazed at the two, through the attainable to the unattainable, till he blacked out.

He had forgotten to wind his wristwatch and didn't know how much time had passed since he had left the taxi, so he turned and started for home. After a few steps, he went behind a bush and vomited; he felt relieved. After another half-hour's walk through narrow, sunlit lanes that crisscrossed a hillside of fruit trees in bloom, he arrived at the house. They lived on the first floor. In the garden, to the right and left of the front door, stood two white lilac bushes. He went up the front stairs.

No one answered the bell. There was no nameplate on the door. He went downstairs to the caretaker's flat and knocked at the door.

"Good morning," he said to the woman who opened the door. She, too, looked thinner and had aged.

"Are you looking for anyone?"

"I am B.," said B. "Is my wife still living here?"

"My God!" said the woman.

B. looked upon the floor. "Is my wife still living here?"

"My God!" said the woman again. "So you've come home?"

"Yes, home," said B. "Is my wife still living here?"

The woman let go of the knob and leaned over against the doorpost. "You've come home," she repeated. "My God! Of

course she's living here. And didn't she know that you were
coming home, either? My God! Yes of course she lives here."

"My son, too?" asked B.

The woman responded. "He's fine," she said. "He's in fine
shape, strong and healthy. Good God!"

B. said nothing.

"But come right in," said the woman, her voice shaky.
"Come right in! I knew you were innocent. I knew you'd come
home some day."

"But they didn't open the door," said B. "I rang three times."

"Do come in," said the woman again. "There's no one
home. The other people are also away."

B. said nothing. He looked upon the floor.

"Your wife is at work, and Gyurika is at school," said the
woman. "Won't you come in? They'll be home in the afternoon."

"Are there others in the flat?" asked B.

"Very decent people," said the woman. "Your wife gets
along very well with them. Good God, so you did come home!"

B. said nothing.

"I've got the keys to the flat," said the woman after a while.
"Perhaps you'd like to go upstairs and rest a little before your
wife gets home."

On the wall two keys were hanging on a nail. The woman
took one and shut the door behind her.

"Perhaps you'd like to go upstairs and rest," she said.

B. glanced down at his feet. "Are you coming, too?" he asked.

"Of course," said the woman, "I'll show you which room
your wife lives in."

"In which room does she live?" asked B.

"Well, you know, the other people are four altogether," said
the woman. "They have the two rooms. Your wife moved into
the maid's room with Gyurika. But they share the kitchen and
bathroom."

B. did not answer.

"Shall we go on up," asked the woman, "or would you rather wait here with us, till they come home? Just come in and stretch out on the sofa till they come home."

"They share the kitchen and bathroom?" asked B.

"Yes, that's right, they share them," said the woman.

B. raised his head and looked right at the woman. "Then I'm allowed to have a bath?"

"Naturally," said the woman, smiling and putting her hand on B.'s elbow convincingly. "Of course you can have a bath, why shouldn't you? It's your flat, isn't it, and as I said, the kitchen and bathroom are shared. I'd be glad to make up a fire for you to warm the water, since we have a little of the wood left over from the winter in the cellar, but for all I know the others keep the bathroom locked in the daytime."

B. said nothing. He glanced down again.

"Shall we go upstairs, then, or would you rather stop in at our place?" asked the woman. "Do come to our place, I'll be in the kitchen and won't disturb you at all. You can lie down on the sofa and maybe even have a nap."

"Thanks," said B., "but I'd rather go upstairs."

THE MAID'S room was tiny and faced north, as maids' rooms usually do. The window looked out on an ornamental tree and to the left you could see a dark hilltop covered with pines. The foliage in front of the window made the room seem dark green. As soon as he was alone and his breathing had quieted down, he recognized the fragrance of his wife. He sat down near the window and took a deep breath. In the tiny room there were, all told, a worn white cupboard, an iron bedstead, a table, and a chair; to get to the bed you had to push the chair out of the way. He did not lie down on the bed. He just sat and breathed. The table was piled with many things—books, clothing, toys. There was also a small hand mirror. He looked into it; it showed what the one in the shop window had shown. He put it back on the table, facedown. He didn't disturb his wife's things on the table. A child's rubber ball with red dots rested on the ashtray. His wife's fragrance lingered over the table, too.

He had hardly sat down when the caretaker's wife came in with a large jug of milky coffee and two thick slices of white bread. He ate it as soon as he was alone. Soon afterward, the ground floor tenant's wife rang the bell. She also brought coffee, bread and butter, sausage and a red apple like the ones he had seen in the small shop in the street. She put the tray on the table. His eyes were moist and she left after a few minutes. When B. was alone, he ate it. He still hadn't wound his wristwatch and didn't know how long he'd been sitting near the window. The window looked out on the back garden where there was no one. The tree had leaves with white borders that rustled lightly in the wind, and the afternoon light glowed on the whitewashed walls of the tiny room.

When he had breathed in so much of his wife's fragrance that he didn't notice it anymore, he went down into the street near the garden gate. Soon afterward his wife turned the corner with four or five little boys around her. She came toward the gate, her steps suddenly slackening. She even stopped short for a second, then ran toward him. B. also started running without knowing it. As they neared each other, the woman slowed, as if uncertain, but soon ran forward. B. recognized the long-sleeved gray woolen pullover she was wearing, which he had bought for her in a shop downtown just before his arrest. His wife was a wonderful blend of air and flesh, unseen and unheard of before, unique. She surpassed everything he had treasured about her for seven years in prison.

When they separated from each other's arms, B. leaned against the fence. A few paces behind his wife stood four or five little boys, with curious, if somewhat perturbed, faces. They were about six or seven years old. There weren't five, but really only four. Leaning against the fence, B. looked at them, one by one.

"Which one is mine?" he asked. At this point she began to cry.

"Let's go upstairs," she said, crying.

B. put his arms round her shoulders. "Don't cry."

"Let's go upstairs," she said, sobbing openly.

"Don't cry," said B. "Which one is mine?"

The woman swung open the garden gate and went running between the two lilac bushes to the house. She disappeared in the entrance. She was still as slim as when they had parted and she ran with the same long, elastic strides as once, when she was a girl, she had run away from a cow with uncontrolled fear in her legs. But when B. reached her upstairs in front of the door to the flat, she had calmed down; only her girlish breasts heaved under her gray sweater. She was no longer crying, but her eyelids were still moist beneath the tears she had wiped away.

"My dearest," she whispered, "my dearest."

When she whispered, each word could almost be taken in one's mouth as it hung in the air.

"Let's go in," said B.

"There are other people living in the flat, too, now."

"I know," said B. "Let's go in."

"Have you been inside yet?"

"I have," said B. "Which is my son?"

Once inside, the woman knelt on the floor and put her head in his lap and cried. White threads glistened in her light brown hair with an alien luster. "My darling, I waited for you. My darling."

B. stroked her head. "Was it hard?"

"My darling," whispered the woman.

B. kept stroking her hair. "Did I grow very old?"

The woman clasped his knees and drew him close. "You are the same as when you left, for me."

"Did I grow very old?" asked B.

"I'll love you always, as long as I live," whispered the woman.

"Do you love me?" asked B.

The woman's back trembled. She wept openly. B. took his hand from her head. "Can you get used to me?" he asked. "Will you ever get used to me again?"

"I've never loved anyone else," she said. "I love you."

"Did you wait for me?"

"I was with you every day," said the woman. "There wasn't a day that I didn't think of you. I knew you would come back. But if you hadn't, I would have died alone. Your son was you all over again."

"Do you love me?" asked B.

"I've never loved anyone else," she said "I'd love you, no matter how you've changed."

"I've changed," said B. "I've grown old."

The woman wept, she pressed B.'s foot close to her. B. stroked her hair again.

"Can we still have a child?" she asked.

"Perhaps," said the man, "if you love me. Please get up."

The woman got up.

"Shall I call him?"

"Not yet," said B. "Let me stay a while longer with you. He's still a stranger. Did he stay in the garden?"

"I'll go downstairs to him," said the woman. "I'll tell him to wait."

When she returned, B. was standing at the window, with his back to the room. His back was narrow and awry. He did not turn. The woman stood in the doorway for a moment. "I told him to pick some flowers for his father," she said, a little hoarse with emotion. "The lilacs are in bloom over on the next allotment, and he should pick a big bunch for his father."

"Do you love me?" asked B.

The woman ran up to him, clasped his shoulders and nestled in close. "My only one," she said.

"Can you get used to me?" asked B.

"I've never loved anyone else," said the woman. "I was with you night and day. Every day I talked to your son about you."

B. turned around, he embraced the woman and looked closely at her face. In the rays of sunset that fell through the window, he saw with some relief that she, too, had aged, though she was more beautiful than the image he had recalled every day for seven years. Her eyes were closed, her mouth partly open and her hot breath touched B.'s cheeks. Thick eyelashes covered the pale skin under her moist eyes. She was meekness itself. B. kissed her eyes, then tenderly moved her away from himself.

"Love our boy, too," she said, with her eyes still closed.

"Yes," said B. "I'll get to know him and love him."

"He's your son!"

"And yours," said B.

The woman clung to his neck. "I'll wash you," she said.

"Good."

He stripped. She made the bed, laying her husband's naked body on the sheet. She brought warm water in a tin pan, soap and two towels. She folded one, dipped it in the water and put soap on it. She washed the whole body down to his feet. Twice she changed the water. B.'s hand still twitched now and then, but his face was at peace.

"Can you get used to me?" he asked.

"My darling," said the woman.

"Will you sleep with me tonight?"

"Yes," she said.

"Where does the boy sleep?"

"I'll make a bed for him on the floor," said the woman. "He sleeps soundly."

"Will you stay with me all night?"

"Yes," said the woman, "every night as long as we live."

Translated by Ilona Duczynska

Two Women

I

IN THE morning, before she pressed the bell of her mother-in-law's small cottage, Lucy stopped when she reached the front door, took the small round mirror out of her handbag, and checked whether her tears had smeared her black mascara. The mirror glinted in the sun, casting a dazzling beam of light that flashed back from her shining red hair. She scrutinized her face with narrowed eyes, with the passionate objectivity of a tracker dog; to be on the safe side, she put on some powder, and retraced the line of her lips with two swift light strokes; she would have resented even Irene, the old housekeeper, seeing her with a tearstained face. From the open kitchen window wafted a smell of buttered toast, and this made her feel a little better. Still standing in front of the door, she "concentrated" for a few seconds more, then, with her customary gesture, scornfully shrugged her shoulders. Up till now—meaning the best part of a year—she had always managed to scrape through the mornings somehow.

To the left, next to the three stone steps of the entrance, the spirea already stood in bloom, spilling its sparkling white flowers like a cascading waterfall onto the narrow strip of lawn. Beyond the fence, four women stood gossiping in the highroad, and about a hundred yards further on, four geese stood motionless in the dust.

"The old lady got out of bed with her left foot today," said Irene.

Lucy planted a kiss on the red, round face of the old house-keeper. "Did she get up?" she exclaimed, laughing. "Has Christ come down and performed a miracle?"

The apple-cheeked housekeeper burst out laughing. The old lady, Lucy's ninety-six-year-old mother-in-law, had been laid low seven years ago with a kind of neuralgia; since then she got out of bed less and less frequently, and never before six in the afternoon, when—in a ratio directly corresponding to her waning strength—she walked the length of the room, at first fifty times, then, slowly decreasing the daily quota, only about ten to fifteen times. She reduced it to ten in the last year, but had not fallen below that figure yet.

"She's been fuming ever since last night about not getting a new cover for her bedpan. Have you brought any savory biscuits?"

"Tons," said the young woman. "I've brought you some money for the housekeeping, too, Irene."

"Tons?"

Lucy laughed again; her laughter was irresistible, you couldn't help laughing with her. "Hell," she said. "I've brought you five hundred for the moment. Will that do?"

"That's more than we want this month," said the house-keeper.

The young woman opened her white, sack-like hand-bag, and started rummaging in it. It was not tidy; the few folded banknotes she had received this morning at the Commission Store for her old, blue, fox stole lay crumpled at the very bottom, beneath the savory biscuits, the little tray-clothwrapped in tissue paper, under her lipstick, her purse and her mirror.

"One-two-three-four-five . . ." she counted, and her finely cut, mobile face, whose expressive features never quite came to rest, looked for a moment deeply serious while she counted the money. "Never mind, we'll settle it if there's any left. You don't have to stint yourself, old thing," she said, and was already laughing again. "Any other trouble?"

"None. Got any cash left for yourself?"

"To stuff pigs with," the young woman asserted. Into the clean, white kitchen where the gleaming whiteness was doubly increased by the glaring sunlight, the acacia, standing in front of the window, sent a bouquet of chokingly sweet fragrance that for a moment suppressed the aroma of hot buttered toast.

"Has the postman been?" the young woman asked.

"Not yet."

"Keep an eye on the mailbox, Irene dear; there will be a letter from America today," said Lucy. "I'd like her to read it while I'm here."

"Oh, she's ringing again," the housekeeper said. There were three or four short, impatient buzzes. "If she's rung for me once since breakfast, she's rung ten times. Her hand work as if it had an itch in it."

"Leave it, dear, I'll go," said Lucy.

STANDING IN the doorway—the opening creak of which did not register with the slightly deaf old lady—Lucy contemplated the thin, pallid face that was framed by a black velvet bonnet tied with a ribbon under the chin. The head had sunk into the huge white pillows, the large, straight, waxen nose protruding from the bony structure of the face, beneath the closed eyelids, seemed to foreshadow the death mask. Not a muscle moved under the light yellow eiderdown, not even the rising and falling of the chest was visible. The young woman had to "concentrate" hard again; her eyes were beginning to fill with tears. Fragile and athletic, she stood on the threshold, her head thrown back on the lovely, long stem of her neck as if the weight of her glorious russet hair were pulling it down toward the ground; her nostrils quivered, her small round belly tensed with excitement. "*Silly goose!*" she said to herself furiously in an effort to gain some strength once again. The sun shone from behind the enormous bed, on the narrow, white face lost between the billowing pillows, that was saved from extinction solely by the black velvet bonnet. The young woman pulled a wry face and impatiently stamped her foot.

The woman lying on the bed opened her eyes and looked toward the door.

"Good morning, Mother," Lucy called, her voice ringing light and gay once more.

"I rang so often, Irene," the old woman complained huskily, and knitting her brows, she looked toward the door again. "Is the buttered toast not ready yet?"

"It's me, Mother," Lucy called. "It will be ready in a minute."

The old woman cast another suspicious glance toward the door. "Who is?" she asked.

ALTHOUGH SHE had lived in Hungary for more than seventy years, the Austrian accent of her hometown, Vienna, had not worn off. She spoke Hungarian fluently, with a Germanic turn of phrase. A Hungarian word, misheard and stubbornly retained when she first arrived, occasionally slipped into her vocabulary and each time this irked her daughter-in-law to uncontrollable laughter. She still read German in preference to Hungarian, and in these last years that she had spent in bed, she had returned to the adored ideals of her youth; she read Goethe, Schiller, and sometimes—with slight boredom—a volume of Thomas Mann, and out of consideration to the country that offered her hospitality, the essays of Gyorgy Lukács on Goethe; these she annotated in her large, masculine Gothic handwriting with innumerable marginal notes and exclamation marks. Her own remarks—mainly quotations from the books read, interspersed with household accounts—she penned in a hardbacked ruled copybook. The books—eight or ten volumes of them—the copybook, one packet of sweet and one packet of savory biscuits, as well as a box of chocolates of which she consumed one chocolate per day, were ranged in precise and predetermined order at the edge of the large bed so that they were easily at hand, and so that it should not be necessary for her to ring for Irene if she wanted any of them. The wireless stood at the foot of the bed, tuned in to the Kossuth station, so that with the aid of a switch fixed to a long flex, put up for her by her son, she could operate it herself, and only had to call for the house-keeper when—according to the scheduled program—the Petöfi station supplied the preferred composition, and the dial had to be switched back. But for the last few months this had happened less and less frequently; the old lady lay prone in her bed for the best part of the day with closed eyes, and it was impossible to tell whether she was dozing, turning over the memories of her youth in her still-agile brain, or speculating on her all-too-brief future. She only came to life when Irene offered her some forbidden paprika potatoes from her own lunch, or when her daughter-in-law called in the morning.

"You—is it?" she said, grumbling, slightly lifting her head from the topmost lilac silk pillow. "Haf you bring me the little salt cakes?"

"Of course I have," laughed Lucy, and opening her sack-like handbag, she cautiously lifted out the little tissue-clad par-cel. "And what else have I brought for you, Mother?"

"For surely, flowers," the old woman said discontentedly; her features, however, smoothed out instantly and her eyes, her still lovely dark eyes, lit up with delight when they fell on the small bunch of gold pansies. "You will never learn to economize?"

Lucy stepped right in front of the bed, rolled her eyes up so that only the whites showed, and extending her forefinger, began to admonish the old woman with it. She kept it up until the latter started laughing.

"All right," she said. "I say the same thing every day because you makes every day the same thing. You not to bring me flow-ers every day. You to buy me tomorrow eau de cologne."

"And what else have I brought for Mother?" Lucy asked, diving into her handbag again. She poked around in it for a long while, watching the old woman intensely in the meantime.

On the old face sudden senility appeared, the moronic reflection of credulous, open-mouthed infantile curiosity. Out of the dark cavity of the mouth glinted her one remaining tooth.

"Well, give it here," she said, losing her patience after a while. "Or have you got it lost?"

When she saw the little embroidered tray-cloth Lucy took out of the tissue paper she flushed with pleasure. She was demanding, but at the same time childishly grateful for the smallest service. "Is good," she said, "you now to bend down and to kiss me." She slightly lifted her head, and pursing her bloodless lips, clasped one of her bony hands on the full white neck of the young woman, drew her down and kissed her forehead noisily. "It's beautiful," she said. "But where from you take so much money?"

"I earn it, Mother," Lucy said cheerfully. "You know what a prodigious whore I am."

The old woman looked at her with round, uncomprehending eyes for a while, then suddenly started giggling, and lifted a threatening finger.

"Whore?" she said. "Ach, go away. I shall tell you to Janos when he comes home, and you will get two such big boxes on the ear." She turned her black-bonneted head toward the bedside table and looked at the bedpan standing on the lower shelf. "You to cover it up," she said. "It is lovely. It is high time, too, because in the afternoon comes Professor Hetenyi, and Irene will get excited and maybe will forget to put it away like the last time, and then here we are."

"The Professor's seen worse than that before," said Irene, appearing suddenly in the open doorway. "And anyway, what makes you think he'll come this afternoon?"

Wrinkling her forehead, the old lady looked toward the door. "She always eavesdrops," she whispered reproachfully to her daughter-in-law, but as her deaf ear could no longer censure the volume of her voice, her subdued hiss sounded as if she had bawled the old housekeeper out.

"Of course she wasn't eavesdropping," said Lucy quickly. "She's brought you the buttered toast."

"That I should be eavesdropping . . ."

Lucy winked at the old housekeeper like a conspirator.

"That I'm eavesdropping . . ."

Through the open window came a loud cackling of geese.

"That *I'm* eavesdropping . . ."

Lucy burst out laughing. "Don't have a stroke, Irene dear. If you go on like this I'm sure you will. Come on, let's have that toast."

"That is why the Professor comes today afternoon," said the old lady from the bed, angrily, toward the door, "because he was not here already for very long, for at least a month, and he has promised that he will come once every month. . . ."

"He is coming this afternoon," said Lucy, teasing, "because Mother is in love with him, and is expecting him every afternoon; so that she can chat with him about Goethe—and she doesn't want the Professor to look at her bedpan while they're talking, why, that's only natural, Irene dear, isn't it?"

"What do you say?" asked the old woman, blushing. "What do you say?" When it suited her, the old lady could go stone deaf in a second. "Why must you always so whisper so that one cannot hear one's own voice?" Lucy laughed outright, and the geese in front of the house started cackling again. "What do you say?"

The reason Professor Hetenyi had not been to the little cottage for so long was that he had died four months ago, but this was a secret closely guarded from the old woman, who was not able to keep count of the passage of earthly time any longer.

"It's no use denying it, Mother," said Lucy, "that you are in love with the Professor. Otherwise, for whom else would you learn all those quotations from Goethe by heart?"

The old woman had in the meantime fitted her dentures into her mouth, and was now crunching the toast. "*Dumme Gans,*" she said, "for whom . . . ? for whom . . . ? for myself. I'm eating the toast for myself, too."

Lucy sat down in the little armchair next to the bed that was upholstered in yellow silk. She crossed her legs. "Tell me, Mother," she said, "is the Professor really so witty when he speaks German?"

The old lady didn't reply, but continued to munch her toast disdainfully.

"Well, he might be witty when he is talking German," went on Lucy. "Actually, he's quite sweet even when he chatters away in Hungarian. If only he weren't so ugly."

The old lady still did not notice that she was having her leg pulled. "Not everybody can be as beautiful as you," she said, and a slight flush spread over her forehead.

"Am I beautiful?" Lucy asked.

The old woman stopped pushing the food around in her mouth, and her old eyes, seasoned with the experience of nine decades, fastened attentively on her daughter-in-law's face, every sensual particle of which was bathed at this moment in the sunlight and scent of acacias streaming in from the window.

"If only were you so clever," she said querulously after a time.

"As clever as whom?"

The old lady started rotating her food again and did not answer.

"As clever as the Professor?"

"*Dumme Gans,*" said the old woman.

The young woman laughed cheerfully. "Oh, I nearly forgot, the Professor rang yesterday," she said. "He only came up for the day from Szeged so he couldn't come to see Mother, but he sends his respects. He says Mother will live for a hundred years, so not to worry, there will be many more times when they can see one another."

The old lady went on eating, but cast a suspicious glance at Lucy from the corner of her eye. "He told me, too, that I will live one hundred years," she muttered after a while. "Did he now say the same on the telephone to you?

Resting her head on the sun-drenched back of the armchair, the young woman closed her eyes.

"You not now making a fool of me?" the old woman inquired.

Smiling with closed eyes, Lucy nodded.

"How? . . . What? You now a tricking me?" the old woman asked incredulously.

"Of course," said Lucy.

THE OLD lady looked at her with large naïve eyes. Now she really did not know what to make of the professor's prediction. But whenever Lucy laughed, then—however put out she was—she ended up by laughing with her daughter-in-law, with quiet, perplexed chuckles at first, her bony, austere face assuming an expression of fatuous simplicity—then more and more relaxedly, with more honesty and with the good-humored realization that she was laughing at her own expense—the tiny sting in her left brain only stabbing her memory hours later and sometimes only the next day.

"You are now really fibbing me?" she asserted gaily.

Lucy jumped up, bent over the bed, and with her fresh young mouth planted kisses all over the hard old face trembling between the pillows.

"How can you think that I'm telling you a fib?" she exclaimed. "Haven't we worked it out a few days ago who is still going to be alive on Mother's hundredth birthday, and whom we can invite, and even what dress I am going wear? We said my low cut, red silk one, don't you remember?"

"We haf not choose the white silk with the low cut?"

"Where is that by now?" sighed Lucy quietly.

"What haf you say?"

"Nothing, Mother."

"All right," said the old lady. "Then you give me soda water now. Has to you the professor really said on the telephone that I will live one hundred year?"

WHILE LUCY was rearranging the crumpled pillows in the bed, and the old lady cautiously groaned from time to time from the remembrance of the neuralgia of seven years ago, Irene came into the room again, and with a jealous glance at the quick skillful hands of the young woman, removed the little wooden tray with the empty glass and plate on it.

"Aren't all these books a nuisance for you, Mother?" asked Lucy, smoothing the eiderdown. "You can only read one at a time!"

"But I am reflecting on the others," the old woman said severely. "You not to touch those ones, either. Have you learn the German lesson?"

As she did not receive any reply for quite a while, she turned her narrow head toward the young woman, fixing her with a reproachful gaze. The gaze became a stare, losing its focus and purpose, and lasted for so long that it seemed to have lost all relation to subject and object alike, and was now glimmering on its own with aimless radiance, like an orb in the ether. Then, suddenly, it became affiliated with the earthly world again.

"What is Janos going to say," she said accusingly, "when he comes home and you not speak German yet?"

"Janos . . . Janos . . ." Lucy mumbled. "He'll be lucky if I haven't forgotten Hungarian by then."

The old woman looked at her again. "What do you say?"

"I'm tired of Janos," muttered Lucy, but of course the old woman caught that. "I'm tired of Janos," Lucy repeated slightly louder to make sure she would be heard. "How is it that whenever one mentions Janos you always hear it, however quietly one speaks, Mother? I'm sick of your son, Mother."

"You are now fibbing me again?" the old woman asked, her mouth slightly twisted by laughter.

"Of course," said Lucy.

The old lady didn't know what to say. But her eyes, resting on the face of her daughter-in-law, were so anguished and so guileless that Lucy could not bear it for long; she raised her head and smiled. Immediately and gratefully the old woman smiled back.

"Tell me, Mother," Lucy inquired, "how was it when you lived in Savanyukut?"

The old woman reflected, "Savanyukut . . ."

"Yes," said Lucy, "you know, when the whole family had to sleep in one room."

"And?"

"Oh, you know," said Lucy, "when you all had to sleep in one room and your other son was peeping."

"Poor Gyuri? You did not know him anymore."

"Yeah," said Lucy, "I mean Gyuri. When in the evening you had to get undressed, Mother, and told the children to turn toward the wall."

"Ach," said the old woman. "I haf told you about that before."

Lucy smiled at her again. "But I don't remember it very well. When was it?"

"Ach, very long ago," the old lady sighed. "Maybe it is fifty years."

"More than that," said Lucy. "How old are you now, Mother?"

"Ninety-six," said the old lady proudly.

"There you are!" Lucy exclaimed triumphantly, "and when you lived in Savanyukut, and could only get single room for the night, you were still quite a young woman, weren't you? That must have been at least sixty years ago."

"Sixty?" the old woman mused. "Then was I thirty-six?"

"Just about," said Lucy. "Now tell me, how was it with that spying?"

"Well, what happened . . ." the old lady started, then stopped abruptly, and shot an uncertain glance at her daughter-in-law. "But I haf told you that already."

"But if I don't remember it very well," complained Lucy. "I

only remember that it was evening and the children were already in bed, and that you wanted to undress. Mother, you must have been very beautiful as a young woman."

"Yes, I was very beautiful," said the old woman simply. "You know, at that time became fashionable those big hats that you had to tie down with those silk or velvet ribbons . . . how do you say . . . under your chinbone, and my husband, he gave me as a present such a very wide moiré ribbon, and when I tied that down under my chin every young man turned around after me in the street."

"I'm sure they did," said Lucy. "And not only the young ones, either. Professor Hetenyi would have turned around, too, if he had known Mother at that time."

The old lady smiled modestly. "Oh, go away," she said, suddenly sternly, "maybe the professor was not even alive then."

"Maybe," said Lucy. "Anyway, what happened then?"

"When?"

"Well, about the spying?"

The old woman ran her bony finger over her black bonnet. "Do you know," she said reminiscently, "that this bonnet has been made from that very wide ribbon that my husband gave me then?"

"But this is velvet, Mother!" Lucy laughed merrily. "And you received a silk moiré ribbon."

"Never mind," said the old woman, flushing. "Maybe that one was velvet. Well, what you want to know?"

"Well, Mother," Lucy said, "what I would like to know is how you undressed that time in Savanyukut."

"Everybody had to sleep in one room," the old woman began, and her voice sounded slightly muffled from crossing the crippling distance of sixty years in the dimension of time; even her eyes lost some of their luster. "What happened was that everybody had to sleep in one room and the children were already lying in their beds, and I wanted myself to undress. Do you know, all the ladies wore corsets in those days, long corsets from here to here, and that my man had to lace it up, and that I haf not wanted the children to see. Oh," she said impatiently, "I haf told you all this before."

"But if I don't remember it, Mother," Lucy said. "All I remember is that you told the children to turn toward the wall."

The old lady nodded distractedly. "I told them."

"And when you started to undress, you looked behind you to make sure that the children really had turned to the wall."

"Yes," said the old lady, "I stood there in my petticoat."

"Sorry, not in a petticoat," interrupted Lucy, with lips twitching with laughter, "but in pants, in long pants, down to your ankles with lace at the bottom."

The old lady laughed, too. "Yes, in pants."

"And when you turned to look, you saw that Janos was honorably turned toward the wall, but your younger son . . ."

The old lady burst into laughter again. "Yes, Gyuri was espionaging."

"Yes, he was espionaging," said Lucy. "He was lying on his tummy and he was ogling Mother with one eye."

"He had long golden hair," the old woman said softly, "lovely, long golden locks and he was espionaging from behind them into the room."

"And then?"

"What then?"

"Then what happened?"

The old lady did not reply.

"Oh, do go on, Mother," said Lucy, "because I don't remember all of it. You put a large towel over the side of the cot. . . ."

"Of course, I did put one over it," the old woman said vaguely.

Lucy giggled. "And then you saw from the mirror that Gyuri was lifting the corner of the towel and peeping from behind it."

"Yes, he was peeping," said the old lady, and in order to be able to laugh more comfortably, she took her dentures out of her mouth and placed them in the glass of water standing on her bedside table. "He was peeping out and grinning off his head."

"While Janos . . ."

The old woman suddenly glowed with the memory. "While Janos?" she said quietly, "he just lay there, turned toward the wall and did not move."

"He was very scrupulous even as a little boy, wasn't he, Mother?" asked Lucy, watching the old woman closely.

"Yes," said the latter, very slowly and decisively. "He is a very honorable man."

She closed her eyes and there was silence in the sunlit room, broken eventually by the deep hooting of a horn that came from outside the window. The old lady opened her eyes again, and fixed them on Lucy. "*Dumme Gans,*" she said loudly and deliberately, "you belief that I do not see that you remember better than I? Yes, he was all that scrupulous even as a child—is that what you wanted to hear?"

"Like hell I did," Lucy said quietly, but the old lady did not hear it. She was watching a wasp that was circling above the little bunch of pansies that stood on the bedside table; craning her neck, she was watching it with her head turned sideways, then—forgetting her neuralgia—she propped herself up on her elbow, and, popping her spectacles on her nose, her mouth half opened with rapt attention.

"YOU LOVE Janos?" she asked hoarsely, after a while. Exhausted, she sank back on her pillow and took her glasses off.

"Like hell I do," said Lucy.

The old lady knitted her brows with disapproval. "All right, you not to fib me now," she said huskily, "because I now was speaking in earnest. If you love Janos you tell him when he comes back from America that he should not be so obstinate."

"Why, Mother?" Lucy asked with interest.

The old lady did not answer. She was staring into space, her mouth half opening again with inward excitement. "Never mind," she said. "You just tell him that."

"But why, Mother?" asked Lucy again.

Again the old woman made no reply. She lifted her head a little, tried to include in her vision the wasp droning above the pansies, observed it a little while, and then let her head fall back onto her lilac pillow.

"Once I was watching such a wasp," she said in a muffled voice, "that was buzzing, too, like this one above such yellow pansies, then sat down on one and because it was very heavy the pansy quickly turned her head and bent deep to the ground. You know, if it had not bent down then perhaps its . . . what you call it—stem would have broke."

"Is that what I am to tell Janos?" asked Lucy.

"Yes," said the old lady.

"It's too late," muttered Lucy.

"What do you say?"

"I haven't said anything."

"You don't have to," said the old lady. "You just tell him that."

"Why don't you say it to him, Mother?"

The old lady lifted a hand, and let it fall wearily. "It will be a very long time before he comes home again," she said, staring fixedly into space again.

Fortunately, Irene came into the room again; her pleasant round face shone as if clad in its Sunday best; even her white hair sparkled in the sunlight. The old lady spied the letter she was holding at once. She sat up, opened her mouth, but no words came.

"There is a letter for you," said Irene, winking at Lucy.

The old lady took a deep breath. "From Janos?"

"How should I know?" said Irene, coming up to the bed. "I haven't read it."

But this time the old lady was not to be taken in by the indifference of the tone; as if an earthquake had shaken and transformed her whole being within the space of a second, her eyes dilated, and the cavities of her long bony face filled out, color crept into her cheeks, and her breast was heaving under the light yellow eiderdown. The weight of the excitement brought her soul up to the surface, into the pupils of her eyes, her colorless nails, her scanty, electrified white hair. She extended both of her trembling hands; with one she grabbed the letter, with the other she clasped the old housekeeper's neck, pulled her head down and kissed her. She felt so faint that it was minutes before she could open the envelope, tear the letter out of it, and smooth out the typewritten pages. "Give here the magnifying glass, Irene," she said, panting.

She put her spectacles on, and holding the magnifying glass in her shaky hand, stopping from time to time as if she was out of breath, then, with a deep sigh, starting again, she read the four closely typed pages, which for the next week she was going to take out every day and read, from the first letter to the last, over and over again.

"THIS TIME I'll try to make up for my short letter, although I have even less time than before because . . . and this is the great news . . . I'm just putting the finishing touches to my film, in another month it will be ready and then I shall come home. This is the news I wanted to tell you first to compensate for the long wait you had. The first night of the film will be a month from today in a New York film theater that holds thirty thousand people. It is just being built on the outskirts of the city on top of a high mountain and has to be completed for the first night because they want to open it with my film. From the roof you can see half of America down to the Cordilleras and the Andes, not to speak of the Atlantic Ocean, which is just as blue here as the Adriatic at Abbazia, where we were together one summer. The theater is going to have an airport of its own because all the rich people from all over the States will be coming here, flying their own airplanes, and from the city,

meaning New York, there will be a special helicopter service
for the audience, costing one dollar per head. They are preparing great festivities for the first night, but I'll come back to that
later; first, I want to reassure you that in spite of all the work
I'm in the best of health and very happy about being able to return home soon, and although I work ten to twelve hours a day
I reserve one hour every day for sport because I don't want to
get fat. I box, fly a plane, walk and swim. Of course, you will
ask, where do I swim? In my own swimming pool in the park.
That's a story for itself.

"You know, Mother, that until recently, I stayed in the
largest hotel of the United States, the Waldorf Astoria; I had a
suite of twenty rooms on the hundredth floor from which again
you could see about half of America. But I had to keep so big a
staff, about six secretaries and a dozen typists and so on, that
there wasn't enough room for us all although in the end I had
beds put up even in the reception rooms, in bunks like the ones
you saw on your honeymoon! However, the reporters who kept
coming from all parts of the world pestered me so much that
we decided to move out and keep our address secret. So, about
a thousand miles from New York, we rented a XVI-century castle, every stone of which was imported from France separately,
and rebuilt here, of course with every modern comfort, in the
middle of a hundred-acre park that has several swimming pools
and an airport as well. The house is air-conditioned, and now
we have enough space because the castle has so many rooms
that even my black valet and my hairdresser have a suite of their
own, and my groom a small cottage next to the stable. Oh, I
forgot to tell you, Mother, that I go for an hour's ride every
morning before breakfast, I have a lovely white mare called
Darling, and I canter away on her, leaving even my secretaries
behind. At these times I'm followed only by the six secret police officers detailed for my safety by the film company, but
they ride a hundred paces behind me. If we should have anything to do in New York we can fly there in less than an hour in

our own red-white-green jet plane, and can get back before lunch, because, as you know, Mother, I insist on my afternoon siesta, so I can be fresh and rested for work in the evening. *My address is secret, so I can't tell even you, Mother, please give your letters to Lucy as before, and she will send them to my old address, the Waldorf.*

"All these distinctions I've been overwhelmed with are most embarrassing; I only write about them because I know they please you, Mother, and this will make up to a small degree for the distance that separates us. Still, this will come to an end soon, and I shall be home again. Unfortunately, I'm unable to send anything of real value to you, Mother, for the moment, as I shall only receive my salary after the film is finished, and anyway, you would have to pay too much duty at home. So, for the time being, you will have to content yourself with the bits and pieces I can send through Lucy. But I have already earmarked a large silver-gray luxury Ford for you; I shall bring it home myself, as well as a radiogram with a thousand records and a superb wireless on which you can even get the North Pole. Although they don't play Beethoven there!) For Irene, I'm going to buy a little five- or six-roomed villa somewhere in the neighborhood, but I'm not telling anyone what I have for Lucy. There is a large brown bear here in the garden, about twice as big as Irene; we are very fond of each other, so maybe they'll sell him to me—although I have no idea where we could keep him at home. He looks rather like that big bear we saw together in Vienna when you took me to the zoo in Schoenbrunn when I was ten. Do you remember? And the same evening we went to see Offenbach's *Helen of Troy*, and I laughed so loud during the performance out of sheer joy that the whole audience was looking at me—do you remember that, too?

"Oh, I still owe you the description of the festivities they are planning for the first night. Don't speak too much about them, because they are partly a diplomatic secret. I don't suppose I need to tell you that all the radio and television companies of the States are going to arrange for a live transmission so that at least fifty million people will see the film. They are expecting one or two hundred reporters, and the best-known radio commentators, among them the world-famous Mr. Smith, and, of course, the representatives of the European Press and radio companies are going to be present, too. Pity Budapest won't be able to receive the transmissions.

"They have invited a lot of celebrities in my honor. I'm saying that just to please you, Mother, not to boast. Mrs. Roosevelt, the widow of the late President, has undertaken the chairmanship of the festivities, and invited her friend, Queen Wilhelmina of the Netherlands, who has accepted the invitation. The President of the French Republic is also coming with his whole family, and representing the Queen of England will be her son, the Prince of Wales, whom you, Mother, will no doubt remember. He was in Budapest once and rather liked our apricot brandy. The foreign minister of the Soviet Union is coming and Hungary will be represented by the Minister of Culture; the German Chancellor and the King of Greece are coming—the only thing they are wondering about now is whether or not to invite Franco. The Maharaja of Jaipur has accepted, and is bringing his whole court with him, also his favorite white elephant, who of course cannot be dragged up to the mountain, so they will have to build him a separate stable at the foot of it, all of white marble and air-conditioned, and also some cottages for the elephant keepers. The elephant has a pure gold saddle studded with pearls and precious stones. . . ."

BY THE time the old lady finished the letter, reaction to her excitement had set in, and she fell asleep quite suddenly. It was possible to talk freely now for if she did not see lips moving, she did not register voices, even if they spoke next to her ear. She slept quietly, without a sound, her bony face transformed by the magic of happiness. While she was still on the whole in full possession of her senses, and occasionally—as far as her naïve disposition permitted—even capable of suspicion, she was quite prepared to believe the most fantastic things of her son; his talent, his strength, his courage, his genius, all were beyond question.

Irene giggled. "Again she didn't notice that the letter was posted in Budapest," she said.

Lucy jumped up from her chair, went to the window, and from behind the bed, so that she should nor even see it in her dream, stuck out her tongue at the old woman.

"What did you write?"

"A lot," said Lucy. "I laid it on thick."

"She won't talk about it today," said the housekeeper, "but tomorrow she'll ring for me at dawn."

"Well, why shouldn't you have some fun, too?"

They were both silent. The sun climbing to its zenith had left the room, the old lady's face was now in shadow. Only the mirror of the large wardrobe standing at the far end of the room reflected the sun's rays, the beveled edges dissecting it to the seven colors of the rainbow, and throwing a trembling veil of colored light onto the wall. Above the bunch of pansies, the wasps hummed sleepily.

"You won't be able to stand this much longer," said Irene, looking with compassion at the young woman.

"Like hell I won't," said Lucy.

"Well—not for ten years."

"He's done one," said Lucy, "there are only nine left."

Irene nodded. "The old lady won't live that long."

"No," said Lucy, "but as long as she lives, I want her to have everything."

"Professor Hetenyi promised her she'll live to be a hundred. That's four more years."

"Possibly," said Lucy. "Come over here, Irene dear, and have a look how lovely her face still is from this angle."

The old woman slept so soundly and so happily that Lucy decided she would not wait for her to wake up. But before she had reached the door, the old lady behind her opened her eyes. "Where are you going?"

Lucy turned around, laughing. "I was going to hop it, Mother."

The old lady said nothing; she looked at the flexible, slim figure of her daughter-in-law for a long time. She lifted her head a little, and smiled gently.

"How lovely your red hair looks in the sun," she said. "Like an English Princess."

Lucy flushed. "Well! Is it really lovely, Mother?"

"Really," the old lady said. She nodded a few more times, then called Lucy to her. "Will you kiss me, please? No, not there, on my forehead. I want you to. You are very lovely and very good."

"Well, really!" said Lucy.

"There's something I want to ask," the old lady went on. "Why must my son Janos have secret police by him in America?"

Lucy swallowed hard; her eyelids began to flutter.

"Well, every famous person is surrounded by secret police in America, Mother."

"All right," said the old woman, relieved. "Is good." Suddenly she laughed in a thin old voice. "Do you want one bear? One very big bear so big as two Irenes. *Mein Gott*, what an idea—only he can have an idea like that." She laughed until the tears came to her eyes. "Now you go," she said, suddenly impatient. "Tomorrow I will tell you the letter."

But Lucy had hardly reached the door before she called her back.

"Now," she said, "you nearly forgot to pull out the hairs on my chin, and this afternoon Professor Hetenyi is coming. You please take the tweezers out from my drawer. And the new bed-jacket because Irene will not give it to me. You to put it on me, please. You see," she said proudly, while looking at her bare arm, "you see how it is nicely smooth, there is no wrinkle in it only where I bend, here by the elbow."

"The young ones have wrinkles there, too, Mother," said Lucy.

The old woman looked at her.

I I

THAT MORNING Lucy arrived at her mother-in-law's cottage later than usual. Opposite the door four geese were cackling in the sun-flecked sand—the four women already had gone home to cook the midday meal.

The door was opened by the white-haired, square-set housekeeper. She did not allow the visitor to enter at once; she planted herself in front of Lucy, and with her small sharp eyes set in her round apple face she scrutinized the young woman's features for a long time.

"Well, aren't you going to let me in?" Lucy asked, laughing.

"What's wrong?" asked Irene, blocking the doorway.

"Nothing," said Lucy. "Why should there be anything wrong? Aren't you going to let me in?"

The old housekeeper did not move from the doorway.

"There is nothing wrong—why should there be?" Lucy repeated.

"Why didn't you bring any flowers, then?" she asked.

Lucy laughed. "Aren't you sharp! I didn't have time. Well, let me in, blow it. I'm late as it is."

"You didn't have time?"

In the clean white kitchen, where the gleaming whiteness of the furniture was enhanced by the blazing sunlight, the jasmine, from the edge of the lawn, sent a bouquet of chokingly sweet fragrance. Turning her head from side to side, Lucy sniffed the air. "I can't smell any buttered toast," she said. "Has she eaten it by now?"

"Ages ago."

"Is it that late?"

"Nearly midday," the housekeeper said.

"Irene dear, go and pinch yesterday's flowers out of the vase," said Lucy, "and bring them out here. I had no time to buy any today."

"Are you broke?" the housekeeper asked.

Lucy did not reply. "Look, just pinch yesterday's flowers," she said, "and give me some tissue paper to wrap around the stems. What sort of flowers did I bring yesterday?"

The housekeeper shook her head. "I cant pinch them because if she never notices anything else, she'll notice if the flowers are missing, sure enough. You brought white carnations."

"Bring them out," said Lucy. "I'll put some lipstick on them."

Irene laughed. "Would you like a glass of brandy?"

"Yes."

Irene went to the kitchen cabinet and opened it. On the lower shelf of the top part, which was edged with a white doily strip, the soup bowls, meat plates and dessert plates shone in separate groups, the last group a little lower than the rest. The meat, vegetable, salad and sweet dishes were piled upon one another according to size, the great urn-shaped soup tureen was in the far corner. They were all decorated with a narrow gold band that glinted in the sun.

"She broke another dessert plate yesterday," the housekeeper said, while from among the glasses, cups and saucers on the top shelf she took a lead crystal liqueur glass and filled it with brandy.

"What's the matter?" she asked as, turning around with the full glass in her hand, she saw that Lucy, her head resting on the kitchen table, was crying soundlessly. "I knew . . ."

Annoyed, the young woman threw her head back. "What did you know? Tell me, what did you know?"

The old housekeeper watched her silently.

"Well, is it surprising if I cry," sniffed Lucy, "if they break my inheritance to pieces? That's the fourth dessert plate that's missing. Or did she leave the china to you?"

"She did," said the housekeeper quickly and decidedly. "And the silver, too. What's wrong?"

"Nothing."

"No money?"

"I made seventy-four forints last week by dyeing nylons," she said. From her white handbag she took her handkerchief, powder, lipstick and mirror, and threw them down on the table in front of her. There were a few specks of powder on the mirror, which she wiped off with her handkerchief, and then raised it to her face; with the heartbreaking intensity of the eternal struggle for existence, she examined each feature with infinite care. Moving the mirror from side to side, she smoothed her greasy eyelids with the tip of her forefinger, sucked her lips in and pressed the upper lip to the lower a few times. Then, wetting her forefinger, she passed it once or twice over her eyebrows. Creation, without which there is neither life nor death, had been completed. Looking into the mirror once more, she cast a last glance at her heavy russet hair; this was Sunday.

"I only had to work two days and two nights for it," she said, the last tremors of creation reverberating in her voice.

The housekeeper pulled up the little kitchen stool where— under the worn paint—the texture of the wood was beginning to show through, and sat down next to her. "I could lend you some," she said. "My husband got his wages yesterday."

"Go to bloody . . ." said Lucy. "The hairdresser offered me eight hundred forints for my hair only last week—that should do for two months' rent as it is."

"Is there no news?"

"None. My mother-in-law?"

"She was asleep when I looked in a few minutes ago."

Lucy's eyes filled with tears again. She could not even put up any resistance to herself anymore—she was finished.

"What's the matter with you?" Irene asked.

"Nothing. I'm jittery. Leave me alone."

"Got your period?"

Lucy laughed suddenly. "Sure. That's the least of my worries."

"Well, what then?"

"The bailiff has been again," the young woman said. "Came at nine and plagued me till eleven."

"But he's already collared everything."

"No."

"What d'you mean?"

"I mean he hasn't confiscated everything."

The old housekeeper folded her hands in her lap. The geese broke into a frightened cackle in front of the house.

"As soon as he left," went on Lucy, "the family of the concierge came up, all three of them, father, mother and the little girl, and sang Verdi's *Requiem* for me."

"What?"

"Nothing. I'm playing the fool," said Lucy.

The housekeeper stood up, then sat down again.

"When I was a little girl," said Lucy, knitting her brows, "I once got lice at the convent in Majsa. The Mother Superior ordered my hair to be shorn off completely, and it took a year until it grew anyway near halfway respectable again. In that year I felt more or less as I feel now."

The housekeeper was silent.

"Funny," said Lucy. "I just remembered, the Mother Superior came from Vienna, too. And I was often hurt because she always spoke German with Lilla Bulyovsky and I didn't understand it."

"She made you bald? Cut off all your lovely red hair?"

"She cut it off because it was red," Lucy said. "And the next day my mother went to the convent with a whip, and had to be forcibly strained from horsewhipping the Mother Superior."

"I thought the bailiff had laid his filthy hand on everything by now?" the housekeeper said after a while.

"He hasn't," said the young woman obstinately.

"Well, what did he leave?"

Lucy made an impatient gesture and bumped her elbow on the table. "No!" she cried in fright, "I don't want an unexpected guest! I don't want any unexpected guests!" Snatching at her elbow with her hand, she pulled the unexpected guest out of it, and turning her palm outward, scattered him into the four winds. "I've had quite enough of them as it is. He hasn't dispossessed me of my furniture yet."

"Of course not," said Irene.

The young woman shook her head with annoyance. "Why, 'of course'?" she asked. "Because I had all the old bills and notes of delivery, and with those I could prove conclusively that the furniture belongs to me and not to Janos. Janos had hardly enough furniture for one room—he didn't even have a decent bed when he married me."

"I know," nodded the housekeeper.

"And now the Ministry has sent Mr. Kulinka along to confiscate everything, and I'm supposed to reclaim whatever belongs to me," said Lucy with tears in her eyes. "He was just spitting zeros all over the place—five thousand, ten thousand, another ten thousand—it was no use begging him and telling him that they would restore the things to me anyway, and would he mind valuing them slightly lower, as I won't be able to cope with the stamp duty. He looked at me mournfully, for he was so sorry for me he nearly cried, then bawled out: one neo-Baroque wardrobe twenty thousand."

"Twenty thousand," repeated the housekeeper, shaking her head.

"What are you groaning about?" asked Lucy. "It's worth it.

I'd get that much for it if I sold it any day. But I won't sell it, not if it kills me—I want Janos to find everything as he left it."

The housekeeper glued her eyes on the ground.

"Stop bawling," shouted Lucy irritably. "What the hell are you bawling about? Just like Mr. Kulinka. We won't frisk you personally, he cried with tears absolutely flooding his eyes, but we'll search every cupboard. . . . Irene dear, find me that old French soapbox we saved."

"Did you bring her some soap?" asked Irene, going toward the kitchen cabinet.

"Yeah . . . and find that empty Czech chocolate-box for me, too, that nice red one," said Lucy, while taking a tablet of soap and a bag of sweets from her handbag.

"She's still got the old ones untouched."

"Well, let her have some more," sneered Lucy. "Her beloved son, Janos, is sending them to her from America," she said sarcastically, while pouring the sweets from the paper bag onto the table, and putting them one by one into the red chocolate-box. She laughed again.

"What's up?" asked Irene.

"Nothing. I'm laughing at myself."

The bell buzzed three or four times in quick succession. The housekeeper looked at Lucy. "Are you going?"

"Not yet. I'll get my breath back first," said Lucy.

"Don't you want to lie down for a quarter of an hour in my room?"

"What for?" asked Lucy. "I'll lie down after lunch anyway, and won't even bother to get up till tomorrow morning. I'm out of work again."

"Why don't you go to the pictures for once?" Irene asked after a while.

"What for? I laugh enough about myself as it is."

THE BELL rang again. Since the time, about a month ago, when during one of her walks along the room, the old lady fainted, fell and broke her ankle, she had become even more neurotic and crotchety than before her accident. Sometimes she rang for Irene three or four times in quick succession; at other times she did not touch the bell for days; she lay in bed without moving, her foot in plaster, her eyes closed, neither reading nor switching on the wireless; the only reason one knew she was awake was that she opened her eyes immediately someone entered the room. At these times the mirror of her eyes was not clouded by the unconsciousness of sleep but by the weariness of a greater distance that drained the hue of life from her waxen skin and allowed the uncontrolled glands at the corner of her mouth to discharge their saliva. She did not speak at once at these times like dozing old people usually do who, like defenseless beasts, want to deny having been asleep, and do so with immediate and loud protestations; she inspected the fact that swam into her vision with a long and penetrating gaze as if tying to decide what strange unknown world it came from. She usually made some small deprecating gesture so as to wave away the welcome guest. Since breaking her ankle, she could not get up in the afternoon and, although not in pain and unaware that her ankle was broken—she thought it only sprained—the quarter of an hour taken from her daily program upset her whole routine and disrupted her small but steady universe. In place of the dead Professor Hetenyi—who was supposed to be furthering his studies in the Soviet Union—a new doctor had to be introduced to the scene and this, too, contributed to her feeling of insecurity. Although she liked the new doctor, Dr. Illes, for some unknown reason, through some unfathomable channels of the nervous system, when she looked at him he evoked the memory of her son, Janos; the stranger intruding on her horizon still disturbed the groove her life had been running in for years now. Naturally, Dr. Illes spoke German well and had an extensive knowledge of the great German classics—they would not have dared to bring the old lady a doctor who did not—apart from this he had a very nice tenor voice, and sometimes sang in concerts; this was something not even Professor Hetenyi could do. Equally naturally, Dr. Illes, following the example of his predecessor, shared, without any reservation, the old lady's admiration for her son.

"Is that you, Irene?" the old woman's voice came from the bedroom.

Lucy jumped up and tiptoed to the door to listen. She moved with the same grace when she was alone as when she was in company, even if only in her mother-in-law's company, who did not see very well now. Her face, complementing her body, acted as well—she grimaced, raised her eyebrows, wrinkled her forehead, and smiled at herself as if to a second person who would watch, observe, and appreciate all this. Incidentally, her ears were so finely tuned that she could just as well have stayed in the kitchen, and would still have heard every word from upstairs.

"It is you, Irene?"

"Well, who else?" asked the housekeeper. "You rang."

"Come nearer, Irene dear, I not see your face," said the old woman suspiciously. "I have rang?"

"Twice."

"I remember not," the old woman said. "Do you not know what I wanted?"

"I'm supposed to know that as well," muttered the housekeeper. "You wanted to ask me what the time was."

"All right," said the old woman. "Tell me, what is the time?"

"Nearly midday."

"Nearly midday," repeated the old woman pensively. "Did I not want anything else?"

"You wanted to ask me what I'm having for lunch."

"What are you having?"

"What's left over from yesterday's braised beef with potatoes and tomato sauce."

"Phew!" said the old woman. "I do not want that one. No noodles with cabbage?"

Irene shook her head.

"Pity," said the old woman disappointedly. "That Professor Hetenyi has strictly forbidden, but I always eat up by the spoonful. Tell me what time it is?"

"Midday."

"I know . . . midday," said the old woman. "But then why did not the young lady come yet?"

This was what Lucy wanted to hear; she grinned contentedly. It seemed the old lady wanted her after all, if for nothing else, to talk about her son. She ran back to the kitchen, snatched up her handbag, had a last look in the mirror, and then ran back to the room.

"Good morning, Mother," she called loudly.

"Is it you?" said the old lady, bad-temperedly. "Why do you come so late? Irene says it's midday already."

"I wrote a long letter to Janos, Mother," said Lucy. "I took it out to the airport so it should go today."

"*Ja,*" said the old woman.

"What have I brought for Mother?" Lucy sang.

"Flowers, for sure," said the old woman. "You never learn to economize. What flowers they are?"

"White carnations."

The old woman turned her head toward the bedside table where she could not see yesterday's white carnations. She looked back uncertainly to the vase in Lucy's hand.

"I put them in quickly with the others," Lucy said. "They wilted a bit on the long journey. And what else have I brought for Mother?" she went on quickly, with distracting tactics. But the old woman did not look toward the handbag; she was still staring at the white carnations. "What else have I brought for Mother?" Lucy repeated more loudly.

The old lady looked at the presents with indifference. "Is good," she said. "French soap? Janos sent it? It smells very nice. You to give it Irene—she will put it away. The sweets, too. You to write to Janos he should not now send anymore because there is now enough."

"Oh; let him send some," said Lucy. "There is never enough of these. Why shouldn't he send any?"

"Because he should economize," said the old woman wearily. "He cannot economize, either. What will happen to you, my child, if you will never learn to economize, not you, not he? One day you will be old."

"Never, Mother," Lucy laughed. "Not while there is lipstick and makeup on the market."

The old woman closed her eyes. "I thought it was already afternoon," she complained, "and that you already gone to home. And it is only midday and I still have to eat that miserable dinner."

Suddenly she sat up and, forgetting her neuralgia, leaned out of bed, fixing the dark rays of her dimming eyes on her daughter-in-law's face.

"Come nearer here, my child," she said.

"Yes, Mother."

"Nearer," said the old woman. "More nearer! Tell me, my child, the truth—when is he coming home?"

"Who?" asked Lucy, frightened.

IT WAS the first time in a year that the old woman allowed her doubts to rise to the surface, and admitted openly even to herself that she had them. It had happened before that she had lost patience and grumbled that her son should leave her alone for so long, but she never doubted his veracity that in a month's time, or in three months, he would come home, and when that time was up (of which, with her faulty sense of arithmetic she could not keep track, anyway), and her son had not yet arrived, then, with a mother's implicit faith, with unquestioning credulity she believed without any doubt that her son was busy and accepted the new time almost at once. This was the first time that she openly rebelled.

"You tell me the truth," she repeated quietly but obstinately. She put her glasses on and, bending even nearer to

Lucy's face, she bore her dark eyes into those of the young woman. "When is he coming home?"

"Well, in his last letter he said that in three months he will definitely have completed his work. One month is now up," said Lucy.

The old woman suddenly fell back on her pillows, and in a thin, old voice, began to cry. The tears dropped one by one from her open eyes, ran down her narrow, bony face—which remained undistorted by their touch—flowed down her chin and under the ribbon of the black velvet bonnet. Lucy had known her mother-in-law for several years, but she had never seen her cry, not even in '56 when the shells nearly ripped the roof from over their heads and the two women stuck it out alone for days in the vibrating room because Irene was with her husband at the other end of the town and did not dare come home. They had no news of Janos for a week then. The old woman was lying more or less helplessly in bed even then, but not a muscle moved in her set face at the sound of the detonations—true, she was hard of hearing, even then—and all day long she kept telling stories to Lucy about her own youth, about Janos, and made Lucy tell of her own childhood, which she spent in the country.

"Please don't cry, Mother," said Lucy, whose heart had stopped in terror for a moment. "Two months is not such a very long time."

"I won't live that long," the old woman said between the two rows of tears that were falling from her eyes. "I won't live till then."

"Oh, Mother, what are you talking about?" Lucy cried with all her strength. "Professor Hetenyi said you will live for a hundred years."

"What do you say?"

"Professor Hetenyi said that . . ."

The old woman turned her tearstained face toward her daughter-in-law. She did not speak, but stared with her guileless, leaden eyes at Lucy's face for a while, then lifted her hand—and let it fall again.

"That's at least four more years," cried Lucy. The old woman looked at the ceiling again.

"Ach—go away," she said. "Maybe Professor Hetenyi is dead as well."

There was complete silence in the room for a second; only the faint sound of whimpering came from the pillows. "All right. Mother," Lucy said with sudden decision, "I'll write to Janos and tell him to come home."

"What do you say?" asked the old woman after a few seconds.

"I'll write to Janos and tell him to come home at once," repeated Lucy in a louder voice.

"When?"

"Today."

Looking at Lucy again, the old woman said, "I don't ask that. I ask when he should come home?"

"At once!" cried Lucy. "You are perfectly right, Mother, he's been knocking around America long enough. I'm sick of it, too."

The old woman's tears ceased, and a deep sigh escaped her. "That he should come home at once?" she asked dubiously, as if not believing her tears.

"I'll tell him," said Lucy, bending over bed, "that if he hasn't finished that goddamn picture by now, he may as well leave it and come home. You're absolutely right, Mother, I'm not prepared to wait any longer, either."

"That he should leave the film?"

"Don't worry, Mother," said Lucy, "if I tell him to come home or else I'll divorce him, he'll be home in no time."

"You divorce him?"

"And how!" Lucy said. "Well, tell me, Mother, is it fair to leave a woman alone for that long? Everyone else would have been unfaithful to him by now except me. . . . Well, what the hell does he take me for?"

"That he should leave the film?" the old woman said again with trembling lips. "Before the first night?"

"Damn the first night!" said Lucy. "He can stuff his first night. I don't want his dollars. He'd better come home before I run out on him."

The old woman sat up. "What you say? That you will run out from Janos?"

"To hell with his dollars," said Lucy. "I know he won't get a cent if he doesn't finish the picture and that he slaved away for nothing for heaven knows how long, but I don't care. I'm not going to stew here on my own any longer."

The old woman sat up quite straight. "If Janos comes home now, then he will not get one dollar?"

"Of course not," said Lucy furiously, watching the old woman from the corner of her eye in the meantime. "So what? I don't want his money. You're quite right, Mother, I'll send him a wire today to come home at once."

The old woman was silent. Then, *"Dumme Gans,"* she said suddenly, her forehead flushing with anger. "And then he has made the whole work for nothing?"

"Made it for nothing," said Lucy, "so what? Work isn't the only thing in life. He's got a wife and an adored mother as well."

"Dumme Gans!" the old women repeated, getting more and more red in the face. "For man the most important thing is his work. You cannot wear on your conscience that Janos did not finish the film. Do you not know that also the Queen of Holland wants to see?"

Lucy shook her head. "I don't care, I'm going to wire him today. You are absolutely right, Mother."

"I'm not right," screeched the old woman angrily. "You being very stupid. Just because I whine a little bit, you do not have to already tear your hair. You shall not write him anything at all."

"I'm not writing, I'm sending a telegram," said Lucy. "Who is more important, Mother, you or the Queen of Holland?"

"That I forbid that you should telegram," said the old woman. Her convulsed face, which the unusual anguish emaciated to even more angular dimensions, loomed for a moment gauntly and threateningly into Lucy's. But the next instant an almost incredible transformation took place; the face softened with affectionate tenderness, and she smiled at Lucy with all the captivating charm and wisdom of her ninety-odd years.

"You listen to me, my child," she said. "I know what is hurting you. I know you feel jealous for Janos. But I know my son, you be quite sure. My son is like I am, he is faithful to the people he loves. It can happen that he will have one or two affairs in America with women—will have one or two affairs in Europe, too, because I had an affair once myself—but in the end my son will tell every woman: Out! You do not have to telegram to him. My son will live to the end of his life with you."

FORTUNATELY, THE bell rang at that moment. Dr. Illes, the new doctor, looked in at the old woman for a quarter of an hour's therapeutic talk. The old woman—by some mysterious process of the mind, she associated the doctor with her son—was very fond of him, and grumbled at him incessantly. The more she grumbled the more she liked him. Her tearstained worn face lit up instantly as she now saw him at her bedside. He was a doctor, that was reason enough for deference; the old lady acclaimed science with all the superstitious veneration of the nineteenth century; but apart from that, the six-foot-tall, broad-shouldered young man with the intelligent smile, appealed to her still sensitive feminine heart through his masculine charm. His balding head reminded her of Janos, his classical literary education—although it could not compete with Professor Hetenyi's—recalled memories of her own girlhood and beaux. They spattered each other with quotations like playful children bathing in a river who splash water into each others faces.

There was only one thing the old lady could not bear with equanimity, and that was the fact that Dr. Illes occasionally sang in church at the Sunday Service at the church of the Inner City, or at Ascension Day at the church of Kristina Square.

"Well, have you been singing in the church again, Doctor?" she asked petulantly, fixing her tired eyes on the doctor's kindly face. "Do you know that I have not been in church for ninety years?"

"Not once?" asked the doctor. "Not even on your wedding day?"

"Not even then," said the old lady. "Only to look at pictures, when my husband took me to honeymoon in France. But I do not understand well the pictures so I mainly just walked around in the church and I looked at the kneeling people praying and I thought, *O, les pauvres!*"

The old housekeeper, who was standing in the doorway behind the doctor, secretly made the sign of the cross.

"I was ten or twelve years old," said the old woman, "and I have a new dress from my Mamma because next day we wanted to make excursion to the *Wiener Wald.* In the evening I prayed for long to God that he should make fine weather so that we can go for excursion and I can wear my new dress. And then next day it rained. Then I was very angry with God."

"And you are still angry, Mother?" asked Lucy.

The old woman slowly turned her eyes toward Lucy. "I said, my child, that I got very angry then. And the next day when my Mamma wanted to take me to church in the morning, I said: No."

"And you didn't go?"

"My Mamma, she was a clever woman," said the old lady. "She waited until next Sunday when there was sunshine and we could go for excursion and I could wear my new dress and was very happy. And then she asked: Are you coming to church again now, Stina?"

The doctor laughed and patted the old woman's hand, which he had been holding all the time. "And Stina was clever, too, was she?"

The old woman smiled. "My Mamma asked: Stina, are you coming to church now? And again I said: No."

For a few seconds there was silence in the room. The sun was shining from behind the bed, highlighting the gaunt face molded of skin and bone.

"I said to my Mamma," the old lady went on, slightly out of breath, "I said: No. I said: I will not ask for help from no one in this world whom you cannot trust. I want to walk on my own feet and head."

"Well, that you've achieved," said Lucy in an aside.

"What do you say?" the old woman asked.

"I said, Mother," Lucy shouted, "that you've most certainly achieved that."

The old woman shook her head. "I don't know . . . I don't know if I achieved. Since I become so old—since then I'm so lonely and helpless. But when I die," she said, "then only my son will hold my hand." She looked at Lucy again. "Not even you . . . I will not want you then, either," she said slowly with a long, penetrating stare at the young woman's face. "The beasts, they want to be alone when they die. If my son cannot be with me and cannot hold my hand then, then I want to be on my own."

Her strength exhausted, she suddenly closed her eyes. The various events of the day had evidently tired her; she withdrew her hand from the doctor's and tucked it under the eiderdown next to the still dependable warmth of her own body. Out of tact for her visitors, she did not turn toward the wall, but pretended deafness, or, maybe, by auto-suggestion, became temporarily deaf, and did not reply to any more questions. But when Lucy, following the doctor, wanted to tiptoe out of the room, the old lady lifted her head from her lilac pillow and called her daughter-in-law back.

"Lucy," she said, clearly and intelligibly, "you please to stay with me a little longer."

Lucy floundered. The old lady hardly ever used her Christian name. "Of course, Mother," she said. "I'm only seeing Dr. Illes out."

"Thank you," said the old lady, "but afterward you come back?"

"Of course I'll come back," said Lucy. "We haven't seen much of each other today."

Despite her tiredness, the old lady kept Lucy with her for a long time. She shared her lunch with her while she herself only ate a few morsels—Irene, too, offered some of her own tomato sauce and braised beef. Lucy ate with such a good appetite and obvious enjoyment, transforming the food so quickly into energy, gaiety, and jokes, that the gastric juices of the other two women began to work at a more healthy rate. They, too, seemed to thrive on what Lucy put away.

"Is it good?" the old woman asked. "First-class," said Lucy.

"The tomato sauce as well?"

"Absolutely. If only I liked it!"

"You don't like tomato sauce?"

"Loathe it," said Lucy.

When they had finished the black coffee that the old lady had ordered specially for her guest, Lucy had to undo her waist-length red hair and comb it in front of the bed before the large, silver-framed mirror of the dressing table. The sun rose and shone directly into the room, now onto the mirror, the white arm that rose and fell in front of it combing the Titian red hair with a large ivory comb, coaxing electric sparks invisibly out of its long glittering strands and scattering them into the room. The old woman looked for a while hungrily at the young, slender neck, the white shoulders gleaming in the sun, drank in the healthy fragrance of the mass of lustrous hair— then suddenly she had had enough, and became weary.

"I thank you, now you go home," she said, almost as soon as Lucy had put the last pin into her hair.

THE NEXT day, the young woman arrived an hour earlier than usual. She rang and started hammering the door with her two fists. "Irene," she shouted, still outside the door, "Irene! I've got a letter, a letter, a letter. . . ." She hugged the housekeeper's neck and laughing loudly, happily, she spun her around and waltzed along the narrow little hall. She was so excited that her teeth chattered audibly while she danced.

"From your husband?" Irene asked.

"He's alive!" the young woman panted. "It's quite sure now that he is alive. I can go and visit him Sunday. It was not a letter that came only, but a printed permission form saying that I can go and visit him next Sunday. If he is permitted visitors, then he must be in good health."

Irene did not answer, but the young woman was so happy that she did not notice.

"Even if he isn't in good health, at least he's alive. That much is certain."

"The old lady is very unwell," Irene said after a time.

Lucy sat down on the kitchen stool. Now she noticed the traces of a sleepless night on the old housekeeper's apple cheeks, the shadows under the eyes, the puffed lids. "What happened?" she asked.

"Well, in the middle of the night I woke up—you know how lightly I sleep—because I heard talking in her room. So I went in and she was talking to herself, but much louder than she usually does; she was even shouting and quarreling with her son. At dawn my husband went to phone the doctor, because by then her cheeks were bright red."

"Pneumonia?"

AFTER THE onset of the illness, the old lady did not lose consciousness for three more days, but, like a poet, by this time she was only concerned with herself. Out of courtesy, and self-discipline, she made an effort to conceal that she had no interest in anything in the world anymore—the last honor her disciplined pride paid to the world of the living—but her efforts were not very successful. She could not hide her indifference very well; the people around her found out soon enough the polite trick she was trying to play.

The inflammation first attacked the left lung, and when they succeeded in subduing it there, the right one; it spread to both lungs again. While she was conscious, the old lady—when she believed herself to be alone—sometimes kept up long monologues, mainly about the small inconveniences of her helpless state. As at the onset of pneumonia the bladder stopped working, she felt very ashamed about having a nurse come twice a day to draw off her water. Later, she became unconscious, and did not speak at all. Lucy wanted to hire a full-time nurse but Irene was having none of it. "What for—so I can look after her too?" she asked. "Anyway, how do I know what she is going to take out of the cupboard when she is alone in the room?" Apart from this, while she was able to speak or thought speaking worthwhile, the old lady herself protested against the constant presence of a stranger. The first time she spoke was on the afternoon of the third day, during the doctor's visit.

She looked at the visitors, Lucy and the doctor, with clear open eyes, but did not return their greeting, and when they sat down by her bed, she kept her eyes fixed on the door as if expecting someone else who was certain to come. Even later, in her unconscious state she kept this posture; when they straightened her pillows and placed her narrow, black-bonneted head on the topmost one, the next instant she turned it toward the door, craning her neck, and whether her eyes were open or closed, her whole blind body was listening to a sound from that direction. In the last days she even brought her right hand from under the warmth of her eiderdown, and, twisting her wrist, placed her palm under her chin at a queer angle. If Lucy cautiously eased it out of its contorted position and put it back under the eiderdown, the old lady, stubborn even in unconsciousness, slid it out the next moment and wedged it under her chin again. Otherwise, she lay as quiet and motionless as a dry leaf in the sunny dust, her breath could neither be seen nor heard, her legs were stretched out one next to the other, the one in plaster touching the other waxen foot. She did not complain even during her unconsciousness; she neither sighed nor groaned; the only time she uttered a little plaintive whimper—so unbefitting to her severe and austere life—was when she was turned on her side so that the doctor, who now came twice a day, could examine her lungs, or the little sores on her back caused by the long stay in bed, could be dusted with talcum powder. She submitted to the injections without a sound; the hypodermic needle only touched the topmost layer of her mortal form.

But on this last afternoon of her conscious life, she did not reply anymore to the doctor's questions or to Lucy's endearments, compressing her lips and fixing her, for the moment, still clear eyes on the door, she remained obstinately silent.

"I might be able to keep her alive for two or three more days," the doctor said to Lucy after the examination. "Is there any hope . . . ?"

"None."

"What is your wish?" asked the doctor, looking out of the window to the sun-flecked lawn and, beyond it, to the dusty road.

"Whatever is better for her."

"It's all the same for her."

"Whatever is better," said Lucy.

"She does not feel anything by now," the doctor said. "Within a few hours she'll probably lose consciousness. With caffeine and strocaine, I can keep her heart going for a few more days. Is there any hope for . . . ?"

"No," said Lucy.

"What is your wish?"

"Whatever is best for her."

After the injection, Lucy went out with the doctor into the hall. They had hardly reached it when the bell rang. This was the first time the old lady used the bell since she had had pneumonia.

"Mother, Mother darling," Lucy whispered, bending over the bed. The doctor was waiting in the hall. The old lady went on looking at the door but clung to Lucy's arm with her hand.

"I did not tell you, my child," she said in a queer, muffled voice, "about the last letter of my son. Do you know he is going to get the Kossuth Prize?"

"He didn't write to me about it yet," said Lucy.

The old woman kept her eyes on the door. "He is going to get it," she said. "Now you get out and send me in the doctor."

The doctor came in and bent over the bed. "Do you know, singing doctor," said the old lady, still keeping her eyes on the door, but with her mouth twisting into an ironic grimace, "do you know, singing doctor, that my son is going to get the Kossuth Prize?"

"Wonderful," said the doctor, "wonderful."

The old woman nodded again. "Is going to get," she said. "It is a secret not but you tell Lucy, my daughter-in-law, that she should be proud of my son."

"Wonderful," said the doctor again.

"Now you go on singing," said the old lady.

After the doctor had left, Lucy sat down in the kitchen with Irene. Her lips were trembling so badly that it was a long time before she could speak. Irene poured her a glass of brandy, put it in front of her and left the bottle out. Lucy put her shaking fingers to the stem of the glass. "Now what am I going to tell him on next Sunday's visit?" she asked.

Translated by Dr. D. Mervyn Jones

THE CIRCUS

THE CHILDREN were bored. It was a stifling hot and dusty Sunday afternoon. The children's bare feet sank ankle-deep into the dust of the great courtyard enclosed by the flour mill to the left and the house on the right. Their eyebrows were gray with dust, and when they spat, dust grated in their teeth.

"What should we play now?" asked Manci. She was sitting on the porch steps staring at the dust in front of her. The other children hung lazily around her, standing first on one leg and then on the other; they were silent. Kalman, the watchmaker's son, wiped dust off his glasses with a large walnut leaf.

The house belonged to them now. The chief miller had left for Pest; his wife had gone to the farm to visit Grandmother, who was gravely ill. The mill was at a standstill. A Sunday stillness hung over the street outside; not even barking dogs could be heard. Traffic had been suspended since noon when a Catholic priest had passed the house, bells of the altar boys growing louder, then dying away in the dense village silence. If anyone went down the street, the cloud of dust balling up behind him as it drifted toward the board fence betrayed his presence no matter how noiselessly he ambled along. All along the street, houses were shuttered against the burning sun, which drove everyone indoors. Only the mill yard was full of children and dogs.

"What should we play?" asked Manci.

They were all alone in the house. They could tear it down, or, if they felt like it, burn it to the ground. There were nine or ten little children and older ones from the neighborhood, as well as Manci, the fourteen-year-old daughter of the chief miller, and her twin brother, Gyula. Until nightfall, when their mother came home, nobody would know if they had axed every piece of furniture in the house or drowned every hen. But for the time being, they were sitting quietly, standing about in the dust eyeing each other.

"What should we play?" asked Manci. "Now we can play anything."

She had large gray eyes whose cold and sleepy stare flustered even some adults as she fixed them with her languidly searching gaze. Not even her mother had ever seen her cry, except from impotent rage. She bore every punishment in silence. But once, when she was ten years old, at a taunt from her father, she had grabbed the kitchen knife on the table and with all her strength plunged it into the palm of her hand. The scar was visible to this day. This summer, for the first time, she sat alone in the yard underneath the mulberry tree, and with her sleepy cold eyes she stared at the yard bathed in moonlight until her mother chased her off to bed.

"What should we play?"

The children were silent.

"We can play anything we want."

"Let's pretend we're having an Olympics," said Pista Deli, the son of the neighbor, a fairly prosperous peasant. A hot-blooded child with a short neck and red face, famous because he would soundly trounce even much older children if they dared look askance at his shortness. He had not yet tried his strength against Gyula, the chief miller's son who was the same age.

"Olympics?" said a girl's thin voice. "It's too hot."

"It'll be hot in Rome, too."

"No, let's not," said Dezso Trenka, the stonemason's son, who lived next door. "Besides, it's boring."

Pista Deli turned toward Manci sitting on the porch steps. She fixed her large, brooding, cold gray eyes on him, looked at him for a while, then shook her head.

"Let's play doctor," said another girl.

"That'll be all right. The patient will die."

"Then we'll bury him."

"Where?"

Again they looked at Manci. The young girl's ivory neck and reddish-brown hair were impervious to the sun. Her face had only a faint pinkish glow below her long, tightly combed hair. And young bespectacled Kalman, scrawny son of the local watchmaker, stood behind the girl, leaning on one of the porch columns and studying the downy nape of her neck in rapt absorption; then a minute later, turning pale, he tore his gaze from her. It was obvious, even from behind, that the girl had nixed the idea.

"Let's play grocer's," said someone.

"Let's play ball."

"Let's play Tarzan."

Manci said nothing. "Let's play Tarzan," repeated a boy's voice. The young girl shook her head. "Today we can play anything," she said impatiently, "even something special."

"Let's give the brood-hen a bath."

"Let's go up to the attic."

The children grew silent. They stared ahead blankly, downcast. Three spotted dogs were lying side by side in the shade of the mulberry tree. One scrambled to its feet, circled the others, then threw itself on its side, tongue lolling, and sighed.

Young Kalman with the glasses stepped down from the porch, taking a deep breath. "Let's start the mill," he said with lowered eyes. "If we get it started, we can grind twenty sacks full."

"What for?"

Kalman blushed and said nothing. The girl looked disdainfully at the silent children. "You're all stupid," she said quietly to the dust at her feet. "You can't find anything to do."

"Go to hell!" said Pista Deli. "Don't you tell us what to do!"

Manci got up slowly, and lazily stretched herself. She smiled and shrugged her shoulders. "Where are you going?" asked Piri Trenka, alarmed. "Wait! I'm coming with you."

"You don't have to," said Manci without turning around. Her legs, covered only to the knees by the short cotton cambric skirt, were girlishly round and as white as her arms and neck. "I'm going inside to read."

Although Busan, largest of the three dogs, was lying with his hindside to the porch, he raised his head and looked back. He pondered for a moment, then got up and, tail wagging, set off after the girl. At this moment, the sharp cracking of a whip was heard from the other end of the porch, short and hard like a gunshot. "You're staying here!" said Gyula, the head miller's son, and again he cracked his short-handled, leather-thonged whip. It was impossible to tell whether the command was meant for his sister or the dog. Both stopped. "You're idiots," said the boy, turning his pale face with the great blaze of red hair toward the children. "Idiots."

"Who's an idiot?" asked Pista Deli.

"You're one, too."

The squat, short-necked child bowed his head; blood rushed to his forehead. "Why am I an idiot?" he said in a muffled voice.

"Ask your Papa," said Gyula, smiling disdainfully and squinting. He turned his long freckled face toward the sun. "Manci is right. If I weren't here, no one would know what to do."

"I know," said Pista Deli.

He turned and started for the gate. With his disproportionately wide back, short legs and arms, he seemed shorter than he really was. Gyula waited till he reached the gate. "Wait, idiot!" he shouted after him in his rather thin, rasping voice. "I need you, come back!"

Pista Deli stopped, but did not turn around. The other children listened silently without moving. On the porch, Manci was also standing with her back to the group, only her head turned out of curiosity.

"Come back!" said Gyula. "I've found something to do."

The circus game the gang was going to play for the first time required every hand, every head. The oppressive heat seemed to suddenly give way; unseen sweat poured down the high-spirited children's backs. Mozsi Beck, the poultry contractor's son, ran home with two companions to fetch empty chicken coops in which to put the menagerie. "Hey, bring your little brother, too!" shouted Gyula. "Your youngest brother!"

"Why him?" asked Mozsi Beck. "He still wets his pants."

"Just bring him!"

"What for?"

"He'll be the ape," said Gyula.

They had to get a handcart, at least two of them, to transport the menagerie. Dezso brought a little trap-like two-wheeled handcart from home; assistants had to help bring it over. Pista Deli stole rabbits from the courtyards, complete with pens whenever possible. If he couldn't find pens, he brought them naked under his coat; they were put in Beck's chicken coops. There were plenty of cats, dogs, even pigeons in the mill yard. But it wouldn't hurt to add one or two more. The mill yard, wearily on the verge of slumber a moment ago, in the blink of an eye roused itself from dusty summer sleep, and man and beast began to whirl around the leader, Gyula, like electrons. The initial excited shouting was succeeded by the tense silence of creative work, broken only by the joyous yelping of dogs thrown into confusion and rushing about in every direction. Young Kalman leaned against the porch and wiped his glasses.

"What did you bring from home?"

"Nothing," said Kalman.

In the village, one seldom came across suitable raw materials for a circus in the household of the watchmaker's widow.

Gyula, sinking his hands into his pants pockets, looked the thin, round-shouldered boy up and down scornfully.

"Go help Pista Deli!"

"No."

"Why not?"

"I don't want to," said Kalman.

Blinking, Gyula turned his long, freckled face toward the sun. "I can't hear you. Speak up!"

"I don't want to," repeated Kalman.

"You don't want to?" asked Gyula, incredulous in a sing-song. "You don't want to. What do you mean you don't want to? I don't understand. I said, go help Pista Deli."

He raised his whip and slashed it into the dust, exactly an inch from Kalman's naked toes. A tiny round cloud of dust rose suddenly in its wake. The boy with the glasses involuntarily stepped back.

"Stop jumping!" said Gyula. "What are you jumping for? I tell you, go help Pista Deli."

The boy with glasses, his face pale, stared at the tiny cloud of dust whirling at his feet.

"Well, what are you going to do?" asked Gyula and his face was still full of surprise.

"He can't go," said Manci, behind his back at this moment. "I need Kalman."

"What for?"

Rather than answer, the girl laughed softly. She had a clear, bell-like laugh. The thick crystal vase that her father had taken in the war from an Arrow-Cross member's house, a man who'd fled the country, rang with the sound of her laughter. Gyula looked at his sister and screwed up his face.

"You need him?"

"What of it?"

Gyula stood for a moment longer, then turned without a word and walked away.

"Are you coming?"

"I'm coming," said Kalman, his ears burning. The young girl had already turned around; she could not see the boy's enraptured look beneath his self-conscious glasses.

"Oh, what a fine game it will be!"

"Yes," said Kalman. "What do you need me for?"

"Oh, they'll be delicious," shouted the girl. "We'll eat heaps of cold, sweet melons."

Kalman quickened his pace. "What do you need me for?"

The girl laughed. "For all kinds of things. Don't you want to come?"

"Yes."

"Then why do you ask?"

Suddenly she shot off. The dust her feet stirred rose toward her tiny waist like a long, light train. Reaching the porch, she turned and waited for the boy striding along slowly and manfully.

"Or don't you want to come?" she said, fixing her coldly pensive, sleepy gaze on the boy's face.

"Now what do we do?" asked the boy.

In the room darkened by the shuttered windows, Piri Trenka knelt in front of the bottom drawer of the large dresser and cautiously lifted the heavy cool sheets and eiderdown cases placed one on top of the other. The plank floor was covered with linoleum; two rows of preserve jars stood on the dressertop, half their contents dried up. The air was cool, musty and made one shiver with pleasure. Kalman had never been in this room before.

"Not there!" said Manci. "There's nothing there."

Even in the gloomy room it was apparent that his face was flushed with excitement. Piri Trenka's groping hands were shaking, her tousled black hair kept falling into her sweating forehead.

"I tell you, there's nothing there."

"Well, where then?"

"In the wardrobe. Maybe on the top drawer."

"Can I help?" asked Kalman, who had visibly drawn courage from Piri Trenka's presence. "What should I look for?"

"As a matter of fact, I'm going to be a bride," said Manci, opening the wardrobe. "There's a bride in every circus; she rides a black horse and leads the procession. The groom follows her on horseback or on foot. Then come the animals and the clowns."

Kalman swallowed hard.

"What am I going to be?" he asked after a while.

"I don't know yet. Do you want to be a clown?"

"No," said Kalman firmly.

"You don't want to be the groom, do you?"

The girl laughed a thin laugh. Her eyes sparkled in the gloom. Piri Trenka giggled. "All right, we'll see," said Manci. "Now come here and take down Papa's linen suit. This will be Gyula's because the ringmaster always wears a white suit."

Kalman was allowed to stay in the room, but he had to face the wall while Manci changed. Among her mother's things, she could not find a white dress to serve as a wedding gown. She had to make do with a gray silk dress for which they dug up a little white lace collar from the top drawer of the dresser. Piri Trenka pinned the dress up all around because it was too long. While Kalman stared at the stains on the whitewashed wall, the young girls were whispering ceaselessly behind his back. From time to time, a suppressed, titillating giggle would burst from the cloud of whispers, tickle his neck and make it break out into goose bumps. The clomping of shoes could be heard on the linoleum. A pair of white stockings and old-fashioned, high-heeled black leather pumps from the dresser turned up on the young girl's white feet, of course, after a thorough foot washing.

"Don't you turn around!" shrieked Piri Trenka.

"I won't," said Kalman standing stiffly beside the wall with burning red ears.

They ransacked the house for a bridal veil in vain; finally

they had to make do with the dirty tulle curtain that Piri Trenka pinned with a few wire hairpins to Manci's reddish-brown curls. But when the bride in the gray silk dress, with the curtain on her head reaching to her waist and her loudly thumping patent-leather shoes slipping off her feet, finally marched onto the porch with shining eyes, there was such a hullabaloo raging in the mill yard that no one noticed her enchanting presence; even less Kalman's wide-brimmed black felt hat, emblem of his rank as groom, which, though it was stuffed with straw, kept slipping over his ears.

Now fifteen or twenty children were rushing about in the yard beneath the burning sun, screaming at the top of their lungs, red faces shiny with sweat. Three handcarts stood in front of the rusty flywheel leaning against the wall of the mill. The two-wheeled street barrow, which Dezso Trenka had surreptitiously sneaked out of his father's house, was behind the carts. In the corner of the courtyard, where three or four old millstones were lying about in burnt-out yellow grass, chicken coops and wicker baskets and larger goose pens were piling up; with tireless zeal, Mozsi Beck and his pals had transported them from the poultry contractor's courtyard. Also, on the millstone slabs the other indispensable paraphernalia of the circus gathered together—ropes, chains, a box of red minium paint, a washbasin, cooking pots and lids, wooden spoons, a sausage stuffer and a large brass trumpet glittering like gold that a member of the volunteer fire department band had, unbeknownst to him, donated to the circus.

Gyula, in his blindingly white linen suit, stood whip in hand on the well wall and directed troop movements. A pair of dogs had already been harnessed to the handcarts, and most of the members of the menagerie were in place. A large red cat was huddled in one of the cages bearing this sign: LION, BE CAREFUL: HE BITES! BEWARE OF LION!

Two large white rabbits posing as polar bears were lying on their stomachs in a small wicker basket, restlessly twitching their noses. There were plenty of birds of prey, eagles, vultures and falcons, exactly as many chickens, geese, ducks as the children could carry to the mill yard. A parrot was screeching in a frenzy of joy above the tiger. The most splendid specimen of the menagerie, the anthropoid ape, was at that moment being led by hand toward the ringmaster by Mozsi Beck when Manci, Kalman and Piri Trenka stepped onto the porch.

"Undress him!" said Gyula, appraising the flawless, superb specimen.

"But he's only wearing these drawers," said Mozsi Beck.

"Those, too!"

Mozsi Beck looked ahead, frowning, a worried look on his face. "What are you going to do with him?"

"Nothing," said Gyula. "We'll lock him up in a cage and we'll put him on exhibit."

"That's not a good idea!"

Pista Deli laughed so hard he had to hold his sides. "Why isn't it a good idea?"

"He'll cry," said Mozsi Beck.

"So?"

"Why should my little brother be the ape?" said Mozsi Beck. "There's lots of little kids around here. I brought ten cages for the circus."

Gyula impatiently cracked his whip. "What are you haggling for?! Everybody brings what they have. If you don't like it, you can go to hell."

Pista Deli guffawed with laughter. Even his neck turned red.

"What are you laughing at?" said Gyula. "It's not funny. Grab him and take off his clothes. We're going to put him in this cage."

They had left the largest wicker cage empty for the ape. Pista Deli jerked the little black pants off the child, then picked him up under the arms and lowered him into the cage through the narrow opening of the lid. All the *artistes* and other employees of the circus gathered around the cage; having heard news of the recent acquisition, they yelled wildly and watched the spectacle. The ape stood up to his armpits in the cage, motionless, clutching the willow twigs of the lid, and mutely he ran his astonished, frightened eyes over the screaming crowd. His tiny, pale face was twisted with fright, but he did not cry.

"Oh! He won't fit," said Piri Trenka.

"Of course he'll fit! All he has to do is pull in his neck."

Manci arranged her bridal veil, which kept slipping onto her nose. With an unconscious, wan smile on her face, her eyes were shining.

"He won't fit if he sits down," said a boy's voice. "Only if he lies down curled up."

Kalman was standing behind Manci. "This should not be allowed," he said surprised and indignant.

The girl kept staring at the cage.

"Do you hear, Manci?"

"Be quiet," said the girl without turning around. "Be quiet!"

Pista Deli clutched the ape, still half-protruding from the cage, and pushed him down by the shoulders. "Sit down," he shouted in his ear as if he were deaf. "Squat down, don't you understand? Damn you, sit down!"

"Slap him!" yelled a voice from behind. "Then he'll sit down."

The excitement spread to the dogs. Busan began to howl, a long-drawn-out sound like a wolf. A smaller dog named Didujka, who could not free himself from his harness, emitted ear-splitting yelps and threw his body to and fro like an epileptic. The two dogs harnessed in front of the second cart also barked and growled in alarm. The eagles and vultures in the cages were gabbling mightily. The lion, its hair on end, stared out into the dust with round green eyes.

The sun had long passed its zenith by the time the procession got underway. Though inside the courtyard it had provided an edifying spectacle, it reached full splendor only when it could unfold its entire length on the street in thick clouds of dust. Andris Kiss, the herald, led the way. His naked upper body had been smeared from neck to navel with dazzling red minium paint. With the gleaming brass trumpet raised to his lips and his father's fireman's hat on his head, he looked like an archangel. On either side of him, a step or two behind, followed drummers who accompanied the trumpet air by beating rhythmically on pots hung around their necks. Meanwhile, they strained their throats carrying out their duties as town criers. At the sound of their voices, the gates opened and filled, and along the length of the street, more and more children, as from a frayed string of pearls, twirled on both sides of the procession.

A few steps behind the herald, the ringmaster marched alone in his blindingly white suit, cracking his whip. He was wearing white lady's gloves and a woman's straw hat, from which a wide red silk ribbon hung down to his shoulders. The bride followed him, also alone in the procession. Unfortunately, her sleek bay steed had gone lame so she had to wobble in the dust on foot. She stepped along with downcast eyes, befitting a bride, looking neither right nor left. Directly behind her, barely a few steps away, marched Kalman, the bridegroom, his glasses glittering bravely under his huge black hat. Unfortunately, apart from his dignified bearing and triumphant look, no clear outward sign indicated his status as bridegroom.

Following the vanguard came vehicles, interspersed here and there with an *artiste* walking by himself. Here, the noise and dust were greatest. The dogs pulling vehicles were barking vociferously; birds of prey were crying and crowing; the personnel designated to care for the lion, tiger and polar bears were yelling at the top of their lungs. Heading the line was the little, two-wheeled street barrow carrying Eszti Bodor, the fortune-teller, hanging onto the sides of the cart with both hands. She was dressed in a flour sack held together under her arms by a thick rope; her head was covered with a large black silk scarf. Four short assistants pushed the heavy cart.

"What's this?" asked the onlookers.

"This is Robinson, the world-famous fortune-teller," shouted the herald who marched beside the cart, waving a national flag above his head. "She tells fortunes night and day, and she'll tell your fortune for only ten cents. A week ago she stated the score of the Hungarian-English game, six to three, and she prophesied the flood. This is Robinson, the world-famous fortune-teller."

The news of the circus far preceded its coming. Old women stood before the gates, shaking their heads disapprovingly and shutting smaller children up in the house. Older girls ran out into the street and, giggling, they watched the pack of children growing more and more enthusiastic marching down the middle of the road. "Of course, it's that chief miller's boy who put them up to it," said a woman. "That brat should be given a good lickin'."

"The girl's the villain," said another woman. "She's the one that stirs them up."

"That's the one!"

"She'll be a great whore someday, that one will!" said the first woman, watching the girl in the white veil.

The head of the procession had already turned onto Rákosi street, when the sound of the bugle suddenly faded away. One wheel of the fortune-teller's cart turned into the ditch with a great thud and Pythia swayed back and forth in the cart. The geese trapped in the crates gaggled piteously as they cooked in the merciless sun.

"They should never have been left alone!"

"The head miller went up to Pest. I saw him at the station this morning. His wife went to the farm to see her desperately ill mother."

Behind the fortune-teller's cart marched Pista Deli. His chest was thrust out and he was swinging his torso stripped to the waist and flexing his arm muscles, showing them off as boxers do. Around his neck, he wore a rusty well-chain that he could break in two with one yank. Unfortunately, the terrifying rattle of the chain was muffled by the howls of the caged wild beasts. Behind him, in a separate cart pulled by two dogs, the greatest attraction of the circus approached, the anthropomorphic ape. Hiding his face in his arms, legs drawn up to his belly, the thin brown body lay motionless in the cage.

"Hey, Laci," shouted a country lad leaning on one of the gates. "What's in that cage?"

"An ape."

"What's its name?"

"Ape."

"But what's its real name?"

"It doesn't have a real name," said a little girl.

The young fellow laughed. "Have you ever seen a cart push the horses?"

Standing in the middle of the street, the children looked at each other. As a matter of fact, the dogs were not really pulling the cart; on the contrary, to make the cart go at all they had to be pushed by their behinds. But this was so only in reality, and reality doesn't count.

"These are good horses!" shouted Sanyi Brio, one of the cart pushers, pertly. "These are good pulling horses. I can barely hold the cart back so they don't run off with it."

The band marched next to the ape cage. Two children on both sides of the cage were using pot lids as crashing cymbals. Two more were carrying a large enamel washbasin on which a third child was drumming as hard as he could with a sausage stuffer, disregarding pieces of enamel flying around. Members of the band who were not so adept at music kept the rhythm by beating on pots and pans or trumpeting into funnels.

When a pack of gypsy children on one of the street corners attached themselves to the procession, the ringmaster beckoned to a drummer in front of him.

"Run back, Peter," he ordered him, "and tell the men to keep an eye on the gypsies, or else they'll steal the eagles and vultures from the cages."

"What eagles?"

"Idiot!"

"Oh, I understand," said the drummer.

"I will whip anyone to a pulp who dares steal anything," said the ringmaster, turning his long freckled face and fiery red hair covered by a little straw hat. He glared severely at the messenger. "Then get back to your place immediately."

"I'm going," said the boy. "Shouldn't we pass the hat?"

The ringmaster gave him a withering look. "Whoever dares to beg," he shouted in his thin, raspy, adolescent's voice, "will be expelled from the procession. And then I will whip him bloody," he added for greater emphasis while he pulled up his white pants with both hands since, in spite of the tight belt, they were continually slipping down to his bare feet. "Come on, move!"

Mozsi Beck marched beside the ape cage. Hangdog, he looked neither right nor left, his ears standing out from his head were burning red from shame. Beside him, one of the acrobats, who had taken a wide red velvet ribbon from the head miller's dresser and tied it around his neck as an emblem of his craft, was uttering cries and turning cartwheels. A seven- or eight-year-old little girl whirled around her own axis until she got dizzy and laughing uproariously, fell headlong into the dust.

The more the troupe advanced, the more easily and enthusiastically it showed off feats and stunts before the wonder-struck audience lining the length of the street. It almost seemed as if the *artistes* were infected with genuine enthusiasm beyond professional skill, and now they were performing difficult and highly responsible work for the sake of the game, as it were, free of charge. When they'd set off, they had timidly side-stepped the council president's wagon and the trotting cow tied behind it. However, by the time they reached the school, they very nearly trampled Kalman Tapodi, the old cowherd of the Petofi Collective Farm who, unsuspecting and defenseless, rode his bicycle toward them down the middle of the road. A few men, pushing wheelbarrows on their way back to the threshing machine after Sunday rest, shook their heads as they drew over to the side of the road to avoid the procession which was growing by leaps and bounds, having absorbed half the village children.

Mozsi Beck, walking beside the ape cage, suddenly broke into a run and passing the strong man, the carriage of the fortune-teller, the bridegroom and the bride, ran up to the ringmaster.

"Gyula," he panted, "we have to take the child out of the cage."

"Address me as ringmaster."

Mozsi Beck's face twitched nervously.

"Don't you hear?"

"Ringmaster, sir," said Mozsi Beck. "We have to let the child out of the cage."

"I don't know what you're talking about. What child?"

"Well, the child."

"I don't hear you. Which child?" repeated the ringmaster.

"The ape," said Mozsi Beck, having pondered a while.

The ringmaster looked him up and down without saying a word. "How dare you step out of line!" he shouted, knitting his brows sternly. "Get out! Go back to your place, on the double."

In the heat of the discussion, both children had unconsciously slowed down, and the bride and groom walking behind caught up with them. "What's the matter with you?" asked Manci.

"We have to let the child out of the cage," said Mozsi Beck.

"Which child?" asked Manci, fixing her lazily pensive eyes on the boy's face.

"The ape," pleaded Mozsi Beck.

"Why?"

"He's crying."

There was a silence for a moment.

"He's crying?" asked Manci.

"His whole body is shaking," said Mozsi Beck. "Even his legs are trembling."

The girl's large gray eyes immediately filled with tears. "Poor little ape," she said softly to herself. "I've never seen an ape cry."

"Get back to your place," said the ringmaster, lashing his whip in front of Mozsi Beck's feet. "If you don't take your place immediately, I'll hit you in the face. About face!"

The boy jumped back and raised his trembling hands protectively. "That not an ape; he's a child," he said, deathly pale. "He must be taken out of the cage!"

"What did you say?" asked the ringmaster.

"That's not an ape," said the boy defiantly. "My little brother is not an ape."

Gyula raised his whip and struck Mozsi Beck. Calculating the blow, the leather thong whistled in front of the child's face and struck his naked neck. Mozsi Beck cried out in pain, helplessly clutching his naked neck. Again Gyula raised his whip. But before he could strike, Mozsi Beck turned and ran off crying loudly.

"Still, the child should be released!" said Kalman the Groom.

Meanwhile, the fortune-teller's cart and Pista Deli, the strong man walking behind her, caught up to the ringmaster's group. In front, the herald with his minium-red torso and golden archangel's trumpet also stopped and turned around, and the two drummers stopped drumming. The procession piled up.

"We must release the child!" said Kalman slowly, firmly, turning his pale bespectacled face toward the ringmaster. "A human being should not be shut up in a cage!"

The ringmaster was occupied with his pants; owing to the sudden movements they had slipped down again. Kalman looked at Manci standing beside him. The girl was smiling mysteriously.

"What are you interfering for?" said Gyula. "You all should have stayed in Auschwitz. Now, come on, everybody go back to your places. Let's go!"

Kalman shook his head. "No. First, release the child!"

"It's none of your business!" shouted the ringmaster, and snatching his whip from under his arm, he whirled it in a wide circle above his head. "Back to your place!"

"First, release the child!" said Kalman in a trembling voice. "I'm not going back until you let him out."

"You're not going?"

Unblinking, the two boys stared at each other. Gyula was taller by a head than the young bespectacled boy; his gray eyes were colder, his muscles more resolute. If it came to a fight, he could obviously make short work of his opponent. Kalman was deathly pale, his knees shaking. He looked at Manci. The young girl with her mysterious smile fixed her dreamy lazy eyes on his face.

"Manci?" said Kalman, swallowing hard. His mouth was full of dust, his back bathed in sweat. He looked at the young girl, who nodded imperceptibly.

"Release the child, Gyula!" said Kalman. "You must not lock a human being in a cage!"

All the children had gathered around the opponents. There was such a silence that even the last row could hear a little girl's excited whisper. Gyula glanced around at the silently waiting children. "Everyone back to their places!" he shouted, and smiling scornfully, he raised his whip. Those standing up front flinched and moved back. The circle widened, thinned out and began to disperse.

"What are you waiting for?" asked Gyula maliciously of the bespectacled boy standing before him. Suddenly he lashed his whip at Kalman's feet, and the thick dust puffed up in a dense little cloud over Kalman's naked toes. Kalman looked around. The others were slinking away. Only Manci was still beside him, standing a few steps away. Obviously, the command didn't affect her. Pista Deli's broad, indifferent back was visible as he slowly ambled by the fortune-teller's cart.

"Release the child!" said Kalman, swallowing hard, his head lowered as though trying to protect his glasses from the raised whip. "I'm not leaving until you release him."

A wagon stopped unnoticed on the side of the road, directly beside them; the dust and the excitement had swallowed the rumbling wheels. A tall woman dressed in black was sitting in the back of the wagon on a plank.

"Gyula!" whispered Manci, covering her face with her hands. "It's Mama!"

The boy suddenly lowered his raised whip and turned around. Shoulders hunched, blinking in fright, he looked at the wagon enveloped in the dense cloud of dust. "Get on!" said the woman sitting on the wagon. Her eyes were red with weeping. She glanced quickly at the gray silk bridal gown, the white linen suit, then turned away without a word. The two children huddled around her feet in the straw, and the wagon set off. None said a word. Instead of the high-laced shoes she'd been wearing when she left home, Grandma's loose, comfortable slipper was flopping on their mother's aching, swollen foot. Manci stared at it for a while with wide eyes, then suddenly burst into tears.

"Did she die?" she asked, sobbing.

She loved her grandmother even more than her parents. Gyula, too, grew pale; all his freckles stood out on his face. The wagon rumbled by the disintegrating circus procession, leaving the monkey cage lingering behind, the sobbing ape sitting beside it in the dust; then, after a few moments, it turned into the mill yard.

Translated by Elizabeth Csicsery-Rónay